Also by Lisa Heathfield
Seed
Paper Butterflies
Flight of a Starling

Lisa Heathfield's books have won numerous awards, including the North East Teen Book Award, the Southern Schools Book Award, the GDST Award, the Fabulous Book Award and the Concorde Book Award. She's also been shortlisted for several awards including the Waterstones Children's Prize (twice), the YA Prize and the Virginia Reader's choice award. Her books are sold across the world.

I AM NOT A NUMBER

LISA HEATHFIELD

First published in Great Britain in 2019
by Electric Monkey, an imprint of Egmont UK Limited
The Yellow Building, 1 Nicholas Road, London W11 4AN

Text copyright © 2019 Lisa Heathfield

The moral rights of the author have been asserted

ISBN 978 1 4052 9386 0

A CIP catalogue record for this title is available from the British Library

68622/001

Typeset by Avon DataSet Ltd, Bidford on Avon, Warwickshire
Printed and bound in Great Britain by CPI Group

Stay safe online. Any website addresses listed in this book are correct at the time
of going to print. However, Egmont is not responsible for content hosted by third
parties. Please be aware that online content can be subject to change and websites
can contain content that is unsuitable for children. We advise that all children
are supervised when using the internet.

Egmont takes its responsibility to the planet and its inhabitants very seriously.
All the papers we use are from well-managed forests run by responsible suppliers.

For my brother and sisters Philip, Lara, Emma and Anna –

for choosing hope and love as your weapons of choice.

They say I am number 276.

And that I can't escape.

They tell me what to do, what to wear, where to go. They try hard to hollow us out, to shrink us, to make us so that we can't exist.

But they don't see inside of me. The part of me that they'll never destroy.

They call me number 276, but that's not my name.

My name is Ruby West. I am fifteen years old.

And I won't let them silence me.

CHAPTER ONE

'Our country was sinking into a black hole, but you
voted for us to save you. We will re-establish order
and we will make you safe. We will make our
country strong again.' – John Andrews, leader of the
Traditional Party

It's his gun I see first. Hard metal tucked into his belt, his fingers
touching the tip.

A soldier, in our street.

I'm behind him now, a few metres away. Close enough to
see how his green uniform has been ironed with a line down the
back, like some weird backbone pushing through the material.
And there's the red slash on his arm to show us he's a Traditional.
As if we didn't know.

His boots are big, but they're quiet on the pavement. He's
quiet. And he's walking so slowly that I have to go past him. He

3

turns and looks at me as I do, but I keep facing straight ahead. I don't want to see his hair, his eyes.

I smell him though, a jolt of aftershave. And he's whistling, quietly. I want to run, but I can't, I must keep walking, concentrate on the houses ahead. I bite my lip, taste my strawberry lip balm.

His whistling stops. I feel his eyes on me, on the undercut above my bare neck.

'The school day starts soon.' It's his voice, speaking to me.

A hand suddenly links through my arm and drags me forward. It's Destiny. She's in my year at school and even though I don't think we've ever even spoken to each other, right now I want to hug her.

'Come on,' she says. 'Or we're going to be late.'

She leads me away from him, away from the soldier and his gun, and we're running around the corner and leaving him behind.

When we're far enough away we slow down and Destiny unloops her arm from mine.

'Thanks,' I say.

She shrugs and smiles. 'No problem.'

'I can't believe that there are soldiers on the streets,' I say.

'It's a bit terrifying.'

'Do you reckon they'd use their guns?'

'Why carry them otherwise?' Destiny says. It should feel

odd to be walking along together, but that soldier has looped a strange thread of fear between us.

'Why do you think they're here?' I ask.

'Apparently it's to keep us safe.'

'From what?'

'Precisely. They'll blame it on the Core Party, as they always do.'

'Because of the protests?'

'They'll pretend it's something like that. My mum's not surprised though. She thought it'd happen as soon as the Traditionals got into power. She's only surprised that it's taken them three months.'

I don't remember seeing Destiny with glasses before. They're nice. The frames are thin and almost bubble-gum pink against her skin.

'My stepdad says John Andrews is actually mad,' I say.

'Your family didn't vote for them then?'

I feel vulnerable suddenly. I realise I don't know for sure what side Destiny is on. Since the election and the new government some people have really shown their true colours.

'No,' I tell her, trying to make my voice sound proud in what I believe in.

'I'm a Core supporter too,' she says. 'Although my mum told me I shouldn't say either way.' There's her laugh again. I wonder how it can be so strong when we're on a street that

5

might have another soldier around the corner. 'She says we haven't seen anything yet.'

'There's worse to come?'

I watch the cars drive past as they always do when I walk to school. The familiar sounds of their wheels on the road, people leaving their houses, a woman pushing a buggy on the pavement opposite. How much can really change? How much bad can a new government really do?

'They made Hannah Maynard go and change her skirt,' Destiny says.

'Who did?'

'The soldiers. They told her it was indecently short.'

'Are you serious?'

'Completely.'

'They didn't put that in their campaign speeches,' I say.

'They're all about traditional values, aren't they? We should've guessed they'd eventually come round to the way we dress.'

'They'll have us in high collars and skirts that touch our ankles.'

We're silent for a bit. Around us it's getting busier the closer we get to school. The gates are still a walk away but even from here I can see two soldiers standing either side of them. I look over at Destiny but I can't read her face – it's kind of neutral.

'Are we still going to go in?' I ask.

'Of course.' Yet when she looks up at me I can see she's not neutral after all. There's rebellion deep in her eyes. 'They're not going to stop me doing anything.'

We're nearly there when I reach up for my ponytail and pull down my hair, letting it fall dead straight to my shoulders.

'Ruby!' I hear Luke call my name as soon as I walk through the door. Whatever the chaos of everyone getting into school, we always wait in the same spot for each other. And after one year, two months and five days I still get that crazy blood-flip when I see him. Even though he recently cut off his curls, he still looks beautiful.

'Hey.' He's leaning against a wall as he kisses me, but I pull away from him.

'Did you see them?' I ask, remembering the soldier's smell. His eyes on me.

Luke puts his arm round my shoulder and pulls me close enough to feel the beat of his heart.

'They're only people,' he says. 'Just in different types of clothes.'

'But they've got guns,' I remind him.

'They're just here to scare us. So don't let them.'

The bell for tutor time rings out.

'Did your dad know they'd be here?'

Luke shrugs. 'He suspected. But sometimes journalists are the last people to find out. People try to hide everything from him.'

'Hurry up, you lot.' Our head's voice ricochets down the corridor, scattering everyone.

'See you in Art,' Luke says, kissing me before I head off to my tutor room.

Mr Hart is looking for something in his drawer. It's only a matter of time before the pile of books on his desk topples.

'What do you think of the soldiers?' Sara asks. I put my bag on the chair and sit on the table, my back to the front of the classroom.

'There weren't any on my street.' Conor swings back on his chair, his new shoes up on the table next to me. He hates them. When the Trads brought in a no-trainer rule in all schools he tried to start a petition, but it didn't get very far.

'My dad told me not to be frightened of them,' Sara says. 'That they're here to do good.'

'What good ever came from people with guns?' Conor snaps at her.

'Don't be so arsey,' Sara says. It's not like these two to fight. 'I thought you of all people would like seeing men in uniform.' She leans over and pulls one of his blond curls and lets it ping back into place.

'Leave it, Sara,' he says, swatting her hand away.

'Settle down!' Mr Hart shouts from the front.

Sara moves my bag so I can sit. Conor takes his feet from the table but doesn't stop rocking backwards.

'Sir,' Sara calls out. 'What's happening?'

'Do you mean right this moment?' Mr Hart asks, adjusting his tie so it goes wonky the other side. 'Or in the country in general?'

'Both.'

Normally at least a few people are still talking, but now it's more silent than I've ever heard it in here.

'Well, right this moment we have soldiers outside our school.' Mr Hart coughs and rubs his hand over the stubble on his chin. 'And the country in general seems to be in the grip of a maniacal political party who want to take us back to the Stone Age.'

'With John Andrews as the caveman,' Conor says.

'As he's their leader,' Mr Hart says, 'it would appear so.'

'Surely, sir,' Ashwar says. 'He's just trying to make a better place for all of us to live.'

'All of us?' Mr Hart says. 'Or just the people like him?'

'By *like him*,' Ashwar says, 'do you mean people who believe in the family unit? Who believe in a safe country?'

'It depends what your definition of *better* is, Ashwar,' Mr Hart answers. 'I'm not sure that dictating how we think and what we do is necessarily better. Take, for example, their proposed law about single-sex schools throughout the country. You do realise that would mean this school will no longer exist as it is? You'd all be split off, divided.'

'It's been proved that they work,' Ashwar says. 'Grades are

9

consistently higher when boys and girls are separated.'

'But it's about choice,' Mr Hart says.

'We've had choice for tons of years and look where that's got us,' Ashwar says.

'Do you actually work for the Trads, or something?' Conor asks and a few laughs scatter about.

'I'm just saying that perhaps it's better to finally be told what to do. To have someone in charge who has the guts to put their beliefs into place.'

'Are you mad?' Conor asks her. Even though we all know she's not. Ashwar is a straight 9 student and probably heading for Oxford.

'I think she's got a point,' James says.

'You would agree with her,' Sara says. 'You just want to know the colour of her knickers.'

Laughter cuts into the atmosphere again and James's face goes so red I think he might explode.

'I think what you have to consider,' Mr Hart says, waving a book in the air to quieten us, 'is why John Andrews and his party are really introducing these new rules. Could it be less about what's *good* for society and more about control?'

'Curfew for anyone under eighteen definitely seems like control to me,' Conor says.

'Or could it be that they just really care about what happens to us?' Ashwar says.

'The Core Party care,' Conor tells her. 'They stand for Champion Of Rights for Everyone, if you remember.

'I hadn't forgotten.' Ashwar glares at him. 'But they didn't get voted in, did they? People voted for the Traditionals. They'd had enough of our country sliding towards oblivion.'

'That's ridiculous,' Conor says. He manages not to shout it, which is pretty impressive for him. For years he was angelic Conor, terrified of spiders and wasps, but since his mum got ill anger sometimes turns him inside out.

'My mum voted for them,' Sara says. 'But she didn't expect them to start telling us what we can and can't wear. Even half *her* wardrobe isn't suitable by their standards.'

'Well, I'm not complaining about the length of her skirts,' Leo says, smirking at her.

'Shut up.' I reckon if Sara had a book in her hand she'd lob it at him.

'Maybe John Andrews is right,' Ashwar says. 'That without the trigger of provocative clothing, rape crime will go down.'

Conor slams his fist on to the desk. 'You seriously believe it's a girl's fault if she's attacked? Because of the way she dresses?'

'I seriously believe that it's a complex topic,' Ashwar says calmly. 'No other government has tried to face it and we're left with a country that's rotting from the inside out.'

'Sir,' Conor shouts. 'You've got to stop her spouting this bullshit.'

11

Mr Hart waves his book from the front again, but this time he looks like he has fury in his veins. 'I think –' he says, his voice raised enough to get everyone quiet, '– that if we voted again now, some of your parents who ticked a box for the Traditionals might change their mind.'

'It's a bit late though, isn't it,' Conor mumbles.

'Yes,' Mr Hart says. 'Yes, it is.'

The only class I have with Luke is art. Sara says I only took it so I could be with him and I think she might be right. I'm rubbish at drawing, but Luke is like the next Picasso or something.

'You okay?' he asks, sitting on the stool next to me. He puts his hand underneath my hair and I can feel his palm against my skin. When he kisses me I wonder if the Trads will stop this too. If they say short skirts lead to promiscuity and teenage pregnancies, what will they think of outright kissing?

'Everything's just a bit weird,' I say.

'There was nearly a fight in maths,' Luke says.

'So much for the Trads bringing peace and harmony.'

Miss Mason bangs her giant paintbrush on her desk. It's her way of getting our attention and somehow it's always worked.

'There's a change of plan for our lesson today,' she says. She's wearing her long hippy dress as usual so she'll be fine with any new rules the Trads impose. 'The whole of Year Eleven are having an assembly in the hall.'

'Now?' someone asks.

'Yes.' Miss Mason goes to the door and opens it. 'In silence though. Other year groups are still working.'

'Miss, I really want to finish my still life,' Kaylee moans.

'I'll open the room at lunch for anyone who wants to make up the time.'

'No thanks,' Conor laughs, walking across the top of the tables to get past everyone.

'Off there,' Miss Mason tells him and he jumps down, using Kaylee's head to support him.

'Wanker,' she says, swiping at him.

'Language,' Miss Mason says.

'The Trads will knock your head off if they hear you say that, Kaylee,' Conor says.

'I said silence,' Miss Mason shouts.

'What's going on, miss?' Luke asks as we pass her.

'I've just been told to get you all to assembly,' she says as she flicks off the light and closes the door behind the last of us.

There's a soldier standing at the front of the hall. It looks wrong that he's here inside our school. Next to him Mr Edwards, our head, paces up and down, directing people where to sit, filling up the chairs from the front. Luke squeezes my fingers before he lets go of my hand.

Normally in assembly there's so much noise, people shoving

13

and shouting, calling out to each other. But there's something about the soldier that sews all our mouths shut. All except Tristan.

'He's fit,' I hear him say.

'Shh.' Sara yanks his arm. Since the Traditionals have come into power they're suddenly very vocal about what they really think of gay people. They say it's a choice and they've made it clear which way they want people to choose.

Luke and I manage to sit together and when everyone is inside, the big double doors close and we all look to the two men at the front.

'Good morning, everyone,' Mr Edwards says. I can tell he's nervous as he exaggerates looking at his watch. 'Yup, it is still morning, just.' A few of the teachers around the edge try to laugh, but there's nothing from any of us. 'Right, well, I'm going to hand over to Chris Stewart, a member of the Traditional Party.' Mr Edwards steps to the side, his hands strangely clasped together. I've never seen him fade in the presence of anyone before. He normally struts around like some sort of demented peacock.

'Thank you,' Chris Stewart says. He clears his throat, his hand balled in front of his lips. 'I'm very proud to be here as a representative of John Andrews and the Traditional Party.' He's older than the soldier on my street this morning. And he doesn't have a gun, but that doesn't make me feel any better. 'As you all know, this is a very exciting time for our country,

14

because for too long we've been at the mercy of people with weak vision and weak focus. We are different. We bring change. We're determined to restore our country to be the great place we know it can be.' He looks so smug standing there, as though he's expecting us all to jump to our feet and high five him or something. 'The Traditionals are not just a party of words but of actions. Already our policies are working. Since we came to power three months ago, violent crimes are decreasing. With us leading you, I promise that your quality of life will continue to rise.'

He's convincing, I'll give him that. I know a lot of people will be lapping this up, oblivious to how much will be destroyed for this so-called life. Like our voice, our freedom. I nudge Luke gently with my arm and he nudges me back. Thank God for his sanity in this madness.

'We know,' the soldier continues, 'that much of the country voted for us. People knew it was time for change. And we believe in the importance of solidarity. We know that you want to be as proud of the party you voted for as we are proud of you. Therefore, from today, you are all instructed to wear a band on your arm depicting your allegiance.'

Mr Edwards takes a step backwards. It's obvious that he didn't know this was going to happen.

The soldier's smile doesn't seem friendly to me. 'Some of you look confused,' he says. He looks like a snake. 'Let me explain it more clearly. You are about to come up here and choose a band of either the Traditionals or the Core Party. You will wear that band at all times.'

There's not even a murmur. Two hundred silent students. I glance around, but everyone just stares at the front.

Two soldiers appear from the side door carrying a box each. And both are carrying guns slung over their shoulders. They put the boxes on a table. Across the front of one there's the red slash against the green of the Trads, the other has a rectangle of purple with four yellow upward steps. One soldier slices a knife across the top of one box, then the other.

'The decision of which band you choose must be your own,' Chris Stewart says from the front. 'Don't be influenced by your friends. And if your parents were foolish enough to vote for the Core Party, know that you don't have to follow them. They may be frightened of change, but this is your chance to stand up to them, to be your own person. Break free of their chains.'

'What an idiot,' Luke whispers so quietly that it's probably only me who hears it.

'The front row first,' Chris Stewart says. No one moves until he points to the girl on the end. 'You,' he says. 'Come and choose your band. The rest will follow in silence.'

She's a new girl. I don't know her name, but she goes straight to the Traditionals' box. She reaches in, pulls out an elasticated green band and pulls it over her school jumper to the top of her arm, turning it so that the red slash is clearly visible. Chris Stewart pats her on the back and she smiles up at him as though he's some sort of hero or something.

It's Shaun Williams next and he doesn't even hesitate before he chooses the Trads. Then James and Ashwar from my tutor group and Tristan. He's not laughing now as he pulls the green band up his arm.

I don't know if they all really want to, or if it's the men holding guns behind them that make them do it.

Sara is first in the second row. I know her mum voted for the Trads as she wanted a change. She said other governments had led us nowhere and she wanted to give someone else a chance. Her dad couldn't decide so he hadn't voted. But Sara? She's been my best mate since our first day in this school and her head is screwed on right.

She gets to the front and hesitates. She looks at Stewart who watches her, before she walks past the Core's box and puts her hand into the one for the Trads. I drop my head down. Luke reaches over for my hand and this time he doesn't let go.

I don't want to see any more of it. I don't want to believe that it's happening. So I close my eyes. Are they doing this with Year Eight? Are they going to make my sister choose?

'I'm not ashamed.' The voice that makes me look up is Conor's. He's pulling a purple Core Party band up his arm,

17

positioning it so that the yellow steps are visible for everyone to see.

'Ignorance is not something to be proud of,' Chris Stewart says, glaring at him. I think Conor is going to say something else, but the soldiers with the guns stand straight and he walks back to his seat.

There are a handful of people in the rows in front who have the purple band. The logo of the steps are meant to represent walking up to a brighter, better future, yet not enough people seem to be listening. Or are they just scared? I wish my dad was here, as he'd tell them not to be intimidated. But he lives so far away now that he might not even know this is going on.

It's my turn. Our line stands up and I follow Jen along the length of chairs. Luke is behind me. The air, all of the sounds, seem to have been sucked from the room as we walk to the front. I can't tell which I feel more – defiance or fear. But there's never any doubt about which I'll choose.

I don't look at the soldiers, at their empty eyes and loaded guns, as I pull the purple band over my wrist and the sleeve of my jumper. The material it's made of is stretchy and clings to my arm. I twist it so that the steps face out and as I walk back to my seat I keep my head held high. I look calm, but if you sliced me open now you'd see my heart struggling to keep up with its beating.

I sit down and for a while I don't look at Luke. I know his dad is a strong Core supporter as he goes to meetings with my mum and my step-dad, Darren. And I know Luke's thoughts and that he'd want to choose that. But did he? With bullets so close by, did he stay strong to his beliefs?

'Look at me, Rube,' he whispers. I do. He has a purple band on his arm.

I want to smile, but I can't.

In the corridor, everyone is strangely quiet. No one quite looks in each other's eyes.

'I want to find Lilli,' I say to Luke. 'She's normally in the canteen at first break.'

'I'll come with you,' Luke says, putting his hand in mine. I try not to see people's arms, but there are far, far more green bands than purple. I've never felt vulnerable in school before, but I do now. It almost feels like being dropped in the sea and circled by sharks. I have to remind myself that everyone is just the same as they were this morning. No one has really changed.

At least it feels normal in the canteen. It's not as busy in here as it is at lunchtime, but there're still lots of people talking and plates being thumped on to trays. Luke and I walk past tables, towards the one where Lilli and her friends are huddled together. They're the girls she came up from primary school with. The Tight-Knits they used to call themselves, before other kids took the mick.

Lilli is laughing but stops the moment she looks at me. She moves her arm back, but I've already seen the green band.

'She chose the Trads,' I say to Luke, pulling him to slow down. He looks confused, but when he glances at Lilli I know he sees it too.

'Ruby,' he says, putting his hands on my shoulders. 'She would've felt alone in there and just copied her friends.'

'But she's not a Trad.'

'I know. But this is what they want to happen. They want Core families to rip themselves apart, so they can show proof that we're the bad ones.'

'Darren'll be furious.'

'He won't. He'll understand,' Luke says. 'And if she falls out with him then she'll need you by her side.' He bends down to kiss me. 'You can do this.'

My sister's table is completely quiet when we get to it.

'Hey, Lils,' I say, hating the fact that my voice sounds so forced happy. 'You okay?'

'Yes,' she says, but she doesn't look it.

'What are you eating?'

'Just a doughnut.'

Her skinny arm has that green armband clamped round it, but I concentrate on looking at her face instead.

'Enjoy it,' I say. 'I just wanted to check you're all right.'

'Yeah,' she says. 'I'm fine.'

'Good. Love you, Chicken Bones,' I tell her, faking a smile. She doesn't make a fuss that I just called her that in front of her friends. Instead, she looks like she might cry, which'll be far more embarrassing for her than some stupid nickname. So I pull Luke away with me.

As we walk out of the canteen I look around. Hannah Maynard has a green band on. Her boyfriend, Tre, who I know is a Core, has a Trad band glaring from his arm. By the door we pass Hunter Melville. He's kind of like the boss of Year Eight. He puts his arm out to show me as we walk by. A Core. I smile at him, genuine now. At least there are bits of surprising light in this grim day.

I don't see Sara again until lesson four. I've wanted to text her, but Mr Edwards has clamped down on phones so bad recently that I don't want to risk him taking mine for a few days. Sara's sitting in her usual seat, the empty chair next to her waiting for me.

'Hey,' she says.

'Hey back,' I say. 'Have you been hiding from me?'

'No.' Her face is shocked and tells me she has. 'It's a weird day.'

'Yeah.'

Miss Hajiev walks into the classroom. She has the green band with the slash of red on her arm. So they're even getting teachers to do it too.

'This thing doesn't change anything,' Sara says, pointing to the Trad band on her own arm.

'Course not,' I say.

'Right, class,' Miss Hajiev says. 'You've homework to hand in, I believe.'

There are groans from people as the air tries to click back into its normal place.

'I bet it's only for a few days.'

'Yeah,' I say. But the word just balances there. It doesn't step into a patch of truth.

I wait for Luke after school. I want to feel more confident and look everyone with a Trad band in the eye, but instead I keep focused on the floor as I stand here, scuffing my shoe backwards and forwards until I make a strong line in the dust.

A gob of saliva lands in front of my foot. I look up and Shaun Williams is standing so close, with bully sunk deep in his eyes.

'Core scum,' he says. People glance over, but no one stops.

'Rather that than be a Trad,' I say, pulling my bag closer on my shoulder.

'You can't hide it any more,' he says. 'So you'll just have to keep watching your back.'

'Or what?' Luke says, appearing at my side. He's at least a foot taller than Shaun, but Shaun is wider.

'You'll have to wait and see,' Shaun says.

Luke just laughs. 'We'll look forward to it. Now 'scuse us, we've got better places to be.' And he grabs my hand as we start to walk away.

'What, like a Core meeting, or something?' Shaun shouts. 'I wouldn't risk going to one of those if I was you.'

I look back without even meaning to. Shaun raises a finger at me and slices it across his neck. I want to think of an insult, but my mind fills with nothing.

'He's not worth it,' Luke tells me. And at least we're together as we hurry away from the school, away from the weird day, from friends who are suddenly strangers. Through all the streets, only stopping when we get to the low wall that runs along the side of the disused railway track.

Normally we're not that careful as we jump over the bricks that lead to the overgrown slope, but today I don't want anyone to see.

'Do you think it's a good idea?' I ask. Part of me wants to get home, even though Mum isn't back from work for another hour. Maybe I should be there with Lilli – but what are we going to say to each other now I know what she chose? Will she hide the band under her bed and lie to Mum and Darren?

'There are no rules about where we can and can't go,' Luke says, looking around before he walks slowly through the long grass. 'Yet.'

I follow him. We always try to zigzag to the bottom, so

there's no path to give us away. Not because we've ever been frightened of being caught before, but just because this is our place and we don't want anyone to find it. Today, I just run down, needing to get to the bottom fast enough. Luke holds up the broken barbed-wire fence and I crawl underneath, holding it for him until he's through.

We hold hands as we slip behind the line of trees and walk further down until we're on the track. I never step on the metal bits, even though it hasn't been used for years. Instead I walk on the piles of leaves in between.

For the first time since this morning's assembly I feel as if I can breathe normally. I reach up to yank off the purple band on my arm and stuff it into my bag. Down here, with the branches of trees touching each other above our heads, life feels normal again. There are no soldiers. No strange rules being introduced. No jealous guarding of some national identity. We can say what we want, wear what we want. I start to roll up the waistband of my skirt, so ridiculously high that I know my knickers show.

'If I like short,' I say, 'I'll have short.' Luke turns to look at me and he nearly falls over.

'Ruby.'

'Yes.'

'Don't do that to me.'

'I'm not doing anything to you,' I say. 'I'm doing it for me.'

And I brush past him, swaying my hips as I hook up my bag on my shoulder.

Our hut is there as it always is. Something solid in this madness. Something hidden and secret and us. I think it was something to do with the trains – maybe a signalman's hut. Luke says it was for a rabbit-shooting man. There was an animal skeleton inside when he first discovered it after he moved to our town and that was all the evidence he needed to create a bogeyman in rabbit skin.

I spin the numbers on our padlock until it opens and am about to push on the door when Luke puts out an arm to stop me.

'Close your eyes first,' he says.

'What for?'

'You'll see.'

And so I do and I'm expecting to feel him kissing me, but instead I hear him rustling in his bag.

'Okay,' he says and when I open my eyes he's holding a necklace. It has *Ruby* spelled out across it in small looping letters. 'For you.' And he laughs. 'In case you hadn't guessed.'

Everything else is silent around us. 'It's beautiful.' And I really mean it.

'As are you.'

He puts it around my neck, his arms leaning lightly on my shoulder as he does the clasp.

'Thank you,' I say. 'I love it.' And I kiss him, taking every drop of the dread and confusion of the day and making it disappear. My hand finds Luke's Core band and I yank it from him. I don't want to open my eyes and see it there.

We stumble into our hut and I kick the door closed.

'Wait,' he says and he pushes me away.

'I don't want to,' I tell him, but he ducks away and goes to the table by the wall.

'I want to draw you first. Like that.'

'In my knickers?' I raise my eyebrows at him.

'No. In your skirt like that.' He's all serious now, like he gets whenever he's near his art stuff. He grabs his sketchbook from beside the wall. 'If they really are going to ban short skirts, I need something to remember it by.'

'That just sounds like an excuse.'

'Maybe,' Luke says and smiles that smile that he knows will make me do anything. 'Seriously, Rube. You look beautiful. I need to catch that.'

I put my hair back into its ponytail and feel the softness of my undercut, before I hold the necklace Luke gave me and trace my fingers along the letters of my name.

'You know, I love you more than popcorn,' I tell him.

'With sugar or salt?'

'Both.'

'Good. Just checking.' And he gets his sketching pencils from his bag.

'Are there any biscuits left?'

'A few, I think.'

They're in a tin that his grandad used to keep his ration book in. His dad was going to throw it away, but Luke managed to save it and bring it here. It's on the floor next to a bottle of water. The tin is stiff to open and the smell of it always makes me feel a bit ick, but I'd never tell Luke that.

'Do you want one?' I ask him.

'I'm all right,' he says, as I knew he would. He doesn't eat when he's drawing. Something about him not wanting to confuse the senses. I watch as he lights a couple of candles next to his paper. They shine up on to him and make him look carved from stone.

I take the tin with me and go and lie on the rug on my side. It's more of an offcut of carpet we found in a skip one day, but it was brand new, so we carried it between us all the way from Sydney Street, next to the park. I stretch out my legs and have to shuffle up a bit so my feet don't press into the chair. The biscuit is definitely stale.

'Eugh,' I say, as I drop the rest of it back into the tin. 'It's bendy.'

'They're meant to be,' Luke says, his pencil in his mouth as he straightens his sketchbook. 'They're called bendy biscuits.'

He looks up at me and it's always in this moment that he sees me differently. I'm not just Ruby. I'm sort of more than me. I'm every line, every shadow that makes up the person I am. All my imperfections too. My nose that could be straighter, my eyes that I wish were brown. The strange splodge of a birthmark above my knee that is clear as anything with my skirt like this.

'Hang on,' I say and I have to move a bit to get the Core band I threw on the floor. I pull it over my head and it squeezes tight over my eyes, before I leave it around my mouth.

'You're not going to be able to breathe,' Luke says, but I shrug. 'Or speak.' I pull the band back up until it rests on my forehead.

'Good point,' I say.

'Ready now?'

'Yup.'

I'm hoping that me lying here like this might distract him enough from his drawing, but my luck's not in. I could lie here naked and he'd probably still just study me and scribble away, detached yet somehow more involved all in the same moment. Maybe one day I really will strip off completely. See if he manages to keep his concentration then.

'Darren says the Core supporters are planning big demonstrations about the Trads wanting to close our borders,' I say. 'He won't let me go to any though, which isn't fair if your dad takes you to them.'

'Mm.'

'I reckon the Trads should introduce a rule that stepdads

don't have to be listened to. I wouldn't protest against that one.'

Luke is lost in his world of pencil and paper. He has this expression when he draws – frowning but with one eyebrow a bit higher than the other. And he always has one pencil in his hand, one in his mouth. I've warned him about lead poisoning, but he says he's happy to die for his art.

'How can women ever vote for him?' I ask, deciding to reach for the bendy biscuit after all. It's meant to be ginger, so if I ignore the fact that it doesn't crunch like it should, I can concentrate on the taste instead. 'I reckon if they could all vote again tomorrow, loads of women would change their mind. Because it's not like the Trads were completely honest in their campaign, were they?'

'No one ever is.'

'They talked about strengthening the family unit, but there was no mention of banning new mums from work.'

Luke doesn't answer. There's just the faint scratch of his pencil.

'Sara chose a green band,' I say.

'I know.'

'How could she? Her parents voted Trad, but she should know better. I thought she was stronger than that.'

'People are scared.'

'To stand up for what's right?'

'Yes. When there are guns involved. Definitely.'

I take another biscuit. 'These are disgusting.'

'You need to stay still.'

'I'll keep my legs still. Draw them while I'm eating. Or better still,' I say, hitching my skirt even higher. 'Eat my legs while you draw.'

'Rubes.' Luke looks pained. 'It's difficult enough for me to focus as it is.'

'Don't then,' I say. 'Come and join me here.'

'I will,' Luke says. 'When I've finished this.'

I pout at him, but I know it won't make any difference, so I settle myself as comfortable as I can to wait it out.

'I feel bad that I didn't go home with Lilli,' I say. 'If she didn't go to a friend's she'll be at home worrying about what I think. Whether I'm going to tell Mum or Darren.' I pick at the carpet in front of me.

'Are they both at work?'

The door to our hut suddenly slams open. I sit up and grab the Core band from my forehead as a soldier walks in.

'What's going on here?' He doesn't look at Luke, only at me, his eyes going from my face to my bare legs. Luke starts to get up. 'Don't move,' the soldier shouts.

'We're just hanging out,' Luke says, raising his hands with his palms facing out. I don't know how he speaks. My voice has wound itself tight round the trigger of the soldier's gun.

'You're indecent,' the man says to me. My legs burn under his glare and I try to pull the skirt longer.

'We weren't doing anything,' Luke says. I don't look at him again, but I can hear fear flickering in his words.

'Where's your ID?' the soldier asks.

'In my bag,' Luke tells him.

'Get it.'

Luke goes from his chair to the wall. He has to turn his back on the soldier as he picks up his bag. In the front pocket is his ID – the one everyone over the age of thirteen now has to carry. Luke walks the few steps across the hut floor and hands it over. The soldier scans it, before he throws it back.

'Now yours.' He uses his gun to point at me and my brain switches blank. All I can see is how close the trigger is. How I could blink and it will all be over.

'Ruby,' Luke says. 'He needs your ID.' He nods at me calmly, even though panic must be biting every cell in his body.

'Fine,' I say. I stand up and pull my skirt to its normal length, but even though it reaches my knees now, I feel completely exposed. I try to stop my hands shaking as I unzip my bag. I'm determined not to show the soldier that I'm afraid as I hand him my ID, looking him hard in the eyes. He stares at my card, then scans it before he hands it back.

'I'll escort you from here,' the soldier says. 'It's clearly an unsuitable place for two young, unmarried people to be. You won't be coming back.'

If he didn't have that gun I'd thump him. Or at least swear at

31

him or something. Instead, like obedient lambs, Luke and I head towards the door.

'You've forgotten something,' the soldier says. He jerks his head towards Luke's Core band on the floor. 'Or you could put it in the bin and choose the option of a better future.'

'No thanks,' Luke says, as he bends down to pick it up and pulls it up his arm.

'Put on yours,' the soldier tells me. There's a strong part of me that wants to hide it in my bag, to deny my beliefs and make my life easier, just for a moment. But I pull the Core band up my arm too.

'I'll follow you out,' the soldier says.

I hear him close the door to our hut. Luke and I walk side by side, our hands almost touching. The tunnel through the trees doesn't feel safe any more. The air is cold. The soldier walks behind us, his boots heavy on the leaves. I don't think he walks on the railway line, but I wish he would. I wish they'd suddenly turn it on and send a thousand volts through his Trad body.

He's close behind us, but I can feel his gun as though it's pressing on my back. Pressing between my shoulder blades, the tip of it boring into my skin. The bullet released.

'We're okay,' Luke whispers. I nod and look ahead.

We reach the broken part of the fence and I crawl through it, knowing that the soldier watches every part of me. Luke follows and holds back the wire mesh for the soldier, who looks vulnerable as he crawls on his hands and knees. A little boy, just for a moment, before he stands up tall again.

'I've got all your details now,' he says, tapping the scanner at his side. 'Both your names, where you live. Your families.' He looks at each of us. 'We'll be watching you.'

We walk up through the long grass.

'Go straight home,' Luke whispers to me.

'You too.'

I want to kiss him but daren't even touch his hand. Instead, I turn and start to run, my feet hard on the pavement. I don't stop until I'm home.

Mum is already in the kitchen. My blood is still stumbling from that soldier's close breath. She puts down the kettle when she sees me.

'You've got one too,' she says, touching the Core band on my arm. 'They came into work.' She takes off her coat and there's a band of purple on top of her nurse's uniform. 'Apparently it's just in our area, though.'

'What do you mean?'

'We're being used as some sort of trial. If it works they'll make the rest of the country wear them.'

'Brilliant,' I say.

'Did they make Lilli choose?' she asks, as she puts her coat over the back of a chair.

I nod. I don't want to tell her, to even say it out loud, that Lilli chose a Trad band. But Mum can tell by my face.

'Don't be angry with her,' I say. Mum looks knackered as she sits down. 'She only chose it because her friends did. And if it's just a trial for a few days then it's not a big deal.'

Mum nods. 'I'll go and talk to her. I think she's in her room.'

She gets up again already and it looks like she's carrying a hundred weights on her shoulders. In the doorway she stops.

'Ruby, I'm not sure these bands are just for a few days. I think things out there are going to start getting ugly.'

'Like how?'

'I've never known our country to feel so divided and that's not a good place for it to be in. There are all sorts of rumours about arrests and blocking off streets, but with so many lies it's hard to know what's true.'

'The Core Party speaks the truth,' I say.

'Mostly,' she says, before she goes up the stairs.

The kitchen is usually a bit of a sanctuary for me. Second to my bedroom, it's my favourite place in our house. But now it somehow feels hollowed out and any air that's left slides inside me when I breathe and sits like a dead bird in my stomach.

CHAPTER TWO

'Enough of the swarms of people entering our
country. We will close our doors against the scum
of the world, those who suck our country dry.'
– John Andrews, leader of the Traditional Party

'You're not coming and that's final.' Darren's talking with his
mouth full, which Mum always tells us not to.

'You're not my dad,' I say quietly, but loud enough for him
to hear.

'No, but he's your stepdad, so that's the next best thing,' Mum
says. 'Besides, we need you to stay home to look after Lilli.'

'But I want to come.' Tonight's demonstration is apparently
going to be the biggest local one yet. The armbands they gave
out earlier have unsettled the Core supporters and people want
to protest before the Trads have a chance to make the rest of the
country wear them.

'Well, you can't.' Darren has finished his meal in about one second. I don't think he means to slam his fork down quite as hard as he does. 'Nothing is worth putting you girls at risk.'

Lilli might lap up this violin talk from him, but it doesn't work with me.

'Then how come it's okay for Mum to go with you?' I ask.

'Because we'll be fine,' Mum says. 'And it's better than us sitting back and doing nothing. We have to stand up to them before things go too far.'

'Dad would let me go,' I say, but even though he's a hard-line Core supporter I'm not sure he would.

'Well your dad's not here,' Mum says, taking my sharp words and throwing them back so they hurt me instead. 'And if he chooses to live hundreds of miles away then he loses the right to make day-to-day decisions.'

Darren stands up. He's usually the one who makes us all wait until everyone's finished eating. Even on those nights when he wants to rush off to the gym.

'Will the protest make a difference?' Lilli asks. She looks so young. When I was twelve all I had to worry about was whether my hair was the right length.

'We've got to try something to make them listen,' Mum says. But she must know that even if we all had megaphones and shouted from the tallest hill, the Trad's ears are so bunged up with their prejudices and their egos that they'll never hear us.

'Don't answer the door to anyone,' Mum says. She's all wrapped up for winter, even though it's only September. Maybe she feels protected underneath her coat and scarf.

'Just stay inside and watch a film together,' Darren says, putting his hand on my arm. He's frightened, I can tell. Underneath a weird energy that's fizzing off him there's something deeper that he's trying to hide.

'Will it be dangerous?' Lilli asks.

'Of course not,' Mum says. 'It's just a peaceful protest to get our voices heard.'

'You said it might be a risk,' I say to Darren.

'We'd just prefer you to stay here and look after Lilli,' he tells me.

'I don't think they'll be expecting so many of us,' Mum laughs, as if she's just going to a party or something.

'They've got guns, Mum,' I say and her smile disappears.

'They only have them to scare us. They won't use them, Ruby,' Darren says.

'How do you know?' Suddenly I don't want my mum to go. I don't even want Darren to go.

'They've got messed up ideas,' Mum says, 'but they're not murderers.'

'Can't you stay here?' Lilli asks as Mum kisses her on the head.

'We have to stand up for what's right,' she says.

'Come on, Kelly, we've got to go,' Darren says and he opens the front door.

'I love you, Mum,' I say, but I'm not sure she hears as she's already walking down the path.

Darren hugs Lilli, but he knows not to try with me. 'We won't be long, but don't stay up if it's late.' And he waves at us as he runs after Mum.

'Right,' I turn to Lilli, my voice too bright. 'Popcorn and a movie?' She looks at me as though she's waiting for the walls around us to crumble into dust. 'They'll be fine, Lils,' I tell her over my shoulder as I walk into the kitchen. 'They'll be back before we know it.'

I get a message from Luke as soon as I open the cupboard.

Dad and I are going to the protest.

I'm not that surprised. His dad's taken him on protest marches since before he could walk. But it makes me feel even more annoyed that Darren won't let me go.

See you there, I text back before I even think about it.

You're coming?

Yes. I'll look out for you.

I close the cupboard and go into the sitting room. Lilli is already curled up on the sofa.

'Change of plans,' I say as casually as I can.

She looks up from her phone.

'You don't want to watch a film?' she asks.

'We're going to the protest.'

'We can't.'

'Of course we can. Our voice is important too.'

'But Mum and Darren said we couldn't.'

'We'll only go for a bit. If we're back before them they won't even know we were there.'

'I could stay here on my own,' Lilli suggests.

'You know you can't. It's too late.'

'Peggy's next door. If anything happens I can call her.'

'She's like a hundred and fifty years old,' I say. 'She's not going to be much good if you pour boiling water down yourself. Or flood the house or something.'

'That's stupid.'

'It's not. It could happen.' I put out my hand to pull her up, but she stays sitting. 'Please, Lils. I really want to go.'

'What if the soldiers are there?'

'They probably don't even know it's happening. But even if they are there, Mum says they won't actually do anything.' I walk into the hallway and hope she'll follow. 'Luke's going to be there.'

Lilli appears within a second. I think she might love him almost as much as I do. 'Is he allowed to go?'

'He's going with his dad.'

'Will we see him?'

'Hopefully.'

'Okay,' she says and already she's looking for her shoes as I put on my coat. I try to ignore the doubt that's pulling at me as she sits on the bottom stair to tie her laces.

'Mum'll kill you if she finds out you've taken me.' Lilli's spinning a bit from the excitement. This is a big deal for her as she never usually does anything she's not meant to.

'She'd kill me if I left you here.'

Lilli jumps up, grabs her coat and hooks her arm through mine. 'Then you're dead either way, aren't you?'

As soon as we're outside, I know it's not a good idea. Our street seems strangely silent. One car drives past then turns the corner at the end. The lamplights are on even though it's not completely dark.

'Are you warm enough?' I ask Lilli and she nods.

Most houses' curtains are closed, but Bob Whittard's are open and he's sitting in his armchair, so I wave to him when he looks up. He doesn't wave back. He doesn't even smile. It feels like a hard line is being drawn down between those who support the government and those who are against it. Surely it's something we can scrub out now, before it gets too deep?

As we get closer to the park there are more people about. They're mostly as silent as we are as they scurry along towards Hebe Hill. There are soldiers too when I told Lilli there probably wouldn't be any. One is standing at the end of

40

Shaw Street, two more along Beck Avenue.

I hold Lilli's hand tight as we take a shortcut through the alley. It's darker in here and has a strange quiet, as though a lid has been put on the world. Ahead, there's the entrance to the park and there are so many people, but I don't know if seeing them all makes me feel safer, or more scared. I don't recognise anyone, but the determination on their faces is all the same.

'Have you texted Luke?' Lilli asks.

'I will when we're in there.' Although I'm not sure now how easy it's going to be to find him.

We go through the park's gate and have to follow everyone along the path. The flower beds either side are still filled with delphiniums, the first flowers Dad taught me to name. Seeing them makes me miss him, so I text to tell him that we're here to protest against the Trads. I think he'll be proud, but I know I won't get a message back soon. I've learned the hard way not to wait for a reply.

From where we are we can see people covering the top of the hill. Someone is holding a megaphone, but their words aren't clear enough yet. I feel better now that we're here. I'm excited more than scared and I think Lilli is too, judging by her wide eyes and smile as she looks around.

'Can you see Mum anywhere?' I ask.

'Shall we hide if we do?'

'Perhaps.' I know Mum would be angry, but maybe she'd

41

be a little bit pleased that we're protesting too.

There's a crowd in front and behind us. I didn't know there were so many Core supporters in our town. They've probably travelled in from a bit further away, but I'm surprised so many people want to show it. I wonder if some of them have come over to our side since the election? Since the government's ideas have got crazier and crazier. I can't imagine that everyone who voted for the Trads will be happy with restricted internet use and having their relationships monitored.

It's almost single file again as we curve around the edge of the playground. I used to spend hours here, being pushed on the swing by Mum and Dad, then me pushing Lilli, then friends pushing each other and being told to leave. There's no one there now. The swings aren't moving, there are no shadows on the slide. Tomorrow there'll be children laughing again, but for now we walk past with hardly a word.

There's more space around us when we get to the hill. Hebe bushes are planted in random clumps for us to walk around. Their colour matches the purple of the Core symbol, so it seems that nature is on our side too. I reach out to touch the flowers. They look a bit like thistles, but they feel like feathers. If it was daytime there'd be tons of bees on them.

'There are lots of people here,' Lilli says, looking up at me.

'How very perceptive of you, Chicken Bones,' I say and she thumps me.

Three men are at the top and they must be standing on some sort of stage. They stick out above everyone. Two of them hold the purple Core Party flag, with its yellow steps going up the middle. The other has the loudspeaker and now we can hear his words. They rumble through the crowd in front of us and light a fire round my bones.

'We won't be forced into silence!' the man shouts. 'We won't be ruled by bigots who love only to hate.' The people around us are even louder now and I start to cheer with them. 'We will champion your rights because each and every one of you has a right to free speech, a right to freedom of movement. A right to freedom!'

I'm glad we came here. It's good to feel a part of this, to feel we might finally make a difference. That things really might change.

'Our rights should be at the core of our society.' His words thunder from him as people cheer again.

I look up into the sky. It's a clear night and stars are beginning to reach out. Thousands and thousands of them watching, looking back at us. It makes me feel part of something even bigger.

'We want to live in a tolerant country!' The man's words jump among us, landing on our hands, our ears, our skin. They skim up to the leaves and I imagine the wind picking them up and taking them to whisper in strangers' ears. To let them see.

Let them believe too. 'A country that does not judge. Does not turn away those who cry for our help. We champion the rights of everyone, regardless of your class, your faith, your sexuality, your roots.' The roar from the crowd is thick enough to touch. My arm stays in the air like everyone else's. 'It's not a solution to cut down those who cry for help. Instead, we will listen. We will care. And we will rebuild our society from the foundation up. We won't cease in our fight to champion the rights for everyone.'

'Champions! Champions!' My voice joins in with the chant, but Lilli stays silent, her arms by her side.

We're getting pushed forwards. More people must be coming from the back.

'Core Party for peace!' the man with the loudspeaker calls above us all.

Suddenly we're pushed so far forward that Lilli stumbles and I only just manage to pull her upright again. The crush is instant and people start to scream.

'It's okay,' I tell Lilli. 'They'll make space.' But it's getting difficult to speak.

People scramble on to the stage and the man with the megaphone falls and disappears. And I see now, through gaps in the shoulders, that there are soldiers with plastic shields and they're driving themselves into the protesters, forcing us together.

'I can't breathe,' Lilli says, as more bodies press into us.

There's yelling and it seems so distant as I lose my grip on Lilli's hand. Everyone is pushing us, pushing everywhere, trying to run, but there's nowhere to move. We're all stuck and more people keep pounding into us and there's nowhere for us to go.

My breath is being squeezed from me.

'Get back,' someone shouts. A woman beside me falls and I try to reach for her, but she's sucked under and trampled on.

'Lilli,' I say, but the word is only a pinch of letters.

Mum. Luke.

My sister has tears in her eyes, but I can't hear her crying.

We're heaved forwards, my feet barely on the ground. My lungs are being crushed and there's not enough air.

I see Lilli lifted, pulled up. A man grabbing her with one arm, pushing her over the heads of others.

'Ruby!' she screams, but I can't see her. My eyes hurt. How can there be so much air above us, just out of reach?

We move forwards. I trip over something soft, but the pressure of the bodies around me keeps me upright. People are shouting, desperate. *Get back. Make space.*

We move as a dying animal, down the side of the playground as people pile over the fence, stumbling and falling. There's screaming as we spill forwards until there's space, enough air now.

'Lilli.' My voice is too quiet. Yet my breathing is easier, just splinters in my lungs now. 'Lilli!' I don't want to be crying, but everywhere there are people shouting and none of them are my sister. The man lifted her up and she's gone.

I'm being pushed further along and I look up as a soldier raises his baton and he brings it down on a man. I hear him hit him, a deadening thump on bones and I know I have to get away from here. But I can't get through, because people are fighting back, charging into the soldiers. I'm stumbling over crushed banners and there's nowhere to hide. And everywhere there are the distorted faces of the soldiers behind their transparent shields. Just their eyes through their helmets and they raise batons and they strike out and I'm too close as panic burns my chest.

Someone in front of me falls, clutching his eyes. A soldier has a spray and I see him grab a woman by her coat and she begs as he holds the can close to her skin. And so I run. Past stumbling bodies, through a cloud of terror, wading through cries I've never heard. I'm at the fence with others and we're clambering over it, someone helping me so I don't fall.

I make it to the alleyway, but I've left my sister behind and my phone is ringing and it's my hands that take it from my pocket and my mum's voice is shouting and I tell her that I don't know where Lilli is. Terror seeps from me into the wall at my back.

'Lilli's here,' I hear my mum say.

She's at home.

I run, the phone in my hand, through the streets I thought I knew, past houses with doors closed to me. I see someone running towards me and I know it's Darren and he reaches me and hugs me so tight.

'You're safe,' he says and I don't know whether it's my lungs, my heart, or my head that hurts as he pulls me towards our home. Where my mum is standing in the doorway and she holds me before I'm even inside and when our front door shuts behind us the relief to be safe is bright.

'Jesus, Ruby,' Darren is shouting.

'You said the protest would be okay.' I can't make sense of the words I want to say.

'I never said that.'

'This isn't helping,' Mum says. 'They're back now.'

'Where's Lilli?' I ask.

'In the sitting room,' Mum tells me.

'She thought she was going to die, Ruby,' Darren says.

'But they're both safe,' Mum glares at him. 'That's the most important thing.'

'We could have lost them.' Darren's voice is still too loud. 'You saw it there, Kelly. You saw what those Trads did. They took a peaceful protest and they turned it into a deathtrap.'

'I'm not going to have this discussion now.' Mum goes into the sitting room and I'm left with Darren in front of me, his anger sharp.

'The soldiers were hitting people,' I tell him. 'But we hadn't done anything wrong.' He steps forward to hug me, but I won't let him. Sirens call in the distance. 'Why did they do it?'

'I don't know,' is all he answers.

CHAPTER THREE

'You told us that you'd had enough and we listened.
Enough of broken families. Enough of soaring crime
rates blighting our country. Enough of our people
hungering for jobs.' – John Andrews, leader of the
Traditional Party

I'm awake before my alarm clock and watch the sun start as a
square of light in the corner of my ceiling, until it spreads across
my room. I hold out my hands and stretch my fingers as far as
they can go and then count them, slowly, feeling the sound of
each number on my tongue.

I breathe in until I can't any more. Hold my breath. Hold it.
Hold it. And imagine what it'd be like to not be able to let it out.
My lungs would be crushed until I close my eyes and drift away.

The door opens and I gasp for air.

'Darren doesn't want us to go to school,' Lilli says. She

walks across my room, lifts the corner of the duvet and gets into bed. I shuffle closer to the wall, but still her feet are cold against my legs. She sleeps with them outside her duvet. She likes to face the bogeyman straight on. 'But Mum says we have to go.'

I lean over her to turn on my phone.

'What do you want to do?' I ask her.

'Stay here. But Mum says we can't.'

On cue, the door opens and Mum comes in, the purple band clear on her arm.

'Up you get,' she says, opening the curtains so roughly I'm surprised she doesn't pull them down. 'You can't be late.' As though everything is normal. That life hasn't just spun away into a black hole.

'Lilli doesn't want to go,' I say.

'There are a lot of things none of us want to do,' Mum says. 'But we have to.' She's sorting through the pile of clothes on my chair, finding my school clothes. 'This could've done with a wash.' She holds up my sweatshirt.

'Are you going to work?' I ask. Lilli and I don't move from the comfort of my bed.

'Of course. It's an ordinary day, Ruby.'

'How can it be?'

'It has to be,' she tells me.

My phone beeps, but Mum grabs it before I have a chance.

'I'll take this downstairs. You can have it when you're dressed,' she says and she's out of the room before I can challenge her.

'Just for the record,' Darren says. 'I don't think any of you should go.' He's standing next to the fridge, both hands round his mug of coffee.

'You're not helping,' Mum says, as she grabs her car keys from the side.

'And you're not thinking straight, Kelly,' Darren tells her. Mum stops and stares at him.

'The only people not thinking straight are those bloody Trads, Darren. If you want to take out your frustration on anyone, take it out on them.'

'And get a bullet through my head for my trouble?' Darren's words snap out of him and make everything go still.

'So we just crawl into our holes like they want us to?' Mum says. 'Don't go to work, don't go to school, just stay in our homes and wither away until they completely destroy our country? Is that what we should do?'

'I don't know any more,' Darren says.

'Well, I do,' Mum says, wrapping her scarf round her neck. 'School is the safest place for them.'

'How do you figure that out?' I haven't seen Darren look this furious in ages.

'The Trads are going to be on their best behaviour after last night,' Mum says. 'They may have managed to twist the truth about the protest, but they'll be hard pushed to keep people on their side if they hurt kids in a school.'

Darren visibly winces.

'What do you want to do, Ruby?' he asks me.

I look at them both standing there and memories of the protest whittle dread into me. But I know I'll be frightened anywhere.

'I want to go,' I say. Maybe Mum's right and we'll be safer there. Or perhaps I've just conditioned myself to say the opposite to Darren.

'That's sorted then,' Mum says, as she storms out of the room and I follow her. Darren comes into the hallway.

'At least let me drive you and Lilli there,' he says to me.

'If you have to,' I say.

Mum grabs her bag from the hall table before she opens the front door. Something makes her stop still.

'What is it?' Darren pulls the door wide open. Someone has painted a giant *C* across the wood, going from the top all the way to the bottom.

'Who's done that?' Lilli asks.

Mum shakes her head in that way she does when she's trying to be strong.

'I'd hazard a guess it'll be the Traditionals,' she says.

'Why on our door?'

'I bet it'll be on the door of every Core household,' Darren says.

'I don't want to go to school,' Lilli says quietly.

'You don't have to,' Darren says before Mum can speak. 'I'll stay here with you.'

Mum nods. 'Okay,' she says, less determined now.

'Ruby?' Darren looks at me. Part of me wants to stay here with Lilli, to stay safe behind the walls of our home where no one can touch us, where I don't have to wear this stupid purple band for everyone to see. But Mum is going to work. And I want to see Luke.

'I'm still going to school.' I need something to distract me from the nightmare our country seems to have stumbled into.

'Could we clean the paint away later?' Lilli asks Darren.

'I doubt they've made it that easy for us,' Mum says as she steps outside.

I've never known our school to feel like this, as though even the walls are watching and judging. And there's a strange link between all of us wearing Core bands. People I've never spoken to before smile and nod at me in the corridor. And people who I thought were vague friends look away.

Never before in my life has it been awkward between Sara

and me. But now a strange, invisible wall has been stacked up between us.

'Hey,' I say.

'Hey.'

And that's it. The scariest thing in my life happened to me yesterday, but I can't even talk to her about it. She should be the first person I want to tell about the protest. She'd be able to put it right somehow, find a way to even laugh today, but she seems distant. I can't tell if it's because she doesn't want to know, or is scared to ask if I was there.

'Did your parents tell you not to talk to me?' I ask, attempting a smile.

'No.' She shakes her head.

Mr Hart comes in late, his purple band strapped to the outside of his jacket. He doesn't have to tell us to be quiet. We already are. He's halfway through the register when James puts up his arm, a green band clear to see.

'Sir,' he says. 'Doesn't what happened last night prove something?'

'And what exactly is that, James?' Mr Hart's expression is cold. If he wasn't a teacher I think he might thump him.

'That the Cores are out of control and violent. That if they came into power it'd be a joke.'

Violent? It was a peaceful protest until the Trad soldiers waded in.

'I don't find anything to laugh about,' Mr Hart says, 'when people have ended up seriously injured.'

'All through faults of their own,' James says.

We weren't at fault. We were only there protesting – doing nothing else.

'So you believe everything you read on the internet, do you?' Mr Hart says.

'Those riots were real. There's no way they were staged by the Trads.'

'From what I understand, they doctored the footage,' Mr Hart says.

'Doctored?' Ashwar asks.

'Edited it,' Mr Hart tells her. 'The news only showed a half truth. Probably not even that.'

'They're not going to broadcast a blatant lie,' Ashwar says.

'Aren't they?' Mr Hart glares at her. 'You've all heard enough about fake news.'

'I know what happened,' I say. 'Because I was there.' I feel every single person in the classroom turn to look at me. My skin blazes red.

'The Cores faked those images,' someone shouts from the back.

'They didn't.' My voice is shaking. I don't want to remember, I don't want to ever be there again, but I have to let them know the truth. 'Everyone was calm, but then the soldiers started attacking us.'

'You provoked them,' James says.

'We didn't,' I say, feeling stronger now. 'There wasn't a riot or anything. The Trads started it and we were crushed.'

James claps his hands slowly. 'Nice one, Westy. You're pretty good at twisting real events.'

'That's enough,' Mr Hart says.

'Oh, so now *you're* trying to silence the truth?' James says. 'I'm simply pointing out the lies, but you won't let me have my say?'

'What I won't let,' Mr Hart says, anger spinning around him, 'is a bully stay in my class.'

'Are you sending me out for voicing an opinion?' James smirks. 'An opinion that is, in fact, the truth?'

'I'm simply giving you a warning.'

'I wonder what the Trads would think if they found out a teacher was calling them liars, sir,' James continues. 'That you're accusing them of editing footage of the protests. I reckon they'd be quite interested to know.'

'This conversation is ending right now,' Mr Hart tells him. 'I've a register to finish.' He's trying to stay calm, but his jaw is tense. I think his hands are shaking too. 'Jermain,' he says, glancing up.

'Yes, sir.'

'Lucy.'

'Yes.'

Sara nudges my arm. 'Were you really there?' she whispers.

'Yes.'

'Was it frightening?'

'Yes.' I can see the real Sara in her eyes. The worry for me, the confusion. 'Can we hang out at break?' I ask. 'We could go to the oak tree?'

She doesn't smile, but at least she nods.

'I think what James has forgotten to point out, sir,' Ashwar says, as soon as the register is finished. 'Is that the Core supporters started riots this morning too and they got completely out of control.'

'They were a direct response,' Mr Hart says, 'to the unprovoked attack of citizens last night.'

'It was self protection,' Ashwar says.

'The Trads weren't under any threat,' I say. But it's barely loud enough for anyone to hear.

'What I don't understand, Ashwar,' Conor says. 'Is how come your family vote for them?' He's swinging back on his chair, but Mr Hart doesn't pick him up on it. 'You're Muslim, right?'

'None of this is about religion.' Ashwar's eyes are steel on him.

'No. But some of it's about race,' Conor says. 'By tightening the borders, they're basically saying they only want Brits living here. If they'd done that before your parents or grandparents or whoever arrived here you wouldn't have been allowed in.'

Conor lands the front legs of his chair heavily on the ground. 'How can that be okay?'

'I don't have to agree with everything they stand for,' Ashwar says.

'But it's a pretty major thing,' Conor carries on. Mr Hart watches from the front of the classroom. His arms are crossed, but his Core band is still showing.

'It's worth it for the other policies,' Ashwar says. 'Did you know that that seventy per cent of A and E departments are taken up with drunk people at weekends? Seventy per cent, Conor. How can that be a good use of public money?'

'There are other ways to deal with it than banning drinking in public and increasing the legal age,' Conor says.

'Are there?' Ashwar looks around. 'No other government has wanted to tackle it and see where it's got our country. Nothing is getting better. It's getting worse. We need a change and we might not like all of the Trad's policies, but it's a small price to pay if the rest of it is working.'

'Is it?' Mr Hart asks. 'As Conor brought up the subject of immigration, let's talk about that.'

Cameron yawns loudly from the back.

'Am I boring you, Cameron?' Mr Hart asks him.

'Just a bit,' Cameron says and people around him laugh.

'I can see nothing boring in people being forced from their homes.' Anger is beginning to tick through Mr Hart. 'They've lost everything: their communities, their families, their way of life. They don't *want* to leave everything they love. They don't *want* to trek hundreds of miles carrying everything they own on their backs. They don't *want* to put their children in blow-up dinghies and set out across an ocean that might drown them all. They do it because they have to.'

'But what about our country?' James challenges him. 'If the Core Party had it their way we'd let them come here and wreck *our* way of lives and *our* homes. That's not exactly right, is it?'

'These people don't wreck our homes, James. They actually boost our economy, but that never really gets reported, does it?'

'Perhaps because they don't boost it enough,' James says.

'So what would your solution be?' I ask James.

'We should just send them back.'

Send them back? As if they're objects, not people.

'I would hope,' Mr Hart says, 'that if the roles were reversed and it was our homes and families blown apart, that we would find compassion somewhere. That people would help us and let us in.'

The bell cuts him off. There's a longer pause than normal before we all get up.

I get a message on my phone as I walk out of the classroom. *People are believing the lies*, Luke texts.

I know, I reply. *I'm scared*.

Don't be.

Meet at oak at break? Sara coming too.

Okay.

Someone smacks the back of my head. It's hard enough not to be a joke, but there are too many people pushing in front and behind me to know who it was. Shoulders, elbows squeeze down the corridor to first lesson. It's the same as always but everything has changed. The crush of it unwinds memories of last night and although I can breathe now my lungs remember. The splinters still thread through them and I have to push past people, get out of the way, to reach a space where I feel safe.

It's starting to rain a bit as I walk to the oak tree. The sky feels tight, dripping down headaches the way it does before a storm. I think Sara might use it as an excuse not to turn up, until I see her legs sticking out from where she's leaning against the trunk the other side.

'You're here,' I say when I get to her.

'I said I would be.' She doesn't look angry, but there's an edge to her words.

'How are things?' I sit opposite her, cross-legged. The leaves above us are umbrella enough for now.

'A bit odd,' she says. She picks a blade of grass and its roots come up too.

'I used to think those were a fairy's legs,' I say, pointing to them.

Sara laughs. 'You always were a bit strange.'

I want to tell her that there's a part of me that still believes it, but she's shredding them apart already.

I hate this awkward feeling that's sitting between us now.

'Luke's going to be late,' I say. 'Aldridge is having a go at him about homework.'

'Okay,' Sara says. And the wall goes up again. Somehow I have nothing to say to a friend who I can usually talk with all day and night.

I watch the rain falling.

'You don't have to support the Trads you know,' I say, 'just because your parents do.'

'Same back to you,' she says.

'But I believe in what the Core Party says.'

'All of it?'

'Most of it.'

'So why can't people believe in most of what the Trads say?'

'Because they're wrong.'

'So says you.'

'And so says you up until recently.'

'Can't I change my mind?'

'I don't think you have,' I say. 'I think you're supporting the Trads because you're scared.'

'Scared?' Sara does a laugh that isn't really one.

'Yes. Like we all are. Since the soldiers came with the guns.'

She pulls up a clump of grass this time. Too many fairy legs to count.

'You know they now say they're going to really limit our internet.'

'Mum says that's good. We can actually chat like in the olden days.'

'I'm serious, Sara.'

'Well, what would the Core Party do? Make us use it until our brains explode?'

'They don't think banning the internet is the solution to cutting depression. They want to do active things, like put more money into mental health.'

'Can we talk about something else?' Sara asks. I know she feels the fracture that's opening up between us.

'But what about the Trads putting up the age of consent?'

'It's to cut teenage pregnancies,' Sara says, but I know her heart isn't in it.

'More like it's to cut all the fun from our life.'

Sara breathes out as though she's fed up with me, fed up with it all. 'Can't you tell me something I want to hear about?'

'Like what?'

'Like why is grass green?' she says. 'If the bottom bit in the earth is white, how come the top bit is a different colour?' Sara crosses her legs and we sit opposite each other with our knees almost touching. She's like my mirror. 'Because surely, if they're exposed to the sun all the time, they should be bleached-white. Or at least a bit sucked-dry yellow from the wind and everything.'

'I do actually know the answer,' I say. Sara's laugh is genuine this time. It makes me want to hug her tight and tell her that we're going to be okay.

'I thought you might, mega-plant-brain.'

'It's not really green,' I tell her. 'It's the chlorophyll in them. It absorbs all the other colours and has no use for the green so sort of chucks it out again.'

'Of course it does.'

I hold Sara's hands, one and then the other. 'I'm not going to let all this Trad and Core stuff make us fall out,' I say.

'Nor am I,' Sara replies. She puts up her pinky finger and hooks it through mine as we used to do at primary school.

The thunder is so sudden that we scream. We're laughing as we jump up and grab our bags. And I don't care that the rain really starts on us as we run back to school, because I've got my best friend by my side, our fingers still linked.

'Love you, Starry,' I shout.

'Love you right back, Rudey,' Sara laughs, wiping under her eyes so that the rain can't paint mascara down her cheeks.

'Do you want a lift, Luke?' Darren asks him.

'I'm all right, thanks.'

'You'll get soaked,' Darren tells him.

'I like the rain,' Luke smiles. There's a soldier close by so I know he won't want to kiss me, but he squeezes my hand. 'See you tomorrow.'

'Yeah.'

'Get in, Ruby,' Darren says through the window. 'I'm blocking the traffic.'

But it feels wrong to just leave Luke like this. Since we've started going out, I don't think we've ever said goodbye without at least a hug. So I lean in to kiss him, just quickly, but enough to feel his lips on mine.

A car horn behind us ruins it.

'Ruby,' Darren shouts.

I don't bother to check if a soldier has noticed us before I get into the car.

'Not your wisest move,' Darren says as he starts the engine.

'They can't lock me up for kissing my boyfriend.'

'You might just have to play along with them for a bit,' Darren says, as he starts to drive. 'Until things settle down.'

In the mirror I can see Luke walking away, his bag on his back.

'What if I don't want to?' I ask.

'They've got guns, Ruby,' Darren says. And it's enough, that one small word, to pull me right back into reality.

CHAPTER FOUR

'We're not just a party of words, but of actions. We
will take back the reins of our destiny. We will fix
our nation.' – John Andrews, leader of the
Traditional Party

'Ruby.' Someone is shaking my shoulder. 'You've got to wake
up.' It's my mum's voice, but I turn away from her, curl the
duvet closer to me and feel my dream try to find me again.
'Ruby.' She sounds urgent this time, enough to make me open
my eyes. It's still dark.

'What is it?' I'm not late for school. It's definitely still night-
time outside.

'You've got to get dressed.'

'Why?'

My bedroom door kicks open and a soldier stands in the light
from the landing. My heartbeat blocks my breathing.

'It's okay,' Mum says, but her hand on my shoulder is shaking. I see now how she's already wearing her clothes and her coat. 'I'll help you.' She stands up and looks straight at the soldier. 'You don't have to watch.' Her voice is calm, before she walks across my room and pushes the door. The soldier moves his foot forwards so she can't shut it completely, but at least he turns his face away.

'I don't want to get up.' If I lie down and close my eyes then none of this is happening.

'You have to,' Mum says, pulling the duvet from me. The shock of the cold wakes me fully.

'What's going on?' I whisper.

'I don't know. They just came to the house and said we have to go.' She turns on my lamp. The light makes me blink. Makes this all too real.

'Where's Lilli?' I ask.

'Darren is with her now.'

'But she chose a Trad band,' I say. 'They can't make her go anywhere when she's not even a Core.'

'We are, though,' Mum says calmly. 'And it seems that's enough.'

'And you're going to let them do this?' I grab Mum's hand as she opens my drawer.

'What are our options?' she asks. I don't know whether she's going to shout at me or cry.

My arms feel empty of everything but fear as I take off my pyjamas and pull on my underwear and Mum passes me my jeans.

'Where are they taking us?' I ask.

'I don't know.'

'And for how long?'

'I don't know, Ruby.' If she wasn't whispering she'd definitely be shouting at me.

She passes me my black T-shirt, but I open my cupboard and pull out my new pink one and my white hoodie and grab my trainers.

'You can bring a small bag,' Mum says.

The soldier pushes open the door.

'Time's up,' he says.

Mum takes the bag from my chair and starts stuffing clothes inside it. I pick up the charm bracelet Sara gave me and check I'm still wearing my new necklace from Luke. I reach for my make-up and purse and put them in the bag too.

'Don't forget the armband that you chose,' the soldier says. I look up at Mum and she nods, passing me the purple strip of material to pull up over my sleeve. I feel like I've trapped it over my mouth instead.

'We're okay, Ruby,' Mum says. She puts her hand on my shoulder and I know she wants to steady me, but I can see everything she's thinking in her eyes. 'Here.' And she picks up my phone from next to the bed. I put it in my pocket before we leave the room.

Lilli and Darren are waiting at the bottom of the stairs. My sister's face is stained with shock. On her arm is the Traditional band, bare and gloating. I'm trying to find something to say to her, anything to make her less afraid, but I know all that'll come out is lies.

'Give me your phones,' the soldier says.

Darren looks at him steadily. 'I need it for work,' he says.

'Give me your phones,' the man repeats, putting out his gloved hand.

My mum takes hers from her bag, Lilli gets hers from her jacket and they put them in his waiting palm.

'Yours?' The soldier nods at me.

'I don't have one.' I stare at him, but he simply adjusts the strap of his gun.

'Give him your phone,' Darren tells me.

I need to text Luke. I've got to tell him what's going on.

'Do as he says, Ruby.' Mum speaks quietly.

I feel hate more than anything as I take out my phone. I want to slam it into the soldier so hard that I break his bones. Instead, he curls his fingers round my hand before I have the chance to grab it back.

'Next time,' he says, 'do things the first time you're asked. We're going to instil discipline into this country, even if it kills us.'

There's a coach waiting outside our house. There are no lights inside it, but I can see the shapes of people. It's all too quiet. We should be kicking, screaming, saying we don't want to go, but those guns silence us.

Mum climbs the steps first and Lilli goes next. She looks like a little child again, with sleep still ragged in her hair, and I want to pull her back and take her away from here to keep her safe. But I don't. Instead I follow so close behind her that she has no choice but to keep going into the coach.

I recognise some of the people sitting in the rows. Mick Alum, who used to cut Mum's hair. Ron and Saskia from a few doors down with their three young kids. One's only a baby, strapped to Saskia's front. Everyone's faces are the same, painted with disbelief, as though we should all blink and wake up.

The doors of the coach close. Mum sits with Lilli, so Darren and I sit across the aisle from them. I'm closest to the window and can see our closed front door, the scrawled *C* painted across it. Darren puts his hand on top of mine and even though I need him to calm me I yank my hand away.

I stare out at the houses and streets I know so well. Behind the windows and doors people are sleeping. They don't know that we're being taken. I want to bang so hard on the glass that it smashes. I want to scream so loud that I drag every single person from their dreams. But I can't and it's this that squeezes my lungs again so tight that I only have space for tiny breaths.

'I'll look after you,' Darren says. 'I'm sure we'll be back here before you know it.'

I won't look at him. I don't want to see in his eyes what he really believes.

The coach stops and I watch as an elderly couple are led from their house. They get on the coach and talk loudly as they walk down the aisle. They're either genuinely unafraid or they're good at pretending.

'Good evening,' the man smiles, as they make their way to the back.

'This is a bit of an unwelcome surprise,' the old woman says, before I hear them shuffle into their seats. They've somehow brought a bit of light with them. There's humour lapping around their words and it makes me feel human. And strong.

When we stop again, I see a soldier banging on a door daubed with a C. He waits, bangs again and a man opens it in just his pyjama bottoms. He has shock and terror sliding over his face as he steps back inside.

It's only a few minutes before he reappears with a woman by him, her bleached-blonde hair still shaped by her pillow. He keeps his arm round her as they walk to the coach and somehow I'm now one of the shadows watching as they come up the steps, bewildered.

'There are places here,' the old woman calls from the back. 'You're very welcome to them.'

They walk towards her, their fingers clasping hard to each seat they pass.

'That's it,' I hear the old woman encourage. 'Nearly there.' And I wonder if she realises that this nightmare is real.

We stop for a woman with two children. She carries one of them, a sleepy-looking boy with his legs wrapped round her waist, arms gripped tight round her neck. The other child is crying as she's dragged along. She's wearing her pyjamas under her coat. When the soldier picks her up to bring her to the coach she kicks out and Darren and I stare as the soldier holds the girl from him, as though she's stinking rubbish.

Her screaming is louder when she's put in the coach. It's as though her mouth is actually in my head, the noise taking up all the space.

'Shh, Amalie, shh,' her mother says. The girl sits down in the aisle and I hear her start to sob now.

'Get her up,' the soldier says behind them, as the coach doors close.

'Come on, Amalie.' The mother's voice is angry now, as her other child clings to her.

'Move her,' the soldier says, flecks of panic walking up his words.

My mum stands. Darren tries to grab her, but she ignores

him and goes to bend down next to the little girl.

'Come on,' I hear her say. 'I've got two daughters I'd like you to meet.' The sobbing becomes stilted. 'They're tired too,' Mum continues, 'but we'll sit you in a seat and when we stop you can play with them. Okay?' When she stands up, she's holding the girl in her arms.

They walk towards us, the mother behind, the girl's tears caught in hiccups now.

'This is Ruby,' Mum says.

'Hi,' I say, knowing that my smile isn't right.

'And Lilli.'

The little girl nods.

'You can sit with your mummy back here,' Mum tells her. 'And you can sleep for a bit more.' They're too far back for me to see now. 'It's a bit silly being in a coach in the middle of the night, isn't it?' she laughs lightly.

'Thank you,' the other woman says.

When my mum sits back down again the forced brightness drops from her face completely. Darren reaches across the aisle to hold her hand. He doesn't let go.

My body wants to sleep, but I can't. I keep wanting to message Luke but remember they've taken my phone. I lean my head on the window and there's the relentless sound of the wheels. Sometimes someone coughs, breaking up the muffled noises of breathing. The fear that floats above all our heads sinks down to push into my stomach. It stays there, digging deeper.

Darren is staring past me through the glass. The motorway is dark apart from the street lamps dotted along the side. And the few other cars that are around to overtake us.

'Where do you think we're going?' I whisper.

'I'm not sure,' he says, his eyes fixed on the trees that rise up on the bank outside. The smudge of them dips, grows, breaks apart. It's too dark to tell what type they are. They're clumped together like we are. They're just trees. We're just Core supporters. 'But I think it's possible that the Trads are taking us to a place where we can't cause trouble.'

'Are they allowed to?'

'They're allowed to do anything,' Darren says. 'They're the ones in power.'

'But they shouldn't be.'

'You know that and I know that,' Darren says. 'But until enough people open their eyes to what they're really like then we might not stand a chance in hell.'

'That's not what you said before and it's not what my Dad told me. He says there's enough of us to make a difference.'

Darren looks at me. He seems a hundred years older than he was this morning.

'That was before John Andrews got voted in, Ruby,' he says quietly. 'Now everything's changed.'

*

Outside the coach windows it starts to get lighter. There are still clouds stacked on top of each other, but they turn from black, to grey, to dirty-white. I don't see the sun until it's pushing its way between them, almost halfway up the sky.

Lilli has leaned over so far that she's lying in Mum's lap. Her eyes are closed, but I don't think she's asleep. I can see we're going past the outskirts of a city, bricks upon bricks holding in so many lives I know nothing about. I wonder how many of them are Core supporters. Have coaches stolen them in the night too?

We overtake a car and I look down at the man driving. His hands are on the steering wheel and his coat is on the seat next to him. I'm close enough to see a ring on his finger, but he doesn't look up. He doesn't notice us.

'Help,' I mouth to him, but he doesn't see. And then he's gone.

We're driven even further north. Buildings almost entirely disappear, replaced by hills. Mist hangs out of reach of the grass, touching gorse bushes and alder trees.

'A deer,' I hear someone say from in front of us.

'Can we go and see it?' A child's voice.

'Not right now.'

The deer doesn't move as we pass. Maybe it thinks that if it stays still then we won't see it. That it'll be safe.

74

The old man from the back walks past us down the aisle, swaying into people a bit as he steadies himself.

'Excuse me,' I hear him say, but there's no reply. From here, if I sit up straight, I can just see his face with the grey hat on his head. 'My wife and I weren't told to bring food with us. Could we stop somewhere to buy something for breakfast?'

'We're not stopping,' the soldier replies.

'It won't take long,' the man continues. I'm amazed how he can keep his face so kind. 'Just a service station, so we can get a sandwich or something. A cup of tea.'

'Sit down,' the soldier says.

'But my wife is hungry.'

The old man might not look frightened but the tension hovering above us all thickens.

'Just go back to your seat,' I hear Darren whisper so quietly that I must be the only person to hear it.

The soldier stands looking down at the man.

'Don't you understand English?' he asks.

'I understand English perfectly,' the man says, his warm smile disappearing. 'I'm beginning to think that it's you who doesn't understand.'

The soldier grabs the man's collar, pulls his face close to his own. 'Give me your name.'

'Mr Jesenska,' the man says and he's frightened now.

'Get off him,' the old woman screams from the back.

Darren jumps up to stop her as she tries to run to the front.

'No,' he says. 'This won't help.'

'I'm fine,' Mr Jesenska says, as he pulls himself from the soldier's grasp. 'I'm finished here.' He doesn't rush as he walks back. He nods at Darren. 'Thank you.' Before he takes his wife's hand. 'We're fine Violette.' And doesn't say another word as they sit down again.

It feels different in here suddenly. We had seemed a bit more settled, but now it's all changed. That fog of confusion is back. And I'm hungry, but it's not just that making my stomach so painful. I want to curl up with a hot-water bottle on it. I want to be back in my bed, the curtains closed so I can start this day again and make it different.

'You okay?' Darren asks, tapping my arm.

'What do you think?' I reply. Mum glares at me, but I don't care. Right now, I genuinely, really don't care, because someone has taken over our world and shaken it so violently that all the pieces have broken off and are floating down again so wrong and I don't know when they're going to be put right.

'I'm hungry,' Lilli says to Mum. It's way past when we normally eat breakfast, but I'm more thirsty than anything. Mum looks in her bag, but all she has is half a packet of salted peanuts.

'Better than nothing,' Darren says.

'Do you have a drink?' I ask.

'No. I've only got these,' Mum says, pouring a small pile into Lilli's palm.

'Will they make me more thirsty?' I ask.

'You need to eat,' Mum tells me, passing them across the aisle so I can have a few. It's funny how normal they look, sitting in my hand. If I squint, I could even be eating snacks on a school trip.

I'm feeling sick, so I suck the first peanut. The salt is sharp against the roof of my mouth and I was right about it making me want a drink. My tongue almost sticks to it. I try not to crunch it as I look out of the window and count the trees to try to distract me, but my teeth bite into it before I can stop them.

I eat the last ones without stopping.

Outside now there are huge hills that might even qualify as mountains. A river runs at the bottom of one, but it's like torture seeing all that water there, unable to drink it. I heard once that the mind is so powerful that if you think something enough it's like it actually happens. So I force myself to look at the water as it moves over the rocks. I kneel down next to it and put my hand into it. I can feel the cold, really feel it, wet on my skin, as I scoop it up and drink it. But when it gets to my mouth it evaporates.

I thump the seat in front of me and thump it again.

'Don't,' Darren says, holding my arm down.

'I need a drink,' I tell him.

'They won't get you one.'

'I don't care.' I glare at him. My stomach hurts, my head hurts, the saliva in my mouth feels like glue.

'Well, I do,' Darren says.

I yank my arm from him and chew on the silence instead.

The coach finally pulls off the motorway. It winds its way along smaller roads. The hills are closer to us now and they calm me somehow. The packed earth and stones, how they're so solid and immovable.

Someone behind us is sick. The smell sticks to me and makes bile tick at my own throat. I wait for us all to start, but no one else does. I suppose none of us have much food inside us, since we missed breakfast and there's no sign of lunch. The children on the coach are strangely silent, but a baby is crying, the sound of it grating around me.

I try to think of something else, but all that's in my mind now is Luke at school. How he would've waited for me at our spot this morning, probably right until first lesson started and then he would've texted me and I didn't reply. Will he think I'm ignoring him or will he know something is wrong? I put my head on the window again and let myself cry, because what if he thinks I've left without even saying goodbye?

And Sara? What will she think? Then there are arms around me and I know it's Mum.

'Shh,' she says, kissing my hair. She pulls me away from the window and I curl into her. And I let her rock me, back to my place of safety, back to my childhood. I hold on to her and for the first time in a long time, I don't want her to let go.

The coach stops next to a tall fence and I stare at the lines of barbed wire stretched in layers around the top of it.

'Where the hell's this?' Darren's sitting next to Lilli now, holding tight to her hand.

'An old army barracks, or something,' Mum says.

'Why does it look like a prison, then?' I ask.

A gate opens and I hold my breath as we drive inside. On either side of us there are big derelict buildings. We go past the rows and rows of blocked-up windows. There's overgrown grass in front of them, broken paving slabs spitting up weeds.

'What are we doing here?' I ask Mum.

'I'm not sure yet.' She's got that look she has when she's only half listening to me, as though she doesn't even realise she's speaking.

'Look,' Lilli says, pointing out of their window. I sit up high enough to look out of the front. There are five other coaches like ours.

'That's an awful lot of Core supporters in one place.' Darren smiles now. 'I'm not sure they'll be able to keep us here long without a struggle.'

'Are they going to make us stay the night?' Lilli asks.

'I'll try everything to make sure they don't,' Darren says. I feel better now, seeing the other coaches. Maybe he's got a point and that safety in numbers is a good thing.

A soldier stands at the front of our coach. I try to imagine him without his gun and his uniform. He's just a normal man, underneath it all, nothing to be afraid of. Mum's face says different, though.

'You're all to line up outside,' he shouts. 'We need to do name checks and sign you in.'

'Sign us in?' I look to Mum, but she's staring straight ahead.

'We'd like some food first,' Mr Jesenska calls from the back.

'We'll feed you in due time,' the soldier says.

'*Feed us in due time*,' Mum imitates quietly.

'The children are hungry,' a woman shouts.

'Enough talking.' The soldier's voice hammers down the complaints.

People start to leave and we get up to follow. I pull my bag over my shoulder and try to forget the hunger pains burrowing into my stomach. I thought I'd be pleased to be getting off the coach, but as I get closer to the front, a feeling of dread grabs my ankles until I can't move.

'Come on, Ruby,' Mum says from behind me. She has to almost push me down the steps.

At the bottom, a guard stands next to a table piled high with

80

bags. He has his empty hand stretched out towards me.

'I want to keep my bag,' I say.

'Hand it over.'

'Just do as he asks, Ruby,' Mum says.

I don't want to, but I have to. I throw my bag at the guard and his hands are on it before he adds it to the mound.

'Go over there by that wall,' he says and Mum is quick to give him her bag so that she can stay with me.

'They'll give them back later,' she mutters and I have to believe her.

Darren looks at us as we walk across what must've once been an exercise yard. There are still random poles sunk into the ground, two of them have the Traditionals' flag held up between them. I turn away from it and instead see the length of high-up bars that make my arms hurt just looking at them. The brick wall has iron hooks sticking out of it, so it's difficult to lean back on.

'This is absurd,' Mr Jesenska says, walking slowly with his wife. This close to him, I can see the wisps of his steel-grey hair underneath his hat.

'These Trads will get a shock at the next election,' Mrs Jesenska says. 'You'll see. The young will come through and vote a different way to stop this nonsense.'

'Hurry up,' a soldier shouts.

'We'll go in our own time, thank you,' Mrs Jesenska says.

The soldier looks stunned. People disobeying them clearly wasn't part of their plan. He grabs her by the shoulder and makes her look right at him.

'No,' he says. 'In here you'll go in *our* time.'

'Get your hands off my wife,' Mr Jesenska says, but the soldier stays gripping her. He's hurting an old woman and it feels too wrong. As though we've stepped over invisible tracks into a strange new reality, one that's twisted unsteady and nothing's as it should be.

'We want a society that knows how to be obedient,' the soldier says, bending down so close to Mrs Jesenska that she must feel his breath. 'So when we say jump, you jump. Do you understand?'

'Yes.' She puts her hand on her husband to calm him and I see how thin her skin is, raised veins running over fragile bones. The soldier pushes her into the line. Something tells me not to look at them any more. Look straight ahead and if I want some food soon, just do as we're told.

We wait. I can't remember ever being this hungry or thirsty. I don't know what's worse – the pain in my stomach or my mouth that feels so dry I swear it's been turned into paper.

A child begins to wail. With no warning, it's from nothing to full-scale crying. The soldiers tense. The eyes of the one nearest me overflow with sudden panic.

'Make it stop,' one of them shouts.

There are gentle, soothing words further down the line, but the child's cries still carve into the air. They've taken our bags, there's nothing anyone can give the mum to help.

My feet start to hurt. And I'm tired. My head is stuffed with lack of sleep. I try closing my eyes for minutes at a time and open them quickly, hoping I'm at home. But I'm not. I'm here and in front of me, stretched like witches' skin between two poles, is the Traditional flag, its red slash glaring at us.

I lean towards Mum. 'Why's nothing happening?' I whisper.

'I don't know.'

'Shh,' Darren warns us. Normally I'd chuck him the evil eye, but I daren't barely move my head.

Eventually, a man comes out of the building opposite. He looks different to the rest. His green uniform is a bit darker, with red stripes on his shoulder, and he's definitely got some sort of authority. He's about the same age as my dad, but there's no way they'd be friends. This man has got darkness in him. He stops in front of us and I try to slow my heartbeats and keep my breathing normal. I don't know much about what they want from us, but I know not to show that I'm afraid.

'We're going to register everyone,' he shouts. 'Once we've processed you all, we'll provide you with food.'

'*Processed*. Like meat,' a man murmurs.

'They're going to make us stay here?' I hear someone ask.

'No talking,' the soldier nearest us shouts, so forcibly that his

83

face spatters red. If that happens to a teacher in class it sets Sara and me off, but now I'm a million miles from laughing.

And I feel a million miles from Sara. Will she have any idea where we are? Did anyone see the coaches leave? Or did we just look like a bunch of tourists travelling through the night? I reach my fingers over the bracelet she gave me and find one of the charms. From the shape I can tell it's the paint brush, which Sara chose because it reminded her of Luke. Is she in school now, the Trad band on her arm?

The line finally starts to move. Mum keeps hold of my hand. I'd never have let her at home, but right now I need it. If I can't have Luke then I want my mum.

'Do you think they'll bring Dad here?' I whisper.

'Shh,' she says. She's got a strange look on her face that I've never seen before. A thin layer of distress laid over her skin. Does she know more about what's going on than I do?

It's starting to rain. Not heavy or anything, but enough to feel it. I tip up my head and open my mouth, hoping to catch some of the water, but it only makes me feel more mad as I'm so desperate for a drink. It just jumps these stupid little dots on my tongue.

'I forgot my coat,' I hear someone behind us say. Looking down the line I see two people in slippers. I doubt anyone was thinking straight when they woke us in the night.

We move forwards some more as the rain gets a bit heavier. Mum puts up my hood as though I'm a child. Her coat hasn't got one, but she brought her scarf and she wraps it over her head like a crazy old lady. I don't mean for it to make me laugh, but the noise is out of me before I can breathe it back in.

'Shh,' she says, as she grabs my arm. 'Stop it,' she whispers harshly. But I can't. A wave of it holds on to the back of my nerves and pushes it out of my mouth.

'Quiet!' a soldier shouts, but I'm doubled over so I can't see which one. My hunger joins with the laughter and I've never felt pain in my stomach like it. It should make me cry but I can't stop laughing.

'Ruby.' Mum is trying to make me stand up, but I hear Lilli suddenly laugh, all that worry bursting out of her in a happy sound.

Something hits me on the back so hard that I fall straight on to the ground. Bright terror slams into me.

'Don't you touch her again!' It's Darren I hear yelling as my back burns.

'Get in line,' a soldier shouts and there's a thump and silence. My hands and knees feel scraped from where I fell, but all I can think is that Darren is silent now.

I open my eyes to see Mum bending down beside me. I can feel her arms around me, but she's pushed away by the soldier. 'Move,' he orders.

People are shouting now and all I see are feet not in line any more. A soldier's boots are kicking someone and I close my eyes because I don't want to see it. A shot cracks through the clouds. The echo of it shatters my bones. People are screaming. There's so much screaming that I cover my ears and curl into a ball on the floor.

'Silence!' Another gun shot. And instantly the quiet swoops in and grabs everyone. 'Get into line. Now.' I see shoes moving back into their place. I'm pulled up and Mum makes me stand in front of her. She holds on to my arm and she must be able to feel me shaking. It's the man with the darker uniform who stands with his gun in the air.

There aren't any bodies on the ground. Did he shoot anyone? Was he just trying to scare us? Every last speck of my laughter has disappeared. In its place there's only terror.

When I get to the front, I'm not sure who the man was expecting to see standing here, but he looks surprised. His eyes get under my skin as he studies me for a heartbeat too long. Mum is waiting for me but a guard pushes her to join the line of people already registered.

I keep my head up and meet the man's stare.

'My name's Ruby West,' I say, the words shaking when I don't want them to.

'I didn't ask you,' the man says but there's a smile pencilled on his lips. He looks down at the clipboard he's holding and writes my name in ink next to a number. I see his pen form the letters. He looks up briefly at the purple band on my arm and writes *C* before he presses a full stop hard at the end. 'You are number 276. Remember it,' he says. 'I am the general. We will meet again.' And he puts his hand on my shoulder and I want to scream at him not to touch me, but he holds it there before he moves me to the side. 'Next,' he shouts and I hurry to join my mum.

'What was he saying?' she whispers, holding my hand so tight that she crushes my fingers.

'He just gave me a number like everyone else. I'm 276.'

Mum's eyes blaze hard. 'You are not a number, Ruby.'

'Silence,' a guard shouts. So I keep my words locked inside, where they form thoughts that turn to mud.

When everyone has been processed they lead us across the wet yard into an enormous room. Inside there are rows and rows of tables with long benches stretching along them. In each place there's a bowl of soup, a piece of bread and a glass of water. I've never wanted food so much in my life.

We all rush forwards, sit down wherever we can and start to eat before anyone even tells us. I grab my drink first.

'Slowly,' Mum says, but I gulp it back, moving the water in front of my teeth, to every part of my mouth. I hold the last bit in there until my gums feel normal again.

The soup is almost cold. It's disgusting, with lumps of

vegetables and potatoes in it, but I know I have to eat it.

'You look like animals,' a soldier shouts from where he stands at the end of a table. His sneering laughter ricochets off the low roof, but I ignore him. I feel a bit better, strong enough to face them now that I'm not so hungry.

Mr Jesenska sits opposite me and he puts his spoon into his empty bowl.

'Delicious,' he says, as he kisses the tips of his fingers dramatically. 'I'm ready for dessert now.' And people laugh and start to talk, the murmurs growing until it's like a strange little party in here.

Another man slams through the door.

'Enough!' he shouts. He turns to the soldier next to him. 'Are you incapable of keeping them quiet?'

'No, sir.'

They're so close to each other now that their eyeballs are almost touching.

'Then do your job properly.'

'Yes, sir.'

The officer starts to walk along behind us. There's only the sound now of his boots on the floor and some spoons scraping bowls. I pick up my bread and start to eat it. I can hear him coming closer, so I concentrate on chewing. It's almost impossible to swallow as my throat has closed up. I wish I had more water. He's here behind me as I break off more bread. He doesn't stop, just keeps on walking. I don't look up as he continues down the other side, opposite us.

Chew. Swallow. That's all you have to do, Ruby. Chew and swallow.

And I manage it, even picking up the last crumbs and licking them from my thumb.

They make us walk in pairs. I'm with Mum still as we follow the people in front out of the dining room. I can see Darren ahead of us, his arm protective around Lilli and I'm suddenly so glad that he's with us. His head is leaning towards her and he seems like a wall that won't let anything get through.

We go along a path and through the doors of another building. Immediately there are brick stairs and we go up. It's a strange light, because all of the windows are covered over and the bulbs sunk into the wall are yellow, making everything a bit washed out and faint. I scratch my nail into the back of my hand as we walk. If this is a nightmare I need to wake up. I almost break through my skin, but I'm still here.

The banister is metal, covered with a line of black plastic on the top. I grip on to it and want to rip it free, smash it against the wall. Smash through the bricks to get out of here.

'Ruby.' Mum links her arm through mine.

'I want to go home,' I tell her.

'I know. But to do that we have to stay calm.'

My anger boils inside me as we get to the top of the

stairs. I breathe deeply to try to keep it away as we're made to walk along a dimly lit corridor. The first door we pass is open slightly and I glance into the room. It's crammed full with people. Silent people sitting on bunk beds and on the floor, watching us. I look over at Mum, but I don't know if she's seen them. I pull on her arm, but it's too late, we've gone past.

We're taken to another room. It's big, with bunk beds squeezed in side by side. It's got the same sickly light in here too, with the four long windows all boarded up.

'You stay here until we say,' the soldier says. 'No one is to leave these doors. Do you understand?'

People around me nod.

'Do you understand?' he shouts.

'Yes.'

'We do.'

'Yes.'

The soldier turns his back on us. He walks out but leaves the door wide open. As soon as he's gone, Darren and Lilli find us.

'Are you okay?' he asks and he touches my mum's cheek gently and kisses her.

'We're fine,' she says, but her smile doesn't light up like it normally does when he's with her.

'Why did they take our bags?' Lilli asks.

'To dehumanise us,' Mum says quietly.

'What do you mean?' Lilli's face looks so innocent and no one answers her.

Instead Darren takes the purple band from his arm, bunching it up in his hand.

'I don't think we'll be needing this any more,' he says loudly. 'They obviously know whose side we're on, or we wouldn't be here.' A few people near us nod, but hardly anyone takes off their armbands. I do, though, and Mum. Lilli hesitates before she copies us, her fingers picking at the edge of her Trad band as she grips it and takes it from her arm. If anyone notices that she's been wearing it, no one says.

I stare at the people already in the room. There are men, women, children, just like us. Ordinary people taken away from their homes and put here.

'Well,' a man in front of us says. He's the one whose girlfriend has the bleached-blonde hair. 'Best get settled, then.'

'There won't be enough beds,' a woman shouts over at us, her legs swinging from where she sits on a top bunk. She's right. There must be sixty of us who've just come in and only a handful of empty beds. There's a surge forwards as people suddenly realise. People reach out to claim mattresses, grab for the ladders and clamber to the top. So few people get them and so many of us are left. We didn't even bother trying to move.

It's at least three-quarters of our coachload who don't get a bed.

'They don't seem to have thought this through too well,' a man laughs.

'I'll go and tell them we need another room,' my mum says, moving towards the door.

'No!' a woman on a bunk near the door jumps down. 'They told you not to go out there and they mean it.'

'But there aren't enough beds,' Mum says. 'We need to let them know so they can do something about it.'

'Then you wait until they come back in.'

'You need to listen to her,' an older man tells Mum.

'Just stay here,' Darren says, holding on to her arm.

'Fine,' Mum says. 'But what do they expect us to do in the meantime?'

'Sit on the floor,' someone calls out.

'Make yourself at home.'

'Our home,' the old woman from the coach says, 'looks nothing like this.'

'Come and sit here,' a man near us says. He must know that she's too old to be on the floor. 'We can all budge up and make room for you.'

'We need to have two to a bed,' someone else says.

People move over. I'd prefer to sit with my family in a corner, huddled away from all this, but I don't say.

'Ruby?' the voice is familiar, from a top bunk. I look up and it's Destiny, from school. Seeing her face spins relief into me.

She jumps down from the bed and I go and throw my arms around her, even though we barely know each other.

'You're here too,' I say.

'Yeah. You all right?'

'Do you know what's going on?' I ask.

'Only that they want to keep us away from others for some reason.'

'Will they really make us stay the night?'

'Looks that way,' Destiny says. 'Do you want to sit up there?' She nods towards her bunk.

'Is that all right, Mum?' I ask. The rules seem different here. I don't know what I'm allowed to do.

'Of course,' she says. 'We'll find space over here somewhere.'

Lilli looks up at me.

'You okay?' I ask her. She does a brave smile and nods at me.

'I'll see you in a mo,' I say, before I follow Destiny as she climbs up. 'Have you seen anyone else from school?' I ask as we sit on the mattress.

'I think I saw Peter Eshaw from our year. I'm sure I saw him walking into the place where they fed us.'

'Do you know Luke Stanley?' I ask.

Destiny smiles at me. 'Of course. You and him are together, right?'

'Is he here?'

'I haven't seen him.'

'Did they take your phone?'

'Yeah.'

'Did you manage to message anyone before you left?'

'No chance. They literally grabbed me and Mum, made us dress and forced us out of the flat.'

'Are they allowed to do this?'

'They make the rules I guess.'

She's got the kind of lips I've always wanted – ones that'd leave a proper kiss mark on a window. I wonder if I'd feel jealous of her if Luke was sitting next to us now.

'What number did they give you?' I ask.

'I'm not going to tell you.'

'Why?'

Destiny looks at me, bright fire in her eyes. 'Because I'm more than a number.'

When the door opens, my mum is the first to jump up. She goes straight to the soldier and he visibly tenses.

'There's not enough space for us all to sleep in here,' she says.

'There's plenty of space,' he says.

'There aren't enough beds then,' she says, standing tall in front of him.

'It's all there is,' the soldier says. 'Or would you prefer to sleep outside?'

'What I'd prefer,' Mum says, 'is that you let us all go home.'
My heart starts to beat too fast. I want her to sit back down and
not question it.

'We're okay here,' Darren says, as he gets up to stand next
to her and I think I actually want to hug him. 'Leave it for now,'
he tells Mum.

'Fine,' she says, but she yanks herself away from him and
walks back to where she was sitting. The soldier follows her.

'What's your name?' he asks, standing over her.

'Hermione Granger,' she says, staring him down.

The slap is so sudden that I don't see it before she's on
the floor.

'Mum!' I scream, but Destiny grabs me and pulls me back.
Anger blazes from Darren, but he doesn't move.

'Well, *Miss Granger*,' the soldier says. 'Know that I'll be
watching you.' He moves his leg and I think he's going to kick
her in the stomach, but he just turns and walks away.

As soon as he's gone, I jump down, but Darren is already
helping mum on to the bed, his arms protective around her.

'Why didn't you do something?' I yell at him.

'I'm fine,' Mum says. But her cheek is swollen and stretched
with ugly blue.

'You're not,' I say. I look at Darren. 'You did nothing.'

'What could he have done?' Mum's anger is fired towards me
now. 'They've got guns, Ruby.' She sees now that Lilli has tears

falling silently and she leans over to hold her close. 'I'm fine,'
she says. 'It's just a little knock, that's all.'

That's all? I want to scream. *That's all?*

The whole room is watching. But no one says a word.

CHAPTER FIVE

'You need strong leadership to clear the vermin, to restore your security and your future.' – John Andrews, leader of the Traditional Party

It's been over an hour and no one else has come in. I'm hungry again already. The soup is all we've had all day. I keep hoping Luke or Dad will appear, but then I think I'd prefer it if they didn't. I'm not sure I want them near this place, even if that means I don't get to see them.

Some people are saying we'll be here for a couple of days, others are sure we'll get to go home tomorrow. Destiny's mum, Aba, thinks they're just trying to scare us, so there won't be any more protests.

Mum has barely spoken since the guard hit her. There's a toilet in a tiny room in the corner and she went in there for a while to put some cold water on the bruise. When she came out it was obvious she'd been crying. Lilli just held her hand when she sat back on the bed and hasn't let go of it since.

I'm sitting on the floor next to them, Darren beside me, when the door opens. It's a woman soldier, her blonde hair brushed back in a tight bun. She's got a gun slung across her front.

'The following people are to come with me,' she says and with barely a gap she starts reading from a list. My name is on it. And Lilli and Destiny, but not my mum or Darren. When the woman has finished we all sit and stare at her. It's Darren who gets up and walks to where she stands by the door.

'You can't just take them without saying where they're going,' he says. I feel so relieved that he's here to protect us.

'There's nothing to worry about,' the guard says, her words sucked dry of any emotion.

'They're not going,' Darren says, 'until you tell me where.' He's taller than the woman and she takes a small step back.

'They're going to work in the kitchen,' the guard says. 'You want to eat, don't you?'

'Yes,' a man says. 'We do.'

Mum turns to me. She can't hide that look in her eyes. 'You have to go,' she tells me. 'Just do what they say and look after Lilli.'

Darren puts his hand on my shoulder. I feel safe with it there and want to stay in this room with him and Mum. 'We'll be here when you get back,' he says and I nod at him.

People start moving towards the door. I see Destiny get down from her bunk, so I take Lilli's hand and pull her with me. A woman walks up to the guard. A baby is strapped to her front.

'Excuse me,' she says, 'my name is on the list, but I have to bring my daughter with me as she's due a feed soon.'

'The baby stays here,' the guard says.

'But I'm breastfeeding her,' the woman says. 'She's only three months old, she needs to be with me.'

The guard seems confused about what to do as a man walks up to them.

'I'm her husband,' he says. 'I'll go instead of her.'

The guard looks down at her list. I watch her brain fumble for a moment before she snaps her head up, determined.

'No,' she says. 'This is the list. You –' she points to the mother – 'leave the baby and come with me.'

'I've got some powdered milk you can have,' a woman sitting on the floor offers. Her baby is older, crawling around.

'But she's never taken a bottle.' The mother's panic flutters into me.

'It's okay,' her husband says. He's untying the carrier strapped to the woman. 'She'll be fine. I'll sort it.' He's trying to take the baby from his wife, but she doesn't want to let her daughter go.

'Please,' she says to the guard. 'I've never been separated from her. She's only three months old.'

'You're going to be preparing food,' the guard says. 'You can't do that with a baby stuck to you.'

'I can,' the mother says. 'I promise. I do it all the time.'

The guard holds tightly to her gun. 'I said no.'

It's enough to make the husband take their baby. But the mother is crying and he's clumsy as he tries to wipe her tears and hold their daughter safe.

'You might even be back before the next feed,' he says and it must take all his effort to walk away from her.

'Move,' the guard says and we do. In pairs, we walk out of the room. I try to look back to catch a glimpse of my mum, but she's blocked by the people in the line behind me.

We go along the corridor and back down the stairs. I hold Lilli's hand the whole time. Outside, the rain is heavier and we walk quickly through it, but I want to stop. It's nice to feel it cold against my face, to feel the air on my skin. We go into the place where we ate. The tables are filled with more people and I scan their faces, but there are too many of them and we're marched by too quickly.

'Look straight ahead and not a word,' a guard shouts as we walk on.

A hand grabs mine briefly and lets go. I glance back.

Luke.

I want to break away from the line, run to him and have him kiss me and somehow take me away from here. I need to be back with him in our railway hut, eating stale biscuits as he draws me. But I force myself not to look at him again. I think of the bruise seeping deep into my mum's skin and I know I mustn't give him away.

Luke is close by. It's enough, for now, just to know.

We go through the double doors at the end and we're in a huge kitchen. Already there are people everywhere and there's noise and steam and cooking smells that reach inside me into my stomach until I feel sick. I have to breathe to steady myself, but each breath swills the stink into me again.

'You lot, over here,' a guard shouts. There are long tables pushed together and on the back of them are huge bags of potatoes. 'You peel these until we tell you to stop. You,' he says, pointing to the man at the end. 'Hand out these.' He kicks a bucket next to him filled to the brim with metal peelers. We're each given one. I've helped Mum do this a couple of times before, but I don't think Lilli's ever used one in her life.

'I'll teach you,' I whisper to her.

'Once they're done,' the guard shouts, 'you and you –' he jabs his gun towards the two people closest to him – 'will take them to get cooked over here. Am I clear?'

'Yes,' I say, along with most of us.

'I know that as Core supporters you aren't that intelligent, but I'm sure you can manage this.'

His insult skims above me. Luke is next door. He's safe and he knows I am too.

I take two potatoes from the bag and pass one to Lilli. 'Like this,' I say, but I'm not much good myself. I drag the peeler over the top of the skin, but barely any of it gets caught properly.

'You have to tip it more,' the man next to me says. He has a moustache you should only see in cartoons, twisted up at each end. 'Experiment with it a bit. You'll find a way.'

Lilli scratches away at her potato. Scabs of its skin fall to the table.

'What if they come and check?' she asks.

'I'll give you an almost-finished one of mine,' I say quietly. 'You just keep it with you and when they come over, pretend it's yours.'

'Will I get in trouble?'

'No. You'll be fine.'

'Okay,' she says.

'They can't exactly get angry if you don't do it well,' I reassure her. 'It's the first time you've done it. You're learning.'

'Okay,' she says again. But I know she's not. Under her sweatshirt her heart will be hammering to break through.

And so we peel and I start to get better at it. Curls of potato slide through the metal and land in shapes on the table. I'm so hungry that if they weren't covered in mud I'd eat them. I see a boy further down do it, but he chews it once and spits it out.

Some other Core supporters come round and they sweep our scraps into bags. Lilli concentrates so hard. At home I'd laugh at her, but here I'm begging her to keep going, to get it right.

Would a guard hit her if she doesn't? Hit a child?

The man with the moustache next to me nudges my elbow. 'I'm Stan,' he says. There's enough kitchen noise in here so we can speak. 'Are you sisters?'

'Yes.' People often say we look alike, but I can't see it.

'You've got the same nose,' he says.

'Mum calls it a ski jump,' I tell him.

'I think it's more regal than that,' he laughs quietly. 'Are your parents here?'

'Just our mum,' I say. 'I don't think our dad is.'

'Did he vote for the Core Party?'

'Yes,' I say. 'But he doesn't live with us.'

Stan picks up his curl of potato. 'Look at that,' he says. 'All in one.' He throws it in the air and watches as it lands on the table. 'My dear mother used to say that if you didn't break the peel, it'd spell out the initial of the woman you'd marry.' His laugh sprinkles out of him like glitter. 'I never had the heart to tell her I preferred men.'

'No talking,' the guard at the door shouts. He looks nervous standing there with his gun, fidgeting from leg to leg.

'They haven't got a clue what to do with us,' Stan whispers. 'Amateurs the lot of them.' Under his moustache his mouth

103

hardly moves. 'That one by the door looks so scared I'm surprised he doesn't piss himself.' He lowers his head, so this time his laugh disappears on to the table.

'They're scared?' I ask.

'Can't you tell?' Stan says. 'They're terrified about what to do with us but equally terrified in case we try to escape.'

'That's good, isn't it?' I say. 'If they're scared, they'll all fall apart.'

Stan looks at me steadily. 'Don't you listen in your history class?' His voice smiles but he doesn't. 'Fear is what turns people into monsters. It's the pivot on which the devil himself stands.'

'Look, Ruby,' Lilli whispers from next to me. 'I've done it.' And from her peeler, a perfect curl of potato falls.

The dining room is empty when they walk us back through it. The bowls and the spoons have gone. There's no sign that anyone was ever sitting here.

Maybe I imagined Luke? Maybe I wished too hard to see him? I'm hungry enough for my brain to be working wrong. I scan the table for a scrap of bread to pick up, but there isn't any. I thought they'd be feeding us now, but we're just made to go outside, our stomachs as empty as the room.

Another coach is sitting there. A new group of people line up by the wall. I know Lilli looks at them too and I wonder if she's thinking that our dad might turn up. It's strange how at home I barely miss him any more, but in here everything feels different and I just want to see him. I need him to see where we are, that we're safe, before he escapes over the wall and runs to tell everyone what's going on.

Although, if what Stan says is true – that deep down these soldiers don't really know what they're doing – maybe we'll all walk out of here this evening in any case. After our meal, though. The sight of all that food has eaten further into my hunger.

I keep looking at the line of Core supporters, before we're walking back through the door and up the stairs.

'Do we have to go and sit in that room again?' Lilli asks me.

'I reckon so,' I say.

'It's boring.'

'You're not making it easier,' I say.

'Neither are you,' she snaps back.

At home when she irritates me I can walk away, or be so horrid that she gets up and goes, but here I'm stuck beside her as we stomp up the final few stairs and along the corridor.

I see Luke as soon as I step into the bunk room. He's sitting talking to my mum and Darren, his back towards me. My hunger vanishes, my nerves disappear as I run to him, jumping on his back and wrapping my legs round his waist. I keep my hands over his eyes.

'Guess who?' I laugh.

'Get off him, Ruby,' Mum says, glancing at the door.

But I ignore her and cover his neck in kisses. His smile seeps down to my bones as I move round to his lap.

'Fancy seeing you here,' he says, his arms tight around me. The smell of him makes me want to push him back on the bed and kiss him properly, even with everyone here.

'I'm serious, Ruby,' Mum says.

'Your mum is right.' Luke's dad, Robert, is standing next to us now. 'You can't risk being that close in here.'

Luke moves me from his lap, until we're sitting squeezed in together, side by side.

'Can we at least hold hands?' I ask Mum. 'Or will we get beheaded for that?'

'This isn't a joke,' Darren says. But him getting involved makes my blood burn like it does at home.

'You're not my dad,' I tell him. I'm embarrassed as soon as I say it in front of Luke. He can't see what I've got against Darren and it makes me sound like an eight year old.

'And neither am I,' Robert says. 'But we all know that the Trads won't like seeing you and Luke together in here.'

'But it's stupid,' I say, keeping Luke's hand clasped in mine. I don't mean to sound rude but I'm sure I do.

'It may well be,' he says. 'But they have their vision for their new society and we know now that they'll do anything to get it.'

'Dad thinks they want to keep us here for a while,' Luke tells me. All I can see is his lips that I need to kiss.

'How long is a while?' Mum asks.

'Who knows?' Robert says.

'They can't expect us to come round to their way of thinking just because we're cooped up here,' Darren says.

'That could be exactly what they're hoping,' Robert says. 'Although they must see it'll never work. They can't do this with every Core supporter in the country.'

'Can't they?' Darren says.

'You seriously think that's what they want?' Mum asks.

'Well, they clearly want us out the way. But there's no point just keeping us here and then releasing us.'

'We'd protest even louder when we get out,' Luke says.

'Precisely,' his dad says. 'In which case, we'd better get comfortable. We could be here for quite a while.'

'I knew you'd manage to sneak it in somehow,' I say.

'No one takes away my sketchbook,' Luke smiles. We've found a spot in the corner where we can sit together away from our parents, although we've had to promise them we won't kiss. And we'll separate hands every time anyone opens the door. 'You know Conor was on our coach.'

'Conor's here? Is he okay?'

'Not really,' Luke says. 'His mum's here too.'

'But what about her treatment? She's right in the middle of her chemo.'

'I know.'

'They wouldn't even let her stay for that?'

'No. She looks really ill too.'

'Conor's going to flip out.'

'I know. His mum already had to pull him back from a guard.'

'Where is he now?' I ask.

'They split up our coach,' Luke says. 'Half went in a different room.'

The door opens and the unease in here is instant. 'Line up in pairs,' the guard shouts at us. Instantly people stand up and start doing as he says.

Mum comes across the room to find me. 'You're not to walk with Luke,' she says.

'Agreed,' Robert pulls Luke back, as though he's ten years old again.

'You're going a bit over the top,' I say to Mum.

'If they find out he's your boyfriend,' Mum says, 'they'll separate you completely.'

'Or worse,' Darren chips in.

Worse? They can't do much worse than this. I can barely talk to Luke as it is.

I'm getting more used to the weird light in the corridor, the cold stairs going down, before the shock of natural sunshine as we're led outside. It's colder than earlier and I wish I'd put on my coat, but it's only a short walk to the eating place.

There are so many people in here already, yet none of them are speaking. Just the quick dunking of spoons into bowls. There are more guards than earlier and they look nervous. Too many of us have piled in with nowhere to sit and you can tell that they don't quite know what to do. This must be as new for them as it is for us.

'You!' one of them shouts to the man at the end of our line. 'Move along.' We shuffle forwards and stand with our backs against the wall.

'Eat faster,' a soldier at the end of the table yells. 'Or we'll take your bowls away.'

The heads bend lower, the spoons move quicker. There are some children who screw up their noses at the soup and have hardly touched it.

I've enough time to look at each of the faces and none of them are Dad. But there, almost at the end, is Conor. He nods at me when he sees me and does a smile that doesn't look like his. I want to try and make him laugh, but he looks away and I see him tear off the corner of his bread and drag it through his bowl.

It's like torture with the food just there when I'm this hungry. I've never had so little to eat and it makes me realise that I've never really been properly hungry before. I thought I had, but it's nothing compared to this.

The guards move away everyone who's eaten. They leave the dirty bowls and spoons on the table and two people come out with a huge pan and start ladling out more soup.

'That's disgusting,' I whisper to Mum. 'They're putting it in the dirty bowls.'

'Aren't they going to wash the spoons?' I hear Lilli ask.

'You'll both eat it,' Mum says. 'All of it.'

'Sit!' the guard shouts. I want to ask him what's happened to his proper sentences. Does he think we're not worth more words?

We all push forwards. Somehow I'm separated from Mum, but everyone gets a place. Luke is two people away, on my side.

'Okay?' he mouths at me. I nod at him, too hungry to reply. I soak up soup with the bread and hardly chew before I swallow. It's only lukewarm, so it's easy to eat quickly and every mouthful makes me feel more human again.

I don't use my spoon. The thought that someone else was licking from it will make me spew all the food back up. Destiny is sitting almost opposite. She waggles her eyebrows at me when I look up, so I go cross-eyed. She scrunches up her face like a pig and laughs so suddenly the soup spurts from her mouth. I swear it even comes out of her nose.

'Destiny,' her mum says, clamping her hand over her daughter's. The look on her face makes my bubbling laughter stop sharp. There's terror in her eyes as a female guard steps closer.

'Our food isn't good enough for you?' she says, over Destiny's shoulder.

'It's great,' Destiny says, not looking up. 'I just had an itch.' I can see her nerves folding tight towards laughter again. I stare at her, willing her to be calm. 'A sneeze,' she says and she laughs enough again for the soup to fall off her spoon.

The guard grabs the back of Destiny's head and forces her face into the bowl. The violence is so sudden I can't understand what I'm seeing.

'Let her go,' her mum shouts, pulling back the guard's arm. She's stronger and taller than the woman when she stands up. 'Don't you ever touch my daughter again.'

Destiny is wiping the smears of soup from her face when the male guard opposite points his gun at them. The air is sucked out of the room. There's nothing left for any of us to breathe.

'Take your dirty Core hands off the guard,' he tells Destiny's mum, his voice wrapped in wire. She puts her hands in the air as she sits down. 'And you –' the guard turns the gun on Destiny.

No.

Destiny doesn't blink. Every part of her looks towards the bullet in that metal case.

'You,' he continues. 'Lick up every drop of spilled soup. And when you've finished, you'll clean the table with your tongue.'

Still, Destiny doesn't move.

'Now!' the woman behind her yells, forcing Destiny's head towards the table again.

How can they make her do it? Destiny swallows her humiliation along with the spots and drops of dirty soup. No one looks at her. I think we all want to spare her an audience.

But when they make us leave, I look at her until she glances up. The only thing I can think to do is to put my hand close to my heart. I think I'm telling her to keep strong. Maybe she nods, I'm not sure, before she bends her mouth to the table again.

There are four basins in a row, one toothbrush on each. As the line goes past it, some women stop to use them.

'I'm not doing that,' Lilli whispers to Mum.

'You don't have to,' Mum says.

There's no way I will either. I want clean teeth, but the thought of sharing a toothbrush with a stranger makes me want to gag.

We walk past the basins and stay waiting in line for the showers.

'We didn't bring any towels,' Mum says when we're almost at the front of the queue.

'No one did,' the woman behind us says.

'How are we going to dry ourselves?' Lilli asks.

'You can each use my shirt,' Mum says.

'Did you bring another one?' I ask.

'It won't take long to dry,' Mum says. 'I'll hang it off the edge of a bed and just wear my jumper.'

We move a bit further forward. A woman is holding open the door, so I can see the rows of shower cubicles. Apparently we're only allowed in them for two minutes, so barely even enough time to get off our clothes.

'That one.' The woman guard points me to the empty shower at the end. 'Move.'

Mum strips off her shirt right where we're standing and passes it to me. The guard seems too embarrassed to say anything as she pushes me along the room and I go where I'm told.

I have to be quick. There's nowhere to hang my clothes apart from over the top of the door and I'm sure they'll get wet. I haven't got any soap, but it's nice to feel the warm water on my skin. I close my eyes and let it run over my face, over the necklace Luke gave me and I'm home again.

After this, I'll put on my slipper socks and go downstairs to argue with Darren about me being on my phone. Lilli will complain that she's not allowed to stay up later.

'Out.' There's a banging on the shower door. I try to shake the water from my body so I don't make Mum's shirt too wet, but I don't dry myself enough and it's difficult to get my clothes back on. And I don't like having to use the same pants I've worn last night on the coach and all today. It makes it feel like I haven't even had a shower. 'Out! Now!' the guard shouts again. I haven't time to put on my socks and hoodie, so I grab them and walk out, my hair still dripping down my T-shirt.

'Lilli?' I call.

'I'm in here,' she says. She's two doors down.

'Why do you need her?' the guard asks me. I don't answer and I don't ask for permission as I throw Mum's damp shirt over Lilli's door.

I'm squeezing the ends of my hair when I go over to Luke in the bunk room. Just being next to him makes everything else disappear. If I look only at him then I can pretend that the rest of the room doesn't exist.

'They just made me have the quickest shower ever,' I tell him.

He nods to the group of men over in the corner.

'Dad and your Darren are making new friends,' he says.

'He's not *my* Darren,' I say.

'He's all right, Ruby. My dad likes him.'

'Your dad doesn't have to live with him,' I say, pulling on my hoodie.

'Fair enough,' Luke says. But I feel a hint of guilt, because in here I feel safer every time Darren's near, like he really can protect us.

At that moment he's huddled in the corner of the bunk room with a group of people we've never met before. He's so completely focused and people are really listening to him. They all look very serious. Mum's told him that if he even thinks about trying to break out of here tonight, she'll divorce him on the spot.

'Have you spoken to Destiny yet?' I ask. She's lying on her top bunk, but there's no way she can be asleep with the lights on and everyone talking. 'Maybe we should go and see if she's okay.'

'We don't even know her.' Luke's quite shy in any case, plus she's a girl and a beautiful one at that.

'I talked to her earlier,' I say. 'She's nice.' And however much I just want to stay here with Luke, I know Destiny's on her own with memories of what the Trads made her do.

So I walk towards her bunk and hope Luke will follow. I climb up to the top without asking if she minds. She opens her eyes as I do.

'Budge up,' I say. She sits up to make space.

'Enough for me too?' Luke asks, joining us. It's a bit of a squash, so he keeps his legs hanging down over the edge.

But now I'm here I don't know what to say. I'd wanted to help get rid of Destiny's embarrassment, but I think us just being here has smeared it all over her again.

'You've had a shower too,' she eventually says.

'If you can call it that. A blast of water for two minutes. No soap, no shampoo, or towel.' I smile as though it's funny, but

115

it's not. My hair's dirty, I need to change my underwear and I didn't bring any deodorant, so I probably smell as well. 'I'm so tired now, I just want to sleep.'

'Do you think they're sorting out another room?' Destiny asks.

'Nope,' Luke says, as he takes my hand. 'I reckon this is it.'

'But there's not even enough floor space for everyone to stretch out,' I say.

'Do you think they care?' Luke asks. All I can feel is his thumb drawing circles on my palm.

'Will they bring us duvets at least?' Destiny asks.

'I doubt that either.'

'Great,' I say. I look down at all the people sprawled across the room. There are two babies asleep in arms and a handful of children scattered on laps. Some are playing, stepping over people's legs, but even from here I can feel that the patience in the room is already stretched tight. One man puts up an arm to stop a boy.

'No, thank you,' I hear him say.

'I can't spend the night with only a sheet,' Destiny says.

'Maybe their plan is to send us mad through lack of sleep,' I say.

'Turn us into zombie Trads,' Luke laughs.

'They'd better get things sorted better than this,' Destiny says. 'Or there's no way I'm staying here.'

'Too right,' I say.

And it's good to feel like we have a choice, that we can control what's happening to us. That we won't be beaten.

Mum won't let me sleep anywhere near Luke, so he and his dad couldn't be much further away if they tried. They've got the tiniest patch of floor near the toilet, using their coats as pillows.

People are doubled up on the beds, so I'm head to toe with Lilli on a bottom mattress, the sheet stretched tight underneath us. We're both still wearing our clothes as we've got nothing else. I pull up my hood, but it doesn't make me feel cosy, or safe. Mum is next to us on the floor and Darren is actually under the bunk. He says it'll be darker and quieter there, but it must be horrible.

'I'm cold,' Lilli says.

'Kick your legs like a bicycle,' I tell her, but she doesn't. I don't know whether it's because there's not enough room or she hasn't got the energy.

Someone turns off the light and the room is pitch black. Instantly a child cries out.

'Can we keep the light on?' a woman calls.

'No,' two people shout.

The child doesn't stop crying. There are the sounds of someone comforting it but if anything the sobbing gets worse.

'Ruby?' It's Mum whispering up to me. Her hand pats

the bed until she finds me and starts to stroke my hair. 'Are you two okay?'

'Never been better,' I say. I hate it here in this weird room packed with strangers. But I remember she's on the cold floor. 'Are you?'

'Yes.'

'Do you want to swap?' I ask her.

'No, I'm fine,' she says.

'This is rubbish, Mum,' I whisper. 'I really, really want to go home.'

'I know,' she says. 'Let's try to sleep.'

'I can't without my pillow.'

'You will soon and then maybe things'll be different tomorrow.'

'They better be,' I say.

The child is still crying. At some point it'll wear itself out. It'll stop, but I'm not sure when.

'Could you get him to be quiet?' someone shouts.

'I'm trying,' a woman snaps. 'But it's a bit difficult when he's this hungry.'

I want to text Sara to tell her where I am, but even if I could she'd think I was winding her up. I think of the face she'd pull and how I should be with her, meeting tomorrow under our oak tree. I don't want to cry, there are too many people who'd hear me in here. Around me there's the sound of people breathing.

Someone makes a deep rattly sound with every intake of breath and I have to bite my sleeve to stop myself screaming at them.

Instead I use the sound of the boy's tears and turn it into music, imagine that it's actually something really beautiful. But it's difficult. It's scraping away at me and I want to sleep. I need to sleep.

My mum continues to stroke my hair.

'I can't stay here, Mum.'

'It won't be for long.'

I turn on to my side, but there's barely enough space for me and Lilli. I can feel the necklace Luke gave me nestled against my skin and I reach up to touch it, to feel the letters of my name held in my fingers. And I let the darkness walk slowly over my skin, feel it on my toes, my ankles and it drifts like fog over my body. It settles on my eyelids, pressing them deep enough to try to make everything else disappear.

CHAPTER SIX

'I know there will be opposition to change,
opposition to our vision, but we're ready for this.
We'll embrace the challenges and guide you through
difficult times.' – John Andrews, leader of the
Traditional Party

'You've only got two minutes to be outside, Ruby,' Darren
tells me. The morning has come round too quick and I want to
pull the night back to give me more sleep. My eyes ache and
my body aches and I don't understand how we're here and not
at home.

'Come on,' Mum says, practically dragging me off the
mattress. My clothes feel horrid now and I need to have
something to change into.

'I want my make up.'

'They wouldn't let you wear it in any case,' Mum tells me.

I take my hairband from my wrist and start to put my hair into a ponytail.

'Leave it down, Ruby,' Darren says.

I glare at him. 'You always hated my undercut.'

'You know it's not that,' Mum says.

'It's the Trads who won't like it,' Darren says. 'And I'm not having you singled out.'

'But I need to wash it,' I say. 'I know it looks awful.'

'You'll have to deal with it.' Mum whips my band from my hair so quick I'm too shocked to reply.

'Will we be cold?' Lilli asks.

'Take your coat,' Mum tells her. 'It could be any weather out there.' The windows are so blocked-over from the outside that we can't see a shred of what's beyond them.

The children in here are already running around, even though they must've only just woken up. No one stops them laughing, though. We need it at the moment.

'That was the worst night ever.' It's Destiny standing behind us. 'I can't do another one like that.'

The door is kicked open. 'Line up in pairs. Now,' the guard demands.

Destiny grabs my arm. 'Can I go with you?' She's too far from her mum.

I feel a hand on my shoulder and Luke is standing next to me. Through all of this he helps me to smile.

'I'll go with Lilli,' he says. And my little sister instantly blushes. At home her obvious devotion to Luke winds me up, but here she looks quite cute with her hair all messed up and her eyes half asleep.

Darren holds my mum's hand and they manage to slot in line in front of us as we start moving forwards. I run my tongue over my teeth. My mouth feels so mank that I'd probably even use the shared toothbrush if they give us the chance again.

'Do you think they'll let us shower this morning?' Destiny asks.

'No talking!' a guard in the corridor shouts. There's just the sound of our shoes shuffling along now. I'm too tired to even lift my feet and I've a headache pressing in. I can feel its palm print on my skull.

We get outside and it's pouring with rain, but we all follow the line into it.

'This is crazy,' Destiny says to me. 'What's wrong with these people?'

I want to answer that they're Traditionals, but even at their worst they've never been like this. Before they'd say stupid things and have stupid slogans and policies. But this? It feels like they've slipped into some sort of collective madness.

'It's bloody freezing,' Darren says, putting his arm around Mum and holding her close.

There are already people lined up and more are coming out

of the building. There are so many Cores but it doesn't feel powerful because even though there are far fewer guards than us, their guns make up for their lack of numbers. At least they're getting soaked too. In another place it'd be funny how the water slips down their faces and they can't wipe it away.

The general walks out from the side of the furthest building and just seeing him makes my blood creep strangely. Even from here with the rain streaking down, the red slash on his sleeve is clear. His hands are behind his back and I don't know what he's holding. As he gets closer, he starts to bring one arm in front of him and for a moment everything in my world stops. He'll have a gun. He'll shoot us. The thought is so strong, so vivid, that I close my eyes.

'We were going to check your numbers.' The general's voice rattles through a loudspeaker. I let out such a breath that Destiny reaches to calm me. 'But it's too wet for the paperwork.' His words are distorted, robotic through the raindrops. 'You shall wait here until the weather changes.'

The murmuring among us is instant.

'He really has lost his mind,' Destiny says.

'There's no way I'm staying out here,' a woman says.

'Silence,' the general says through his megaphone. And there is. No one questions it again. No one fights it. I watch as he turns and walks back towards the building, his body disappearing inside.

We wait. The rain drips down the guards' faces and they don't look funny any more. The water hammers down on us and we can't hide from it. I clench my fingers into my palm to try to keep them dry. And I try to imagine Luke's hand there, his thumb on my skin. He's standing two people away, Destiny and Lilli between us, but we feel a million miles apart. I don't even dare turn to look at him.

Even the children are quiet. All but one baby whose wail catches on the wind. Beyond the fence, I see two coaches. The gates open and they drive in. I no longer want my dad to be on them. I don't want him to be here. I need him to be safe, far away.

The coaches come closer and stop. The glass windows can't hide the shock on the faces of the people inside, as they see us standing in the rain. Hundreds and hundreds of us waiting, staring. I watch them as they stumble to their feet. They'll be tired and hoping to get some sleep here. Some food. They proceed down the steps, one by one, reluctantly dropping their bags on to a pile. There are four young children in a row. Two of the girls look like twins and another clutches a rabbit by its ear so its feet almost sweep on to the wet ground. A woman who must be their mother attempts to keep them all together under her arms. They cover their heads to try to keep off the rain.

The next person and the next come down the steps and none

of them are my dad. Maybe they won't catch him. Maybe instead he'll somehow save us.

'I am way too cold,' Destiny says.

'I need food,' I tell her. I wish I hadn't said it, as now I've given my hunger permission to push its way to the front.

'Don't worry, they'll have a fried breakfast waiting for us,' Destiny says.

'That's not funny,' I tell her. But I take it and I start to feed my mind with the food.

The people from the coaches start to join the end of the line. I should look more carefully to see if I know any of them, but the rain is making my eyes ache and it's best to close them. This is what tired really is. Even my blood feels heavy. My bones, my skin, everything is begging me to sit down. And I wonder what they'll do if I try? Will they even spot me? There are so many of us and it's raining enough for them not to see.

So I sit, my back against the wall. If they ask me to get up, I'll tell them I'm too tired. The floor is soaked and I feel the wet crawling through my jeans and my underwear, but I don't care. My legs need to rest. If I'd stayed standing I would've keeled over and that would've been a lot worse.

I feel Destiny nudging me with her foot.

'You're not meant to sit down,' she whispers.

'Just for a moment,' I tell her. I don't like the worry on her face, so I close my eyes again and put my head on my knees.

The cold from the floor joins the cold from the rain and I'm freezing. But still, if it weren't for the hunger, I reckon I could sleep. Even with the rain on my neck and sitting like this, I really could.

I'm pushed hard to the side and put out my hand just in time to stop my face from smashing into the ground.

'Get up!' a guard shouts. I pull myself to my feet and wipe my muddy hands on my trousers.

'I was tired,' I say, though I don't feel so brave now because he's holding some sort of riding whip, gripping its silver handle in his fingers.

'You'll learn discipline,' the guard says. 'You'll run the length of the line and back until I tell you to stop.'

'Run?' I'm not at school. Why do they want me to run?

'You haven't heard me properly?' The guard steps closer and raises his whip until it's touching my cheek. 'I could help by cleaning out your ears with this.'

'Run, for God's sake, Ruby,' I hear Mum say.

The line of leather presses into my skin.

'Fine,' I say, but I don't look at my mum as I know she'll see the fear I'm trying to hide. I won't look at any of them.

I feel every set of eyes on me as I pass, so I focus on the world beyond the fence. In the distance is a mountain and I look at that. I force myself to see how it doesn't peak in a spike. Maybe it's not a proper mountain but it's more than a hill. It's round at the top and joins another, smaller one. They seem very safe. I imagine myself sitting there, hidden among their shape.

My feet pound the wet ground. It's concrete, so it's easier to get a rhythm. At the end I turn around. This way I can see the entrance to the camp. The fence is high, its barbed wire telling me everything. I hadn't noticed the watchtower close to the gate, but it's clear as anything now. There's a guard in it and the silhouette of a gun.

I concentrate on Mum's face as I run back down the line. Her eyes are wild with anger, but her face is stone. Darren holds tight to her hand and he nods at me and says something, but I don't hear it. It's enough though. He's willing me on and it gives me strength.

I know I run past Luke, but I'm too embarrassed to look at him. I'm sweaty and soaked and I know he loves me whatever, but I don't want him to see me like this. I'll have to run past him again and again, looking worse and worse, until the pig of a guard says I can stop.

My legs are beginning to burn as I turn at the end, facing the mountain again. I wish I could look more to the sky but the rain isn't stopping. So I keep going. Running on. Trying to count the sound of my feet on the ground.

'You can do this, Ruby.' This time I catch Darren's words and I use them as fuel.

I'm thirsty, but the water falling on me isn't enough.

The guard doesn't tell me it's over. I've never been good at running far and my lungs feel filled with fire. Someone has lit a match in them and now every breath sparks new flames. A stitch is gripping my side.

I'm sure the rain is weakening.

But now they'll be able to see that I'm crying.

I don't mean to but I look at Luke as I pass. I wish I hadn't. It's hopeless despair on his face. His dad is holding his arm, as if stopping him from trying to help me. I won't look at him again. It's made my heart hurt worse and my tears now are for more than just agony and exhaustion and hunger.

A guard grabs me by the shoulder. I collapse into him and he wipes me away like a piece of dirt.

'You may stop,' he says, pushing me back into the line between a child and an older man. 'Have you learned your lesson?'

I nod, hardly able to hold my head straight.

'I didn't hear your answer,' the guard shouts. 'Maybe you'd like to run again? Or have you learned your lesson?'

'Yes,' I say. My voice squeezes out through my spiky breathing.

'Good.'

When he walks away, the man next to me puts out his arm to hold me up.

'You did well,' he whispers as finally the rain begins to dry.

*

128

I barely notice when the general comes out again. I feel numb to everything, my muscles wound so tight that they block off all feeling. Around me everyone is silent. We all face towards the general as he raises his loudspeaker.

'Welcome,' he says. *Welcome?* His greeting is so out of place that I can't be here. I'm at school, my head asleep on a desk, my legs aching from PE. 'I want you to know that I believe none of you are a lost cause.' I try to blink away his words, but I know that they're real as they touch me and pierce my feet in place on the ground of this exercise yard. 'But, somehow, along the line, you've been broken. And, as you are citizens of our country, it's our duty to try to heal you all.'

Heal us? I'm not broken.

'The people who voted in John Andrews and the Traditionals are very passionate people,' the general continues, his voice waxy and smeared through the megaphone at his mouth. 'They love this country. And we want you to love it as well.'

Is he mad? I did love our country. I still do. The only thing destroying it is the Trads. They're the ones breaking it in the first place.

'I see you as the lucky ones.' The general's smile is made from plastic, stuck on there like a wind-up toy. 'We've chosen you to be the forerunners of this trial. We will show you the light and when you're ready you'll shine that light on the rest of the country. Until all we see is the glow of the Traditional Party.'

129

I glance up at the sky, white as bone. It's too far away to touch. Too far away to save us.

'For now, we will do a roll call. You don't need to concern yourself with anything else.' And he lowers his megaphone. He's finished with us.

There's a strange sense of cooped-up anger circling around us. It slides from my shoulders to grip me. I know there'll be others here who want to escape right now, but none of us can. I shuffle forward with the rest of the line, one step at a time.

As each person is signed off they are sent towards the dining room where, hopefully, there's breakfast. We move slowly. My whole body starts to ache, so I try to imagine soothing my muscles in a bath. It's too difficult to make the water hot, though – the heat from when I was running has flipped so cold that my skin feels like it's covered in ice.

It's our duty to heal you. The general's words echo through me. *A trial.* What trial?

I keep moving forwards, small movements, until finally I get to the front. The general stares at me enough to make me look away.

'What's your number?' he asks quietly, his pen hovering over the page.

'276,' I manage to squeeze through my clamped teeth. He finds it and puts a tick, each second stretched too long.

'You may go.'

And I walk across the yard, through the doors into the room where we eat.

The bench holds me as I sit down. On the table in front of me are two buttered slices of bread and a glass of water. None of us wait to be told to start. I rip off the crust first. It's dry to chew, so I gulp water at the same time.

'Don't eat too fast,' a voice opposite me says. It's Stan, from the kitchen. After every mouthful he wipes his moustache. He nods at me and I wait to put in my next mouthful only when he does. He must chew it a hundred times, so I do too. It's disgusting mush by the end, but it's better for my stomach this way.

'Leave your plates,' a guard shouts. I have to shove the last piece of bread into my mouth.

We go outside and there are two lines formed. It's clear that one is for the women and children, the other is for the men.

'You are going to be working in separate areas,' a guard shouts. I can't see Luke or Darren or Conor, but no one complains, no one says a word.

A hand grabs me and I turn to see my mum and Lilli standing there.

'Ruby,' Mum whispers. 'You're okay.'

'Yes,' I answer, as we're pushed and moulded to stand in the right place. The guards don't seem to mind that there are three of us together and Mum, Lilli and I stay tight by each other's sides as our line is forced to start walking.

We don't go far before we're herded alongside the building nearest the entrance to the camp. This one has windows that aren't boarded up and, although most of them don't have glass, at least they'll let the daylight in. There's no door on the building, so the floor inside the entrance is covered with leaves that have blown in and stuck together and turned to sludge. We're taken past them into an enormous room with a high ceiling and long windows. There's not a patch of furniture, just stacks of boxes in a corner. I haven't the energy to wonder what's in them. The bread was barely enough to touch my hunger.

Mum suddenly leaves my side. I watch as she goes to Mrs Jesenska, who looks bewildered and even older without her husband.

'Stay with us,' I hear Mum say and she brings her over to stand in the line.

A female guard watches from the front of the hall. Her face doesn't seem to be as blank as the other Trads in this place and she looks at us as if we're human beings, not animals to step on. But still Lilli holds my hand. Her other hand is clasped tight in Mum's and she has a look of terror stitched on her face.

'We're fine,' I whisper to her, but she doesn't even attempt a smile.

'Good morning, ladies,' the female guard says. 'We've got some sewing for you to do today.' The murmuring among us is like a wave. Words rising together and dying down when the guard raises her hand. 'This task is unsuitable for children, so they shall all be taken to be educated in the room next door.'

Taken? Educated?

I hold tighter to Lilli's hand. I can feel her shaking.

'There's nothing to worry about,' the guard says. And even though she doesn't seem frightening, none of the children move. 'They won't be able to go at your pace in here and they will slow down the work.'

There are too many questions that I'm afraid to ask. How long will they be gone? Will they just be doing schoolwork? In exactly the room next door, or further away?

Near us, mums keep their arms tight around their children.

'Perhaps you'll be more willing if I show you where your children will be?' the guard says. 'Yes?' And there's nodding, desperate sounds of people agreeing. 'Quiet.' The guard raises her hand just the once and silence whistles through us. She points to a woman with a boy clutched in one hand, another on her hip. 'I'll take you. And you can bring your children.'

I stare at the door that takes them all from the room.

'I don't want to go,' Lilli whispers.

'You won't have to,' Mum says. 'Stand as tall as you can. They won't say that you're a child.'

'You can stay with us,' Mrs Jesenska says.

'What if they ask how old I am?'

'Then say that you're fourteen,' Mum says, her face still straight to the front.

But that's a lie. Lilli is twelve and they could easily check her records and find her out.

The guard comes back in, followed by the woman and her children.

'You can tell them what you saw,' the guard tells her.

'It's just a room. It's right next door,' the mother says, still holding on to her sons.

'Come on,' the guard calls. 'You might even find a biscuit or two waiting for you.'

This is all it takes to make the first children move. And others follow and then more. Because even without the promise of biscuits we can all see the guns, so really what choice do they have? There must be thirty children at least, some barely old enough to stand on their own, but I'm amazed how silent they all are.

Two guards start to walk among the rows of the rest of us. I'm glad that Lilli can't look at my face right now, as I'd know she'd see how terrified I am. All I can do is squeeze her fingers in mine.

But one guard stops in front of her. He's so tall, even taller than our dad. The air is colder just from having him here.

'Your number?' he asks.

'274,' she says.

He taps his thumb on to his belt. 'Age?'

I feel my heart stop as I wait for her to reply.

She breathes quickly twice. 'I'm twelve,' she says.

'Then you're a child.'

'She's not,' my mother says. 'And she can sew. I've taught her at home.'

It's a lie. What if they ask Lilli to show them?

The guard doesn't say another word. He just steps back and holds his arm out in the direction of the door. I want to tell him that she's my sister. That in here I need her next to me.

'Quickly,' the guard says. And Lilli lets go of my hand. She goes on tiptoe to kiss my mum on the cheek.

'I won't be long,' she says, her bravery pressing heavy in my lungs.

And she goes from us, half running down the line. She doesn't look back as she heads towards the open door and disappears through it. The room suddenly feels so wrong. The weight of those taken pushing on to my back until I think I'll fall.

Mum steps next to me and takes my hand. 'She'll be fine,' she says. 'It's just like going to school.' But her words couldn't be less convincing.

Mrs Jesenska nods. 'They'll bring her back.'

There's a burst of laughter from somewhere down the corridor. It's the children. Lilli somewhere among them.

'See?' the female guard at the front says. 'They're happy and it means that you can all get on with your work without interruption. So –' she looks along the rows of women, her eyes finding us out – 'this task today is very easy, even for those non-sewers among you. And you shall learn quickly.' She makes it sound like an order. 'You shall each be given a piece of red material and on it you shall sew your number. You shall stitch it thick enough so that it is clearly visible. It's simple.' She's smiling again, but I don't trust her. What will they do when they find out I can't sew? And I doubt I'm the only one.

We sit in silence as the material, needles and thread are handed out. I look at them in my lap, the slash of red balanced across my jeans.

'You may begin,' the guard at the front shouts.

I stare at Mum and for an awful moment I think I'm going to laugh, but the look in her eyes stops me.

'Just copy what I do,' she says. 'But with your own number.'

The dark green thread feels almost like wool as I lick the end of it and push it into the gap in the needle. I have to look at it closely and pull it through the other side.

'Now knot it,' Mum says.

I do and then I pierce the red material, exactly as my mum does, watching carefully as I stitch the number 276 into the cloth. When I make a mistake, I yank the thick thread free to do it again. And so I stitch and unpick and stitch my identity into the Traditional's material. And there's time now to think. Too much time to wonder how we managed to end up here. I glance at the guards with their guns and wonder if they'd really use them. When they took us from home would they have shot us if we'd tried to run?

I stab the needle roughly into the material. Work until I've got it right, until it's finished.

Those who are good sewers and quick enough do the ones for the men. I wonder whose fingers have turned Luke and Darren into numbers.

'Very good.' The guard from the front nods when all the needles and thread have been packed up and put away. 'From now on, these must be worn on your arms where they are clearly visible.'

The silence among us is thick as Mum leans over, takes the material from me and wraps it over the top of my sleeve. She straightens the number, before she ties the ends tight.

'Fine,' she says. And now I have to tie my mum's number to her arm. I won't look at her face as I fix the material.

There's a sound from the front and the children are rushing through the door. Each one of them wears the slash of red, but their smiles are genuine and they look a million times happier than when they left us. Even Lilli looks better. Maybe they did feed them biscuits after all.

When she finds us, Mum hugs her close.

'Did they hurt you?' she asks, her palms on Lilli's face.

'No. They were nice.'

'Nice?' Mum asks and Lilli nods.

'Silence,' the guard at the front shouts and almost instantly we're all quiet again. 'You're to leave here and go straight to the dining room.'

I look at Lilli's face and wish I could see into her mind. How can the Trads have been *nice*? Has she forgotten that they're the reason we're here?

I get into the line next to her and Mum, my arm gripped under the material stitched with my number. I need to forget it's there, but I don't want to touch it in case I loosen it. Instead I look at Mum's fingers laced with Lilli's and it flares a slice of triumph into me. Lilli is with us. And it'll take more than a few biscuits from them to tempt her away.

Mum and I walk with Lilli between us as we go with the other women from the sewing room to the outside. It's so cold in the wind that for a moment I even forget how hungry I am.

'How was it really?' Mum asks Lilli. 'In the room?'

'I told you already,' Lilli says.

'You just said they were nice to you,' Mum reminds her. 'I'm just interested to know a bit more.'

'They gave us biscuits,' she says.

'What type of biscuits?' Mum asks.

'Chocolate ones. And orange juice.'

I'm caught between jealousy and suspicion.

'Why would they give you that?' I ask.

'They said we looked hungry and because we're growing we need to eat properly.'

'I'm hungry and I'm growing too.'

'We had to sew the numbers too and it was more difficult for us,' Lilli says defensively.

'What about the lessons?' Mum asks. 'They said they were going to educate you.'

Lilli shrugs. 'They just told us stuff.'

'Stuff about what?' I'm sure other women are listening as we walk.

'About what society is like and what it could be like.' She's biting her nails, but Mum doesn't tell her off.

'So they tried to fill your head with lies,' I say.

'It wasn't all lies,' Lilli says. 'They had statistics.'

'They can manipulate those,' I say and Mum glares at me to be quiet, but I don't understand why.

'Lils,' she says calmly. 'You have to understand that they'll try to persuade you away from us. I'm sure we're here because they want to find a way to make us all think like them.'

'They won't take me away from you,' Lilli says.

'Too right they won't,' I say. 'They're feeding you bullshit along with those biscuits.'

'Enough, Ruby,' Mum warns. *Enough?* I haven't even started.

Lilli twists her hair into a rope and starts to bite the ends. I want to tell her that she'll get a hairball, but I don't. I keep each and every one of my angry words inside as we head towards the dining room where, hopefully, there'll be food.

They feed us one sausage each and a spoonful of potatoes. That's it. I never thought I'd be craving a pile of vegetables. I hope they'll bring out more because I'm almost as hungry as when we came in, but when I finish my last mouthful a hand grabs my shoulder.

'276?' the guard asks. His eyes seem hollow.

Mum is sitting opposite me and she puts down her glass of water.

'Yes,' I say.

'Come with me,' the guard says. I feel Lilli freeze beside me as Mum stands up.

'Where are you taking her?' she asks. Silence drops into the room as people stop moving.

'The general has requested her,' the guard says, his fingers tight on me.

'The general?' my mum asks. 'Why?'

'It's the order.'

'She's not going.' Mum looks panicked, but she can't reach me and I can't get to her as the guard pulls me to my feet.

'I'm okay,' I tell her. But I'm not. A stomach ache fires

through me so suddenly that I almost double over.

'No,' my mum says, beginning to run alongside the table, coming around to our side. 'You can't take her.'

'It's orders,' the guard repeats. I don't want him to drag me, so I walk with him. Mum grabs his hand from my elbow.

'You're not taking my daughter anywhere,' she yells in his face.

He slaps her so hard that she falls backwards.

'Mum!' I shout, but the guard pulls me towards the door. I want to tell her that I'm okay, but tears are slicing through my throat and I know they'll come out if I try to speak.

I close my eyes in the daylight as I'm dragged across the grass. I open them only when I'm stumbling too much and think I'll fall. The guard loosens his grip as we walk past the building where we sleep. We go down the side of another building and finally through a door.

We're in an empty corridor, with a grey floor and light blue walls. It feels cold and even though there are windows the sunshine has been snatched away.

'Why am I here?' I ask. But the guard doesn't answer. It's as if I haven't spoken, my words as insignificant as a wisp of smoke. There's only the sound of my feet alongside his, until we stop outside a white door and he knocks.

'Come in,' a voice calls and the guard pushes open the door and gestures for me to go in. The general sits behind a desk, the three stripes across his jacket shoulder. I feel small as he looks up, like he could destroy me just by stepping on me.

'You may go,' he tells the guard and I hear the door close.

CHAPTER SEVEN

'I promise we will work tirelessly to revive our
culture and our way of life. We will restore
our country to a place we're proud to call our
home.' – John Andrews, leader of the Traditional
Party

The general looks at me. If he had a knife to peel back my skin
he'd see how fast my heart is beating.

'I'm not going to hurt you,' he says, looking confused. 'I've
only asked you here to clean.'

To clean?

'I need someone to clean my office,' he continues, gesturing
around him. I can't tell whether his smile is warm, or whether
there's something hidden beneath it. 'It won't take long. It's not
exactly a big space.' His laugh feels out of place, sticky against
my skin. 'You have cleaned before?'

I nod. I can't admit that at home my mum has to nag me to do anything.

'Good. Good. We'll make a start now then. Follow me.' The general comes out from behind his desk. I take a step back as he comes towards me, but maybe he pretends not to notice. 'This way.'

We go out of the room. My footsteps sound faint next to his as we walk a few metres down the corridor.

'We haven't got much, but we'll get more,' he says, stopping to open a cupboard. The room is almost big enough to step into, with floor-to-ceiling shelves. Only one has bottles and cloths on it, the rest are empty.

The general grabs some things, picks up a bucket from the floor and passes them to me. He's awkward and clumsy suddenly. This close, I can smell the sourness of his breath.

We walk back to his office and I think he'll leave me alone, but he sits behind his desk.

'Shall I come back later when you're not here?' I ask. It's the first time I've spoken to him in this room and my voice feels too quiet.

'No,' he says. 'Just work around me.'

'But where shall I start?' I have to be bolder. I have to be strong under his eyes.

'You're a female aren't you? You should know these things.' For a moment I fight an urge to spray the liquid cleaner in his eye. 'The window.' He points to the frame of glass behind him. 'I'm not sure it's been touched since the army were here. You can use the sink in the corner for water.'

I have to walk behind him, but at least his back is facing me. On the wall, though, is a picture of John Andrews – his stagnant eyes fixed on me, that waxy face and soft-lipped smile. There's the sound of water as I fill the bucket. When it's full enough, I carry it and put it on the floor. I've never cleaned a window in my life. I hold the bottle up and pull the plastic trigger. A puff of liquid hits the glass and I press the cloth to it before it drips down too quickly.

One side of the cloth is covered in black almost immediately. I squirt more liquid from the bottle, but I'm not doing much more than smearing the glass with grime. I dunk the cloth into the water and watch it swirl up, releasing its dirt. I rinse it out and try again and it's a bit better this time.

And now that I can breathe properly, I realise where I am. The general's office. He seems to be the man who runs this camp, so there must be information in here about the trial that we're on. I need to look but have to bite back the urge to see everything around me, because if I can get him to trust me maybe he'll leave me alone in here.

'Tell me,' I hear the general say. 'Are you really a Core supporter, or are you simply following the thoughts of your parents?'

I keep the cloth on the window as I try to find the right way to answer. I want him on my side, but will he be able to tell if I lie? I don't want to speak, but I know I have to.

'I am a Core,' I say, my heart beating so hard that my skin hurts, as I force myself to bend down to the bucket and squeeze the cloth clean again. To my left there's a wall with two boxes on a shelf. That's all I can see before I stand up in front of the window again.

'That's an honest answer, which is good,' he says. 'Honesty is very important to Traditionals. Maybe you are more like us than you realise.'

Relief floods through me as I watch my fingers on the cloth. I've still got faint scratches of varnish on my nails from Sara's last sleepover. And I don't understand how I'm at this place. How we all are. How we're suddenly so trapped when we should be at home.

'Why are we here?' I look back at the general. He's eating a biscuit and my hunger starts to rip me open from the inside out.

'Isn't it obvious?' His eyes flick to the half-cleaned glass under my hand.

'No,' I say. From here, I can see curls of hair growing too low on his neck. They squeeze out of puffy white skin.

'The Traditionals are working towards a perfect country,' he says, as though talking to a little child. 'And the only thing stopping us is the Core Party.' He leans back in his chair, the leather squeaking. In front of him is a computer, but the screen is turned off. 'Imagine having a dream so close in your hands, but it keeps getting taken away. You'd want to keep hold of that dream, wouldn't you? You would do everything to eradicate what's in the way.'

'Eradicate?' I feel my fingers grip the cloth and a line of greasy water drips down.

'Maybe that's too strong a word,' he says. 'In essence, we need to have us all thinking the same.'

'Which is why you've set up this trial camp?'

'Yes.'

'You think that by keeping us all here, you can turn us into Traditionals?'

'I know I can. Because I have absolute belief that what we're doing is right. How could anyone not want a safer, happier, more prosperous society?' I think he's waiting for an answer from me, but I won't give him the satisfaction of one. 'I know that you'll see sense. If you do this properly, all of you will.'

Nearer the door there's a filing cabinet. There must be papers inside it, information I need.

'How did you choose which Core supporters should come here?' I ask.

'It's geographical,' the general says. 'We took a twenty-mile radius and tried to get as many as we could from that area.'

They cast a net and I fell in.

'Why our area, though? There are Core voters all over the country.'

'Unfortunately, yes,' the general says. 'But we chose a place where the density was greater.'

Density. Are we some sort of chemical mass, only good to be experimented on?

'And if we take away the influence,' the general continues, 'it weakens anyone remaining.'

'If there are less Core supporters, then it'll be difficult for them to recruit more,' I say.

'Exactly,' the general says. 'We could use the analogy of a table. If you take away its legs, with nothing to support it, it becomes useless.'

'It will fall,' I say, needing for him to believe he can influence me, that I could be on his side.

'Yes. It becomes rubble which we can then use as a foundation to build a stronger table. A better nation that won't fail.'

There are two drawers in his desk, one on either side of him. How easy it would be to step forward and open one of them.

'Are you going to hurt us?' I ask.

The general crosses his arms. 'No,' he says. 'I hope not.'

He turns back to the papers in front of him, but from here I can't see what's written on them. As he picks up his pen I have to concentrate again on scrubbing the cloth roughly along the edge of the window, to where there's a latch.

I could open it. In another life I could just climb out.

'Why have you chosen me to come and clean?' I ask.

The general doesn't answer. A strange feeling slides up me. I shouldn't have asked and it feels like I'm falling. I push the cloth into the bucket, hoping the water will calm my shaking hands.

'You remind me of my daughter,' he says quietly, his back still facing me, his fingers still on his pen. 'She died. Ten years ago. You look like her.'

It's so far from the answer I thought I'd get and now I don't know what to say. I don't know whether I should ask him about her, at least acknowledge her existence. All I do is wash the cloth over the glass again.

Through the window, not far from the fence, there's the loch on the other side. I stare past the barbed wire to see its water completely still, reflecting the mountain rising steeply next to it. It's so peaceful and it helps me.

'What was she called?' I ask, stopping again to look at the general, needing my eyes to show concern.

He puts down his pen. 'Zoe,' he says. 'Zoe Jane.'

'That's nice,' I say. As I watch his mind drift towards her memory, I feel a sting of genuine pity. Because here, like this, his sadness still blinds him.

But it's only an instant and he's back in this room, this office, and now I know he only sees a Core supporter standing in front of him.

'The window looks fine now,' he says, turning from me. 'You can go now.'

Go? I've hardly cleaned at all, but I do as he tells me. I tip up the bucket of dirty water into his sink and slowly clean the rim of dirt from the porcelain bowl, glancing around the room to see as much as I can. There's a small empty table on one side and a wastepaper basket next to the filing cabinet.

'Ruby?' the general asks, as I walk towards the door. It's unnatural to hear my name from him. 'You're not to tell anyone what I just told you. Do you understand?' His voice is cold now, layers of warning clear within it.

'Yes,' I say, before I leave him behind his desk and go from his office.

I'm alone in the corridor. The sound of my footsteps follows me to the cupboard before I click it open. I stand inside it and try to remember every detail of the general's office before I put the bottle, the cloth and the bucket back in their place. I run my hands along the rest of the shelves. Maybe there's a key forgotten here? I kneel down and search on the floor, but there's nothing.

I know I have to go back to the bunk room now, but I'm on my own so maybe I could get *lost* on the way. I could find out what's in the other buildings. For the first time since we've been in this camp I feel a flicker of hope as I step out into the corridor.

A guard is standing here.

'What are you doing?' On the woman's cold face is a pinch of glee.

'I was cleaning,' I say. *Look her straight in the eyes and don't turn away.*

'Cleaning?' she shouts, staring at me as though I'm stuffed full with dirt.

The general's door opens. 'Yes,' he says, not even stepping out. 'That's correct.'

The guard looks from him and then back to me. I know what she's thinking and I wonder if I care. Let her tie herself in knots with the wrong idea.

'And you've finished?' she asks me, a gross smirk twitching her lips.

'Yes,' the general says. 'Escort her back to her room.'

'Yes, sir,' the guard says. It's satisfying seeing her grovelling, but she's ruined my chance to look around. 'Walk in front,' she tells me. Is there a part of her that's afraid of what I might do?

The general goes back into his office and closes the door. The guard and I have only gone a few steps when she grabs me by the top of my arm, gripping sharp enough to bruise my breath. The fear is back, trickling down inside me before I can stop it.

'You're not special,' she whispers in my ear, her lips close enough to touch my skin. 'So don't think you are.'

But maybe I am? I look like the general's daughter. He thinks of Zoe when he sees me. I can use it. I can use him. Maybe his daughter is who I need to get us out of here.

'Why did the general want you?' I don't think my mum's hug will ever end.

'To clean,' I say. I know that other people in the bunk room are listening.

'I didn't know where you'd gone,' Lilli whispers. I can tell she's been crying.

'I'm fine,' I tell her. 'It was a bit weird, but I'm fine.'

'Where did he make you clean?' Darren asks, as Mum brushes back the hair from my face and tucks it behind my ear. I shake it loose, as I always do.

'His office.'

Mum's hand stops. 'Did he do anything to you?'

'No. I just cleaned the window and then was told to leave.'

'And that was it?' Darren asks.

'Yes.'

'Why did he ask you?' Mum asks.

'I don't know.' The lie is easy and difficult all at once.

'You promise he didn't make you do anything else.'

'I promise,' I say.

'Ruby!' It's Luke's voice from across the room. His head is poking out from some sort of den that's been made out of sheets and stacked up coats. Children surround him – the four who I

152

saw climb down from the coach earlier. The youngest girl is sitting on the floor, holding the ear of her rabbit underneath her nose.

'Let her go with them,' Darren says to Mum and before she asks more questions I hurry across the room, stepping over people stretched out on the floor.

'Having fun?' I laugh, as I get to Luke. Among all the horror, his smile is something that's real and true.

'Where were you?'

'Cleaning.'

Luke bursts out laughing. 'You?'

'Yeah, I know.' I want to tell him about the general's office and everything I've seen.

'Were you any good?' Luke asks.

'No. It was odd.'

Destiny's head appears next to him and I try to keep my smile in place as a stone falls heavy in my stomach. Jealousy is definitely an emotion I need to work on.

'Are you going to join us?' Destiny asks, wriggling out her whole body and standing up. I glance at the red material on her arm, where she's tucked her number underneath.

'You're breaking the den,' a boy squeals, as he rushes to the back and holds it steady.

'It doesn't look like there's room for three.' As soon as I say it I know how it sounds.

'Always room for you,' Luke says, jumping up and leaning in to kiss me. I don't really let him and I can't tell whether it's because of Destiny, or because I still haven't brushed my teeth since I came to the camp. It's stupid as all I really want to do is spend the entire day with his arms round me.

'What's wrong?' he asks.

'Nothing.'

'Want to come under the sheet, then?'

It's that smile. It somehow puts everything right. He should be the one who's in charge of the country – everyone would just melt and do whatever he asked.

'Alone?' I ask.

'Alone,' Luke says, taking my hand. 'I have to take this beautiful girl into the den,' he tells the watching children. 'To explain a special mission to her.'

'Can we go too?' I hear a boy ask.

'In a minute.'

There's not much space, but it's enough to hide both of us inside. Immediately, Luke's lips are on mine, but I push him away.

'What were you doing in here with Destiny?' I ask him.

It's a muffled light under the sheets, but it's clear enough to see the disappointment on his face. He knows exactly what I'm thinking.

'Are you serious?'

'She's gorgeous,' I point out.

'And so are you.' I try to speak, but Luke takes my words by kissing me again. 'I don't want to be with Destiny,' he says. And even in here, where I couldn't be further from gorgeous, we kiss again. When we stop he holds my face gently, so I have nowhere to look but into his eyes. 'The only one I want to be with is you.' And I know it's true. Luke is a part of me and I'm a part of him. He's in every cell of mine. And I wish more than ever that we were back at his in his bedroom.

The sheets above us whip back. Luke's dad is glaring down at us.

'Out,' he says.

'Bad timing, Dad,' Luke says, helping me stand up as the children giggle around us.

'None of this is funny, Luke,' his dad says. 'If I'd been one of the guards, you'd be in serious trouble.'

'Sorry,' I say, too embarrassed to look him in the eye.

'I know it's difficult,' Robert continues. 'But you two have to get a grip on how serious this is. If they find you like I just did, they'll separate you. And God knows what else.'

His words drip dread into me.

'Okay,' Luke says. 'We'll be more careful.'

'No,' his dad tells him. 'In this place, you won't do it at all.'

Everyone around us is quiet now.

'We'll go and sit and do a jigsaw puzzle together then,' Luke says. But his dad isn't in the mood. At all.

'Can we still play dens?' one of the boys asks.

'Of course.' Robert smiles down at him. 'But these two aren't allowed in there. Okay?' The little boy nods up at him. 'What's your name?' Robert asks him.

'Zamal,' the boy says.

'Right, Zamal, you're in charge.'

There are so many words in the look that Robert gives Luke and me as he heads back across the room.

Before bed, I'm standing in the corridor next to Darren in the queue for the toilets. I hate that so many of us have to share the same ones and that I can't have more than a few moments on my own. It rattles anger through me, but I know if I start to let it out then I might never stop screaming.

'Why are we even in this place?' I ask Darren. 'We haven't done anything wrong.'

'You're right. We haven't,' he says.

'Then they can't be allowed to do this.'

'I know, but somehow they are.'

I can't tell whether it's Darren or me who's changed, but in here everything feels different. Now I want to speak to him and spend time with him and I feel safe, not irritated, when he's near.

'I was thinking,' I say more quietly now. 'If this really is some sort of trial, surely we can just go along with it all and pretend to be Trads, so they let us go.'

'I wish it could be that easy,' Darren says, as the queue moves forwards a bit. 'They really believe that they can brainwash us into their way of thinking.'

'How will they do it, though?'

'They'll try and wear us down through lack of food and sleep, for a start,' Darren says.

'And stupid punishments like making me run in the rain.'

'You dealt with that really well, Ruby. Your mum and I were really proud of you.'

'What, for sitting down when I shouldn't have?' I smile, as we shuffle forwards again.

'That bit wasn't so great.' Even his face looks different in here. It's like I'm finally letting myself see who he really is. 'Seriously. We have to just go with their rules for now. They're too unpredictable.'

'Is that why you didn't stick up for Mum when they hit her?' I know my words are harsh, but I still wish that he'd at least said something, instead of standing there and letting it happen.

'I couldn't risk stepping in. That guard had my wife on the floor and a gun in his hand. You must be able to see that?'

'I guess.' And I know I do really. I think I just scooped up the anger I felt for the guard and threw it at Darren because he was the only safe option.

'You must never doubt how much I love your mum. It destroyed me not being able to protect her.' He hangs his head down and picks at the skin by his thumbnail. Already it's bleeding slightly. 'I feel responsible that you're all even here. I should've guessed this might have happened and taken you somewhere safe.'

'You couldn't have known. There wasn't a warning or anything. And even if there was, we wouldn't have believed they could do this.'

Darren looks up at me. 'I just don't want any of it to be happening to you. I'd do anything for them to let you all go.'

I put my hand on his arm, something I've never done before. He feels like an anchor now and I need him next to me.

'We'll be out of here soon,' I say.

He nods once and leans his head back against the wall. I rest my head next to his shoulder and look along the corridor, crammed with people as lost as we are.

In the morning, I feel like every muscle in my body is broken. I don't want to be asleep as I'm too uncomfortable, but I don't want to be awake either. I just want to be at home.

After the queue for the toilet, the guards lead us past the sinks in the shower room. We're each allowed to stop briefly and this time I do brush my teeth. I block out the fact that others have used the toothbrush and concentrate instead on the mint taste of the paste and how if I close my eyes, for this moment, at least, I feel clean and normal.

The guard yanks it from my mouth. I watch her as I spit into the sink, before I join the queue to walk down the stairs for roll call.

Outside we stand in line as the bitter wind finds its way too easily through the fence. Darren holds my hand and it's the only thing that helps warm me. Further down I can see Luke. He's talking closely to his dad and when he looks up and sees me he smiles, but it just makes everything that's happening feel even more wrong.

We stand and wait for so long that the cold starts to gnaw through my coat. I feel it rip my skin and feast on my bones. Behind us, Mr Jesenska has his arm round his wife. They both wear hats, but I wonder how they can cope with this at their age.

Finally the line starts to move. Finally my number is checked. I'm too frozen to look back at Darren as I follow the others into the dining room, where a piece of bread and a glass of water is waiting.

After we've eaten, a guard stands by the table and uses his gun to draw an imaginary line between us.

'This half, go back to the room,' he says. 'This half, into the kitchen.'

I want to sleep, or at least curl up on the mattress upstairs, but I'm in the wrong half. And an uneasy feeling hooks into me when I realise I'm not with anyone I know.

I'm pushed with the group into the kitchen, where the steam is thick and warm. Instantly, I feel myself begin to thaw as we stand together, useless, our hands by our sides. None of us know what we should do.

'Where shall we go?' I hear a woman ask.

'Use your initiative,' the guard snaps.

And we scatter among the people already working in here. I want to be close to the ovens where I know it'll be warmest, but as I head there, someone grabs my elbow to stop me.

I yank myself away, but they pull me back by the shoulder.

'It's me.' *Conor.* He's standing here with the number 312 sewn into the red material on his arm. I don't think I've ever wanted to hug anyone so much. But I remember where I am and even though he's only a friend, I can't be close to him in front of the Trads.

'Luke said you were here.' I smile at him.

'Yeah. I heard it was a holiday camp, so I couldn't resist it. Here, hold this.' He passes me a tray before he opens a pack of frozen sausages and tips them onto it.

'Taxing work,' I say.

'It's just about the level I can cope with.' No one has given him gloves and his fingers look frozen.

'Where's your mum?' I ask.

He nods over to the metal sinks lined along the wall. His mum has her back to us, a scarf tied over her head, her number stitched on the slash of red on her arm.

'Is she okay?'

'No. Her next chemo session is meant to be today.' Anger spins from him.

'Will they let her go?' It's a stupid question.

'What do you reckon?' Conor's eyes look suddenly wild and lost.

'Maybe it'll be okay to miss one,' I tell him. 'They could double the dose next time, or something?'

'Yeah,' Conor says. 'Maybe.'

His mum's illness is scooping him dry. His laughter is so, so far out of reach.

We take the trays to the workers by the ovens, before we go to the huge freezer at the back of the kitchen. Icy air drifts out when the woman there opens it and she passes Conor and me more bags of sausages, which we take back to the table.

'I never thought I'd prefer to be doing schoolwork,' Conor says, as he rips open another bag.

'Is this all we have to do?'

'I guess so.'

There are so many people busy in the kitchen that no one notices when we're done.

'Fancy breaking their stupid rules?' Conor asks me. There's that spark of a smile in his eye. The one that's got us both into trouble at school too many times.

'Like what?' I ask. The danger somehow feels diluted with

Conor next to me. I can pretend that we're on a school trip and the only people we have to dodge are the teachers.

He points to the door next to us. 'La porte?'

I nod. 'Après tu.'

'What's that supposed to mean?'

'After you, you doofus,' I say and I push open the door and we're through it before I even breathe.

We're alone in a small corridor. In front of us is a door with a glass window in the top and beyond it is the back of the camp.

Conor grins. 'Shall we?' he asks.

'Would be rude not to,' I say. And he turns the handle to let us outside.

The silence, the freedom is instant. I lean back against the wall and breathe it in, let it wash through my mind and clear all the clutter and nightmares of the last two days.

I only open my eyes when I hear Conor walking away. He's going towards the fence that keeps us in here, its barbed-wire teeth tangled sharp on the top. I don't have to run far to catch up with him.

'What if they see us?' I ask.

'They didn't say we couldn't walk out here,' he says. I suppose he's right, but I know they won't like it.

'Don't touch it, though,' I say, grabbing his arm before we get too close to the fence.

'Do you think it'd electrocute us?'

'Could do. And I don't particularly want a fried Conor on my hands.'

'Should we hide behind that?' Conor points to a blackthorn bush pushed up against the fence.

'If they catch us together there then we really would be in trouble,' I say.

'We could try to escape. They wouldn't be able to see us behind it and we could dig our way to freedom.'

'This camp would be long gone before we got through to the other side.' I wonder which of us I'm trying to convince.

'You think they'll let us go soon?' Conor asks.

'They'll have to,' I say.

'That general guy said it was a trial.'

'Yup. They want to turn us all into Trads.' I laugh. 'Well, good luck with that one, when they can't even get the basics right.'

'What do you mean?'

'Well, you and I were cooking together for a start. Think about it – men in the kitchen isn't exactly in line with what they want from their society.'

'They'll realise their mistakes soon.'

'If we haven't already got out of here,' I say.

'Do you think there'll be an uprising from us, or something?'

'Maybe.' But I only say it to keep Conor positive. I don't think I really believe it, because how would we stand a chance when they've got guns?

Beyond the fence the land stretches out. It's stopped raining and we can see for miles. Past the loch to the horizon topped by a mountain that touches the sky.

'I wish we could walk out there,' I say. It's strange that it's so close, yet we can't even feel the grass the other side.

'Think of all the nature things you'd be able to spot and tell me about,' Conor laughs.

'All the spiders I could throw at you.'

'You wouldn't.'

'You know I would.'

I breathe in deeply, needing to share the air of the distant plants, the leaves, the roots.

'This place reminds me of somewhere we went when I was six,' Conor says. 'When it was the three of us.'

'With your mum and dad?'

'Yeah. One big happy family,' he says. 'Not that I need to tell you about that.' Conor and I both have absent dads, but his is far worse than mine. At least I get to visit mine and he phones Lilli and me fairly often.

Conor kicks at a stone on the floor and it flips up, skimming past the wire and landing on the other side. 'We were camping and he made a show of doing a big breakfast every morning. Eggs, bacon, the works – all on this little campfire. It was great. I loved it.' He doesn't look up at me, only scuffs another stone loose. 'He took me fishing and we spent days just him and me and I thought he was the best dad ever.' He breathes out heavily, letting his memories disintegrate in the air. 'Then when we got home, he fucked off. Literally, the next day.'

'To Cornwall?' I ask. He knows that I get it. He was a bit younger than me when my dad left, but we share so many feelings. I get what it's like to have the bottom literally fall out of your world. To wake up spinning in space.

'He didn't look back.' Conor's laugh hasn't a speck of happiness in it.

'It's made you and your mum close, though,' I say. She's quite quiet when I go round to theirs, but she's really kind and is always there if Conor needs her.

'Yeah,' he says. 'But now she's ill.' I can almost see a pencil drawing the pain on Conor's face.

'She'll get better,' I tell him. She has to.

Conor looks at me and I can guess the words he's going to say. 'Without chemo?'

'We won't be here too long,' I say.

'I'm serious about escaping, Ruby. There's no way I'm staying here for much longer.'

'Do you think it's safe to try?'

'Well it's not safe for my mum to stay here. She needs her treatment to start again.'

'You two!' a voice yells. We both turn quickly to see a

165

guard storming towards us, his hand on his gun. 'What are you doing?'

Conor puts up his hands and I copy him.

'We were just talking,' he says. If he's afraid his voice doesn't show it.

'I felt sick,' I say, as the guard gets to us. 'I needed some air.' Blood pounds in my ears. The mountain and the trees have disappeared. All I can see now is the anger on the guard's face, his finger squeezed tight to the trigger.

'You can't come out here,' he shouts, even though he's close enough to touch us.

'Then we'll go back,' Conor says, cool as anything.

The soldier puts out an arm to stop him.

'Are you together?' he asks.

'It depends on your definition of "together",' Conor says, looking him calmly in the eyes. 'We are standing here together, yes.'

The soldier's teeth visibly tighten. I want to tell Conor to stop. We're not at school now. This man is far more dangerous than a teacher.

'Are you in a relationship?' the guard asks.

Conor looks at me and smiles.

'Nah,' he says. 'Sorry, Rubes, no offence but you're not my type.'

Step carefully, Conor.

'Get inside,' the guard shouts. 'Now.'

We don't run. We don't even walk fast. I follow Conor's pace as we head back towards the building. Towards the door that takes us back into a place I never want to be in again.

CHAPTER EIGHT

'Our great country. Unity for all.' – John Andrews,
leader of the Traditional Party

Something has happened. I can sense it as soon as I walk in. Groups of adults sit close together, talking intensely. Zamal and his sister are crying and our mum is sitting with them on the floor. I go straight to Luke, who's on a bed near them, writing in his sketchbook.

'What's going on?' I ask. He looks up at me and there's something different about him. A deep worry that wasn't there before.

'You know the mum with the four children? They've taken her and her twins.'

'Taken them?'

He closes his sketchbook and moves up to make a bit of space for me.

'The guards came in after dinner and just took them away.'

'Why?'

'I don't know.'

'Could they have gone to that room where they took Lilli when the women were sewing?'

'It felt different to that.' Luke looks bewildered. 'All the children were crying, the ones who were going and the ones who had to stay. Zamal and Rimi were clinging on to their mum.'

Across the room, Rimi is now sitting on my mum's lap, the remnants of tears still shaking her body, her rabbit clasped tight in her hand.

'Why just them?' I ask.

'I don't know.'

I need to unpick the last hour and sew it back together so that none of this has happened. I'll walk through the door and all four children will be playing. And then I'll unpick the other nights – a week ago, a year. To before the time when the Traditionals really started to become a possibility. To a time when John Andrews seemed like a distant nightmare.

The mother and her twins don't come back. Destiny's mum, Aba, has joined Mum on the floor with Rimi and Zamal. She's telling them a story and, although I can't hear much of it from here, it must be exciting as her arms keep circling out and above her head and Rimi is transfixed.

I'm watching Zamal, though, and his fingers are bunched in a fist. He wipes away his first tears, but then lets the others fall. He starts to shake his head again and again, and when my mum reaches out to stroke his hair he pushes her away.

'I want my mummy,' he says, as he kicks out with his legs.

Aba falters, but carries on telling the story. Rimi stares at her brother, her rabbit clutched under her nose.

'I'm sure they'll bring her back soon,' Mum tells him quietly.

'Where is she?' Zamal asks.

'I don't know, sweetheart, but she won't be far.'

It happens so quickly that I hardly realise Zamal has moved, before he's running across the room, grabbing at the door handle.

'No!' Mum shouts, but already Zamal is in the corridor and it's Darren who reaches the door first and disappears after him.

'Zamal,' Rimi cries and Mum grabs hold of her as we all stare at the empty hole that took her brother and Darren. We hear the heavy boots in the passage outside. And then there are Zamal's screams and Darren is shouting and I don't move. I can't. Everything has stopped. My mind is frozen in this place, slowly shattering at the sounds of the guards yelling outside.

Darren runs back in and he's carrying Zamal, holding him safe. Behind them are two guards.

'Stop!' one shouts and Darren does. But he keeps his back to them, shielding Zamal.

One of the guards raises a gun. He points it into the room.

'There's to be order in here,' he shouts, his gun moving in an arc over those sitting on the floor. My mum is there and I can't breathe enough. She doesn't move, keeping her hand resting on Rimi, her eyes blinking.

The silence is long and empty, yet filled with everything. With every heartbeat I've ever had, every blade of grass I've seen and word I've spoken. I hear them all and none of them, as the guard aims his gun at the people sitting and lying there. Some of them close their eyes.

'You'll be obedient,' he says, his gun shaking slightly. 'Or there'll be no place for you in our society. Is that understood?'

'Yes.'

'Yes.'

The words are dragged deep from a place of fear, yet I can't join in as I stare at my mum lying there.

'Good,' the guard says and he starts to back away, still pointing his gun into the room. Both the guards go from us and there's the sound of the door closing.

Darren carries Zamal over to Rimi. I can't see his face from here. I don't know what he says when he kneels down next to my mum. But Zamal doesn't let go of him, his arms staying tight around Darren's neck. And now he's silent.

It's later when a man stands up in the middle of the room. There's a group of people sitting around him, among them his wife with their three-month-old baby. We watch him until one by one we're quiet and silence washes over us.

'Look,' he says. He has to be quiet enough so no one outside hears him. 'We've got a bad feeling about this. I don't want to scare anyone, but we have no idea what they've done with the mum and kids they've taken. They've told us they're safe, but I don't know what to believe.' No one moves as he speaks. 'What I do know is that I don't want to stay here like a sitting target. When you think about it, there are more of us than them. We can easily overpower them and end this before it really starts.'

'Easily?' a man asks.

'We'd obviously have to plan it carefully. We could go at night, when they won't be expecting it and most of the guards will be sleeping.'

'You seem to have forgotten a vital fact,' a woman says. 'They have guns.' Her words sting the air.

'Do you really think they'd use them?' The man looks around, yet no one answers him. 'Because I don't think they would. Imagine what would happen to their reputation. They want this camp to work, but not at any expense.'

'Are you sure about that?' It's Mum who asks it.

'I'm not sure about anything right now,' the man says. 'Apart from the fact that I don't want to stay here any longer. They might only have one or two guards on at night. The perimeter of the fence is huge. They can't watch it all.'

'He's got a point,' someone says.

'Plus –' the man smiles – 'we sneaked out a few knives from the kitchen. They're not quite as clued up as they think they are. We've got a chance here.' He looks around the room. 'So what do you think? Shall we put our heads together to come up with a plan?'

'What if we don't want to be involved?' Mum asks.

'What are our other options? Just stay here like sitting ducks?'

The woman with the baby gets up. 'Those who want to join us can. Those who want to stay, stay.'

'It's not about *wanting* to stay,' Mum says. 'It's about it being too dangerous to try to escape.'

'Let's make a start,' the man says, sitting down again. Some people must believe they can escape, as they go over to join the group.

'Do you think they're doing the right thing?' I ask Luke.

'It's a risk I don't think I'd take,' he says and he hugs me close enough to burn away the grating hunger and dread in my belly, just for a bit.

In the morning, there's a strange quiet in our room. No one speaks loudly of the planned escape any more, but there are whispers stabbing the air. I look around, hoping that Zamal and Rimi's mum and sisters have come back in the night, but they haven't and their absence seems even bigger and more painful than yesterday.

In silence we help tie the red material on each other's arms. When I look at the number on mine, it feels stitched through my skin. When we are done, Zamal holds tight to Darren's hand and Rimi to Mum's. Lilli and I stand close to them as we go from the room.

Outside, I grab the sleeves of my hoodie, rolling them up once to hide the dirt on them. It doesn't make much difference, but it makes me feel a tiny bit better as I get into line. A guard is standing in front of us, his voice shouting through a loudspeaker.

'You are to repeat after me: Our great country. Unity for all.'

I look around expecting at least some people to laugh. No one does. Instead people start mumbling the words.

'Our great country. Unity for all.'

The guard keeps saying it, the sound distorted and unnatural.

I look at Lilli and already she's chanting it, her face tipped up slightly. And I know I have to join her.

'Our great country. Unity for all.' But I keep my voice small, hearing Lilli's lapping over mine. On and on, as we move forwards slowly in the line, until I don't even realise that I'm speaking any more.

I get closer to the front and above the chanting I can hear the general's voice as he ticks the numbers on his list. I reach over for Lilli's hand. When she looks at me I want to give her reassurance that we'll all be okay, but her innocent face hurts my heart so much that instead I think I might cry. I only let go of her when it's my turn to step forwards.

The general looks at me gently. 'Ruby West,' he says.

'Yes.' I'm real. I do exist.

'Number?'

'276.' And I wonder if he sees fragments of his daughter caught in me, before I watch him make a mark next to the number on the page.

Lilli is sitting alone on the bed when I go over to her.

'You okay, squid-breath?' I ask.

'Mm,' she replies.

'I've just had the delightful job of cleaning the loos.'

'Was Luke with you?'

'He's with a group on gardening duty.'

'You should have been with them,' she says, shuffling over to make space for me.

'I doubt I'm missing much. There aren't exactly many plants around here to look after.'

'Maybe you should ask the general for some.'

'I don't intend to stay here long enough to watch things grow,' I tell her. I kick off my shoes to sit cross-legged on the bed. 'Mum says they took you to that room again.'

'Yes.'

'And?'

175

'And what?'

'What did they teach you this time?'

'Quite a lot of things,' she says, but she knows that won't be enough for me. 'It was fun. We played a card game with people on the cards not numbers, so it was easy for even the younger ones to play.'

'People?'

'Yeah. Who did like good and bad things and you had to work it out and build teams.'

'Let me guess, the bad people were the Cores, right?'

She looks hurt. 'No. It wasn't like that.'

'Maybe not on the surface.'

Destiny suddenly jumps down from the bunk above us.

'Room for me?' she asks. She doesn't give us much choice as she climbs her long limbs on to the bed. 'I just made it from my bunk all the way to yours without touching the ground.' She's brought a tiny bag with her, which she unzips and from it tips a few bits of make up on to the mattress. 'They can take away our mirrors,' she says, 'but I want to keep looking good.'

'How come they let you keep this?' I ask.

'I said it was my time-of-the-month kit. They didn't dare look past the tampons to see what was underneath.'

'You're a genius,' I say. 'Albeit a crazy brave one.'

'They're not going to stop me being who I want to be.'

Destiny laughs as she picks up an eyebrow pencil. 'Who wants to go first?'

Lilli looks in awe, as though some sort of goddess has just landed from the ceiling.

'Me?' she asks.

'No,' I say, holding out a hand to stop Destiny. 'The Traditionals hate it, you know they do. They want to ban it.'

'But they haven't banned it yet.' Destiny smiles. 'We'll have to skip the foundation, though, as mine will look mighty strange on your skin.'

'I don't want you to,' I tell Lilli. 'Mum'll freak.' I can see hesitation begin to find its way into her eyes. 'It's not safe enough.'

'It is,' she says. 'I know them better now. They won't really mind.'

Destiny understands the look I give her. 'I think your sister's right,' she says. 'I don't want to put you at risk.'

Lilli shrugs, but she doesn't even try to hide her disappointment.

'When we get out,' Destiny tells her. 'I'll give you a proper makeover. Deal?'

'Deal,' Lilli smiles.

'And until then you two can practise on me.' Destiny passes me a pencil and Lilli some eye shadow. 'I'll do this first.' She squeezes a tube and dark cream swirls on to her finger. 'But you can do the rest.'

'You can't be that frightened of them if you're putting it on still,' Lilli says, as Destiny closes her eyes and rubs foundation into her cheeks and across her forehead.

'Well, I figure that if they don't want me to wear it, then they can ask nicely and I'll take it off.'

'I'm not sure they understand the word *nice*,' I remind her.

'Then we'd better teach them the meaning of it,' she laughs. 'Right, eyebrows first.' She holds her face towards us. 'Do your worst.'

'Okay. Hold still,' I say, as I start to line the pencil over Destiny's eyebrows. 'Lilli was just telling me what they get up to in that room.'

'Where they teach you things?' Destiny asks her.

'They get to do games and all sorts,' I say.

Lilli looks down at the tight blue powder in the tiny compact and she starts to swirl it loose with the mini make-up brush.

'It's good,' Lilli says.

Destiny faces towards her and closes her eyes. 'Your turn. Go crazy with that powder.'

Lilli smiles and starts to colour in Destiny's eyelids. She seems so unlike my little sister, yet more like her than ever. Already she's lost weight, her skin falling closer to the bones in her face, but she seems more vital, somehow, that her essence has been sharpened.

'Did they tell you more about the Trad policies and things?'

178

Destiny asks. 'Some of the stuff they say is quite interesting.'

'They're going to stop knife crime so we all feel safer,' Lilli says.

'That's good,' Destiny says.

'They showed us a film about gangs and things. It was really scary.'

'The younger ones watched it?' I ask, trying to keep my voice as calm as Destiny's.

'Yes, but they told us that things weren't going to be like that any more.'

'I reckon that eye's done.' Destiny blinks. 'How's it looking so far?' She pouts at us.

'Great,' I say.

'Good job, Lilli,' she says. 'Next one, then.'

Lilli concentrates hard. She has the same expression as when she does her homework at the kitchen table and I have to swallow hard to stop myself from crying.

'Any other pearls of wisdom they've told you?' Destiny asks her.

'They said that sometimes apples can look really good but when you bite into them the core is rotten. And they said maybe bits of the Core party are like that.'

'Clever,' I say, trying and failing to keep the sarcasm out of my voice.

'Well, Lilli,' Destiny says, as she opens her eyes again. 'That could be true of any political party or any person. You've got to really look deep into people. You've got to think about everything they say and do and everything they stand for. Not just a bit of it, but all of it. And if you don't like what you see or hear, then you've got to question it. You know you can talk to me, or Ruby, or your mum about any of it.'

Lilli nods as she listens to every word. I feel a bit annoyed with myself that I haven't managed to tell her all this. She's my sister, but I've been so scared and angry about how much she might be believing the Trads, that I've let my words get tangled before I say them properly.

'Now, as you did such a good job of the eyes,' Destiny says, 'you're in control of the mascara.' Lilli looks nervous as I pass it to her, but Destiny just smiles. 'If you go wrong, I'll wipe it off and start again. It's not like we've got anything else to do.'

'Okay,' Lilli says, as she opens the mascara tube.

'Are you doing all this for Luke?' I ask Destiny, before I think to stop myself.

'Doing what for Luke?' Destiny asks. She genuinely looks like I've said the strangest thing. 'You think I fancy him?'

'I don't know.' I feel stupid now. Like a jealous girl in primary school or something. I want to make an excuse about how this horrible hunger is ripping apart my brain.

Destiny smiles. 'I like girls, Ruby.'

'You do?'

'I thought you knew,' she says.

'No.'

'I guess our paths don't really cross at school.' She closes her eyes so that Lilli can start on the mascara. 'But it's even more reason for the Trads to hate me. Imagine, black and gay *and* with make up on,' she laughs.

Lilli stops. 'Are you afraid they'll find out?'

Destiny opens her eyes again.

'It'll take more than their small minds to bring me down. And just for the record,' she says, laughing, 'I don't fancy either of you two either.'

I leave Lilli telling Destiny all about the Tight-Knits and the trouble she and her friends had when they started secondary, but how they managed to stick together. As I cross the room, I think about Destiny's advice to her about prejudice and wonder if Lilli can use it to see more clearly about the Trads.

'Hey,' I say to Darren. 'Room for me?'

'Always room for you, Rubes,' he says, moving up to make space next to him on the floor. I nearly make some smart comment about how I hope I'm not interrupting him as he looks so busy, but I can tell he's not in the mood.

'You okay?' I ask.

'Been better.' There's a bit of blood on his thumb from where he's been biting his nails. It's something he never does at home. 'I never thought I'd actually want to be at work.'

'I never thought I'd miss school.'

Darren laughs lightly, but it makes me more sad than anything. I look over to where Stan is making funny faces to try to entertain some children. He's somehow even got Zamal and Rimi smiling away in the middle of them.

'Where do you think the Trads have taken their mum and sisters?'

Darren glances at them too.

'Do you want the answer I'd give Lilli, or what I really think?'

'What you really think.'

'I'm wondering why the only kids who have been taken are twins.'

'What do you mean?'

'I don't know. It's just something that Mr and Mrs Jesenska said, but I'm hoping they're wrong.' His voice is so quiet that I can barely hear it.

'Darren, what is it?'

He breathes in deeply. 'Twins are useful in experiments.'

'Experiments?'

'If we're on some sort of trial, as they say, who better to test their theories on than twins?'

'Test on?'

'Leave one neutral and try things on the other.'

'What things?'

'We haven't proof of anything, but they may try to alter their thoughts somehow. Really brainwash them.'

'Could they physically hurt them?'

I can tell that Darren doesn't want to answer. 'I think the Trads are capable of anything. The bottom line is that they don't want any Core voters to exist.'

His words are too heavy. My brain literally can't hold them.

'We can't stay here, Darren. Even if there's a small chance they're doing stuff like that we have to get out of here.'

'It's not as easy as that.'

'We could try to escape,' I say quietly. 'Like those people want to?'

'I wouldn't go with them. They're not planning things properly.'

'But you'd try it another way?'

'Perhaps. If I really thought I could do it.'

'How, though?'

'I'm not sure.'

'Are there always guards in the watchtower?'

'I think so, from what I've seen. And there's no break in the fence, or other way in and out apart from the main gate where the coaches enter and leave.'

'When I was in the general's office I looked across the back of the camp, but there's no obvious way out there either.'

'Maybe we just have to keep looking, Ruby. There's got to be something.'

'But what if there's not?'

Darren doesn't answer. Instead he puts his arm around me and, as I curl into him and pull my legs close to my body, I think that if I can make myself small enough I could fall through the cracks of this camp. No guards will see me then as I slip through and roll away.

Luke finally comes back just as we're lining up in the bunk room to go to supper. The skin on his knuckles is bleeding slightly and he feels like an ice block when I hug him.

'I'm glad you didn't come,' he tells me. 'They made us rip up every single bit of weed between paving stones.'

'It still would've been nice to be with you.' But his eyes are so mixed up with an anger I've never seen in him before that I have to look away.

As we're herded down the stairs, I'm wondering where the twins are. Could the Jesenskas and Darren be right? It makes hideous sense and as we trudge outside I'm finding it hard to imagine another reason why they've gone.

At least in the dining room I can concentrate on the food instead, even though there seems to be less of it than yesterday. One sausage each and the smallest portion of potato. I end up sitting opposite Luke and he's got his knife and fork in the wrong hands. I can't work out whether it's because it'll make him go slower, so it'll seem like there's more food. He smears his

184

mash flat and smooths the top with his fork, before he draws something on it.

He raises one eyebrow at me and when he turns his plate I can see that he's drawn a heart. It settles as far as my bones. Because among the hideous strangeness of this place, I've got Luke.

'Eat your food,' his dad whispers angrily to him.

'Yessir,' Luke salutes, his fork in the air, before he scoops up my heart.

CHAPTER NINE

'Too many of you have been forgotten for far too
long. Left to rot among policies that do not work.
You deserve better than this. You have our promise
that with us you will prosper.' – John Andrews,
leader of the Traditional Party

Gunshots shatter my dreams. I sit bolt upright and feel for Lilli
in the dark.

'What's wrong?' she asks, sleep weighed in her voice.

My heart is beating so hard against my skin that it hurts.

There's shuffling, talking in the room.

'It's okay,' I say to her.

More gunshots.

'What the hell is that?' a man asks.

'Jesus,' I hear Darren say and it sounds like he's crawling
from under the bed.

'Someone put on the light,' a woman shouts.

'Are you both here?' Mum asks and I feel her sitting beside us, her hands reaching for Lilli and me.

The light turns on. Mum's arm is tight around my shoulder as I look for Luke. He's there, he's safe, his dad is next to him.

'Ruby?' I hear Destiny call from across the room.

'I'm here. We're fine.'

Fine?

There's distress and confusion on everyone's face. No one stands up. We all just sit and look around. Some children are still sleeping.

Darren is staring into the room. 'The man and his wife have gone,' he says. 'The one who was talking about escaping. And their baby.'

I never knew that fear was something you could touch. But it's walked into this room and it's here in front of us all.

An older man stands up, his hands gentle in the air.

'Let's not panic,' he says.

'Not panic?' It's one of the men I saw led from his house on the night we were all taken. 'Did you not hear what we just did?'

'Yes. But we don't know for sure what's happening.'

'They could have fired shots to scare them,' someone suggests.

'Who else is missing?'

There are voices everywhere.

'Quiet,' a woman says, fierce enough to stop the words. 'Do you want the guards coming in here now?'

The silence is instant, but it is not clean. It's thick and muddy and sits heavy in my ears.

Darren looks up at Mum. 'There are at least seven people missing,' he whispers.

'And definitely the baby?'

'Yes. The baby has gone.'

'They won't have hurt it,' I say. They must have only fired the shots in warning. In a moment, the door will open and the missing people will come back in. And when the baby cries and we can't sleep, no one will care.

I watch the door. I make it open in my mind.

Some people lie back down again.

I wait for the door to open.

'Where are they?' I whisper to Mum. But she doesn't answer.

I don't know if anyone manages to sleep. Mum stays on the bed with Lilli and I. There's not enough room to move when we lie down, but I don't care. I just want to see those people again and the mother feeding her baby.

Darren stays lying on the floor, but he reaches up to hold Mum's hand, his arm resting against the shallow mattress. The light stays on and I'm glad. I don't want to know what the darkness will bring.

My heart won't settle. It's still beating hard enough to remind me that all of this is real.

It's a long time before morning comes. Enough time for me to wonder if anyone from other rooms disappeared in the night and if Conor was among them. Because I know that he's capable of doing anything to save his mum. I try to imagine him asleep instead. I move the gunshots as far away from him as I can.

People are already walking around when the door shoves open. The guard's face has no expression.

'You're to get up,' she says. Her voice is louder than it needs to be.

A man near her stands. The woman next to him tries to pull him back down, but he pushes her away.

'Some people have gone missing,' he says. 'Among them, a mother and child.'

'You have five minutes before you line up in the corridor,' the guard says.

'You didn't hear me?' the man continues. 'Last night there were more people in this room and now they've gone.'

The guard steps over two people to get to him. She reaches up her hand and I think she's going to hit him, but instead she wipes imaginary dust from both his shoulders. He stays still, accepting it, but I can feel his disgust from here.

'You –' the guard says, '– won't speak to me again unless you're spoken to. Do you understand?'

'No,' he says calmly. 'I don't actually.'

'Yes –' the woman next to him gets to her feet – 'he understands, completely.'

Another guard appears in the doorway. The one with the riding whip that's now tucked into his boot.

'From now on,' he shouts. 'You all do exactly what we say, when we say it. Our society can no longer function with disobedience. Those who don't understand –' he glares at all of us – 'will be punished.'

'Three minutes,' the female guard says, stepping back towards the door. She leaves the room but both guards are still watching us. From here, I can see the hand of one, their boots and the ends of their guns.

Darren fixes the red material on my arm, tying it carefully so that my number is clear. His face shows his devastation and I want to piece him back together bit by bit until he's the Darren I know. Luke comes to stand next to me, but without a word Mum separates us and he has to walk behind me. I don't have time to tell him how frightened I am for Conor if he tried to escape.

The sickly corridor light eats into my skin. I match my strides to the man in front to try to calm my breathing as we go out into the bright daylight. It doesn't feel right that the sky is so blue.

There's no sign of the rain, not even a cloud. But there's no sign either of the people who've disappeared.

We're lined up as before. There are so many of us, stretching like a misshapen snake along the tarmac, reaching past the length of the other building. More people have definitely arrived, I'm sure of it. Among the mass of them, Conor has to be there.

We're told to chant their words and so we do.

Our great country. Unity for all. Over and over until they're simply sounds that escape my lips.

Tiredness is gripping tight to my bones. It doesn't let my arms, my legs, my skull escape. It drags the sound of those gunshots with it. Could the Trads have shot them? Are they capable of killing people?

Our great country. Unity for all.

I find my eyes searching the ground for blood. Were they here? Were they killed on this spot? Has any evidence been washed away? I'm sure the gunshots sounded in the building, but did the people still manage to run, did they make it to the outside? I need to think of something else, but the mother is here, running, her baby in her arms. Running to the fence as her back explodes into a crimson flower. The petals scatter. They filter into my brain and make me feel sick.

'Take a deep breath,' Luke whispers from beside me. He squeezes my hand quickly enough for no one to see.

I try to take the rumours and twist them back on themselves.

191

That the guns were shot in warning and maybe the missing people are being held somewhere as a punishment before they're returned to us. But deep inside me, in a place that I know is absolutely true, I'm sure that death has walked into the camp.

It's not the general who starts roll call, but the guard with the whip. The line moves forwards, but those who are signed in aren't led to the dining room. They're being sent back to the building we sleep in.

'Maybe breakfast isn't ready yet,' I hear someone whisper. Hunger is making every part of my body ache and the thought of not eating soon nearly takes my legs from under me.

And then I see him. Conor. He's further ahead of me with his mum, his arm around her, holding her up. I feel guilty at the relief I feel when so many people have still disappeared. But those gunshots didn't take him and seeing him there, walking forward, spreads hope into me.

I get to the head of the line. My tongue is dry against the roof of my mouth, sticking to the number they force me to say, before a guard pulls me to the side.

'You come with me to the general,' he says. This time, I'm not worried, but the memory of those gunshots stops me from asking for food first.

As I walk with the guard, I wonder if there's any way that I could overpower him and take him by surprise, so that I could steal his uniform. But I know I wouldn't stand a chance. Beyond the window in the corridor I can see the blackthorn bush that Conor and I stood near when we sneaked out of the kitchen. *We could dig our way to freedom.* I don't laugh at the thought now. All I think is maybe. Maybe we'll need to.

With the bucket and cleaning things in my hands I wait outside the general's office. Now I'm here, my nerves are spiralling. I know I need to get answers from him, but I'm scared about how I'll ask.

'Enter,' the voice calls. The guard pushes me inside, before he closes the door behind me.

The general is sitting at his desk, the same as before. He looks up and I want to believe that his smile is genuine.

'You came back,' he says.

'I had no choice.' I didn't mean to reply like this. Hunger is tangling my sense. His face changes a little. It stops me telling him that I haven't had breakfast and that my cleaning will be even more rubbish if I don't get food and water.

'Maybe you could dust today?' he suggests. 'I've heard that it's an invisible killer.'

Like you?

But I have to think clearly. Maybe he can admit what's been done to those people. Perhaps he can tell me that they're somehow still alive.

'I'll get started, then.'

'Good,' he says.

193

I stay on this side of the room and begin with the paintings. There are two of them together and they're almost identical, each with a horse staring out, but there's no background so the horses look like they're floating. I wonder if he chose them. My hand still shakes slightly as I rub gently on the front of one. There's no glass on it, so I can feel the bumps of paint through the cloth.

'We've got friends who won't be happy that we've gone,' I risk saying. 'They'll want to know where we are.'

'People know that you're on a rehabilitation programme.'

'But we're not addicts,' I say.

'There's a fine line between ingesting a harmful substance into your body and ingesting harmful views into your mind.'

I pause to show that I'm giving time for his words to settle. 'I hadn't thought of it like that.'

'Sometimes all it needs is a bit of exposure to the correct way of thinking. Re-education.'

'If you'd come into our school, I think you would have been able to convince a lot of us,' I say, as I wipe the duster along the top of the picture frame.

'You included?'

'Maybe. We never had a really good speaker visit from the Traditionals. It would have helped us see both sides.'

'Perhaps it's something I should think about doing,' he says.

'You'd be good at it.' I turn round, wanting him to see his

daughter in me and needing to feel safe in the palm of her memory. 'I find it interesting to talk to you.'

'Good.' I can almost see the smoke of his pride as I reel him in.

'How old was Zoe?' I glance at his computer, but the screen is turned away from me.

'Fourteen.'

Younger than me.

I move to the next painting. Up close I can see that it's not so similar to the other. The horse's head is straighter, its eyes looking further into the distance, far beyond this room, away beyond the horror of last night's gunshots.

'Did she like to ride?

Both the general's elbows are on the desk, his fingers forming a steeple. 'To ride?' he asks. 'No. Zoe was a dancer.' There are two frames on his desk facing him. Maybe one of them holds her picture. 'She had dreams of dancing at the Royal Opera House.'

'Do you have other children?' I ask.

'A son. Older.' He looks up suddenly remembering I'm here. 'You must clean now.'

Our conversation is whipped fast from under me. It makes me lose my balance enough for me to hold on to the wall.

Hunger has found its way into my mind again and now it sits here, taunting me. It gnaws into the silence. I have to go to the filing cabinet, but I can only think of food. I don't move quickly.

I know I'm useless, but the general doesn't shout at me. How strange it is to feel safer in here. Maybe it's because there are no guns on show.

I move the cloth over the handle of the cabinet and open the drawer to supposedly clean inside. There are papers stacked close together and I run the cloth over them, trying to separate them to read any of the lines.

'You can close that,' the general says. He's noticed before I have a chance and as I push in the drawer I feel a drop of hope fall through my fingers. 'You can clean behind it. I doubt anyone has moved it for years.'

I try to pull it, but it's too heavy. So I stand next to it, push it to the side and forwards, enough to fit in a foot behind it. He doesn't help. Even though I'm so tired that it makes my arm shake, he doesn't come to help me.

Behind the cabinet, there's thick dust, but I just want to curl up in the shadow darkness where no one can see me. I'll sleep. Then I'll wake up as his daughter and I'll be free.

Zoe. The thought of her pulls me back to where I am. I have to use her. I have to get the general to trust me. I drag the cloth along the floor, until dirt sticks fast to it.

'Please can I rinse this?' I ask.

'Of course.' And he points to the sink, even though I already know where it is.

I walk across the room and when I twist on the tap I want to drink the precious water but instead I let it spill through the material and disappear.

'Did you teach Zoe about the Traditional beliefs?' I ask.

'The Traditional themselves didn't exist then,' he says. 'But yes, I used to talk to her about politics. I felt very let down by the government of the time and I used to tell her that.'

'Did she agree?'

'She did. We had interesting conversations.'

'So you think she would have been a Traditional?'

'Absolutely.' He says it with such certainty.

I walk back to the filing cabinet. My knees hurt as I kneel on the floor, but at least from here he can't see my face as I clean. He can hear me though.

'My younger sister chose the Traditional band in school.'

'She did?' The general's voice definitely perks up and I feel sick that I've brought Lilli into this room. But I need him to know, because maybe her choice will save her. 'Why do you think she did that?'

Already the cloth is filthy again and I have to go back to the sink. I feel more exposed out in the open of his room.

'She's had a few problems back home with online stuff. Nothing major, but a bit of bullying and things.' I'm not lying now. Lilli and her group were targeted a bit when they started secondary. 'She likes the idea of you monitoring the internet more. She thinks her friends will be happier.'

'I understand her suffering. I had peers at school who didn't treat me well at all. Children can be very cruel. Even in here I've heard reports that some of them are being difficult.'

'It's not easy for them being cooped up,' I remind him.

'Still,' he says. 'They should be easier to control.' When he looks at me, I can feel his eyes picking into my mind. 'You must have heard John Andrews speak of it? How the behaviour of young children must be monitored and adjusted accordingly. They are our future, after all.'

This time I don't hide behind the filing cabinet. Instead I stand next to it and force myself to keep eye contact with him. 'Of course I don't want bullying and I like your idea of a happier society. But it worries me how much it will be controlled.'

'We don't see it as control,' the general says. 'It's more *regulated*.'

'Is that why you're regulating us so much here?'

'That's exactly why. Oak trees aren't grown in a day. We have to try everything we can because we have a real chance to replant the seeds, as it were, in a better soil.'

'So you're sort of like experimenting on us?' I feel myself stepping on to unsafe ground, but I know I have to go there. 'You want to literally change our minds? The way we think?'

'That'd be the ideal,' the general says. 'Yes.'

'How would that work, though? Won't you have to physically do something to our brains?' I'm struggling to keep my face neutral as I think of the twins who've been taken, but he's looking at me so intensely I'm sure he can see into my thoughts.

'We have a chance to cleanse our country of crime, of anti-social behaviour. We can make our nation the cleanest, most pure society in the world. We will create a place where everyone feels safe on our streets, loved and respected in their homes.' He hasn't answered my question and he sounds as if he's reading a manifesto leaflet. There is no emotion, just soulless words.

'You want to make a country that would have been good for Zoe,' I suggest.

'Exactly. It's part of what drives me now, because this is still her society.'

'You're doing what's best for her.'

'Yes,' he nods.

And while he's vulnerable, I take my chance. 'Did they die?' I ask.

'What do you mean?' he looks confused, still lost in his daughter's world.

'Seven people went missing from our bunk room last night,' I say. 'We heard gunshots and they haven't come back.'

His face shuts down. 'They went missing?'

'Yes.'

'By that, I think you mean that they decided to leave the room they were told to stay in, with intentions to leave the compound without permission.'

'Were the gunshots only to scare them?' I ask, my blood beating fast.

'Tell me,' the general says. His fingers once again form a steeple. His nails are too long and I have to swallow back the taste of bile. 'What would you expect us to do? If we're trying to instil the fundamental basics of obedience, yet someone deliberately disobeys?'

My mind has so many answers, yet my sentences get messed together because I know what he's admitting. I know that those seven people, that baby, no longer exist.

'Sometimes we all have to do things we don't like,' he says. 'For the greater good.'

'But how can one human destroy another? Isn't that the one thing that stops us being human?'

'What exactly are you saying?' The muscle in his jaw ticks. I feel him slipping through my fingers.

'I'm just trying to understand.'

'Don't you want to live in a safer society?'

'You know that I do.'

'Then you have to see that you can't have one without the other. For our vision to work, we need everyone to abide by our rules. It's really that simple.'

My body leans against the wall disconnected to the pain of truth in my brain. The general's mouth is moving and I'm forced to listen.

'I have a duty to create a place where Zoe would have felt safe to live.'

'So you kill in your daughter's name?' I whisper.

The general stares so hard that I feel his sight singe into me. He sees my flesh, my blood, my bones.

'Go,' he says. He picks up his mug, places his lips carefully against its rim and drinks.

'But I want to stay and talk.'

'Right this moment what you want is irrelevant to me.' His voice is stiffened with bolts too tight to undo. I've got no choice but to do as he says. I get the cloth, thick with grime, and I don't push back the filing cabinet before I pick up the bucket and leave him.

I feel like screaming when I'm back in the corridor and when I get to the cupboard I want to swing his manky bucket against the wall and rip out his stupid Trad shelves. But I know it's really me I'm angry at now. I needed to get the general onside. I need him to believe in me and to trust me. Instead it feels like I've passed him a gun loaded so full with bullets that soon it'll explode.

Luke and I are hidden behind the furthest bunk from the door, because here at least we can hold hands. I need to be near to him more than ever right now and if a guard comes in one of us can crawl away under the beds. But we're next to the toilet and it stinks.

201

'The general asked you to clean again?' Luke asks and I nod. The mood in here is so different now. No one was given breakfast and a cloud of hunger presses on everyone so heavily that most people are doing little more than lying down where they can find room. 'Are you sure he doesn't want anything else from you?'

'It's not like that,' I tell him.

'How can you be sure?'

I've never had a secret from Luke and I'm not going to start now.

'He chose me because I remind him of his daughter,' I whisper. 'She died when she was fourteen.'

In a normal place the face Luke pulls would make me laugh.

'That's just creepy,' he says.

'Yeah. It is a bit weird. And he's weird. He's really cold, like he doesn't have any emotions.'

'Even about her?'

'She seems the only thing that makes him feel anything. When he talks about her he definitely changes a bit.'

'Is it safe you being there?'

'We're not safe anywhere in here.'

'But will he hurt you?'

'I don't think so. But I could hurt him.'

'Don't be stupid, Rubes.'

'Not physically,' I say. 'But I'm trying to get him to trust me, so he might open up to me about things. I want to know where the twins have gone, if Darren could be right about the experiments.' I don't admit how I messed up today and how the general might not even want me back in his office again.

'I don't think you should. You just need to clean what he asks and then get out of there as quickly as you can.'

'I have to do something,' I tell him. 'They're trying to break us and if they manage to then they'll be able to do anything they want with us.' Luke puts his palm on my cheek and traces along my skin with his thumb. 'You know, I look out of the general's window and I can't believe how close we are to freedom. That just the other side of that fence we could walk away.'

'I imagine myself doing that at roll call,' Luke says. 'I see myself climbing to the top of that mountain by the loch and calling to anyone who'll hear me.'

'There's a blackthorn bush that Conor and I found. We're going to hide behind it and dig our way out.'

'Good luck with that one,' Luke laughs.

'Ah,' Stan says, walking round the side of the bed on his way to the toilet. 'At least a bit of love is still going strong.'

'It'd take more than a few lousy Trads to break us up,' Luke says, looking up at him.

'That's the spirit,' Stan says. He's hopping from foot to foot as he waits for Zamal to come out of the toilet and I can see clearly what he must have been like as a child. 'What I wouldn't give for my own bathroom. And my own bedroom back would be nice. It's the noise in here that gets to me.'

'Do you live on your own?' I ask.

'Yes. In total unwedded bliss.'

'Do you have a boyfriend?'

'I should be so lucky,' he laughs pitifully. 'I was hoping that at least there'd be someone in this room I might find attractive, but if anyone is gay they're not brave enough to admit it.'

'My friend is,' I tell him. 'But as fifteen-year-old girls aren't your thing, that's no good.'

'No good at all,' Stan laughs, as the toilet door opens and Zamal walks out. Stan ruffles his hair as they pass each other and Zamal comes to curl up on Luke's lap, as though he's always been there.

'I'm hungry,' he says.

'They'll feed us soon,' Luke says. But he looks over Zamal's head at me and I know he's not convinced.

'My tummy hurts,' Zamal says. I've never seen tired bags under a child's eyes, but they swell puffy there beneath his skin.

'We'll have food soon,' Luke tells him as he strokes his hair.

Zamal nods and it's a deeper pain I feel as I look at his face, at the innocence embedded out of reach of the Trads. How long will it be before the guards notice it, grip down with their trigger fingers and twist it free?

*

I never knew that hunger could eat into your bones. I can feel its teeth there as it chews and spits, leaving thick jelly that can barely hold me up.

'Don't let them wear you down,' Darren says as we walk in pairs from the bunk room towards the stairs again. I don't know whether he's talking to Mum or us, but there's something sturdy in his voice and it reminds me of the safety of home.

'We won't,' I say as I look back at him and there's definitely pride in his smile for me.

I hold Lilli's hand all the way across the exercise yard to where we have to stand and chant. She steadies me as much as I steady her. It's early afternoon now and the sun has tipped past its halfway point in the sky. They surely have to take us to eat after this.

More people come from inside the doors of the bunk house. So many of them. Some of the children are crying. The sound of it catching on the soft breeze and pushing against our faces.

I see someone I recognise. I hope it's not him. I don't want anyone I know to end up here. But as he gets closer, I know it's definitely Mr Hart from school. I remember him talking about his kids and he's carrying one of them in his arms. He keeps looking back to the woman and child behind him. She must be his wife. She's tiny and pretty and nothing like I expected. They walk towards the back of the line and I watch them until I can no longer see them.

'Is that an eagle?' Destiny whispers next to me as she looks up.

'Shh,' her mum tells her.

I can see it. It's almost impossibly beautiful against the blue of the sky, its wings stretched out as it glides free. It'll be looking for food and I want it to find some for me too. Anything. I'd eat a live mouse right now if it was dropped at my feet.

Our great country. Unity for all.

The eagle takes our words as it heads towards the mountain. In its own time, in its own space. It doesn't know how we need it to peck a hole through the wire fence for us all. And to peck the eyes of the Trad guards so they can't see us as we escape.

Our numbers are checked off before we're herded into the dining room. And now all I know is the soup in front of me. All I feel is the thick liquid as it slips down my throat. My teeth try to find something to chew, but there's nothing. Only the sludge that grazes my tongue, before I swallow again and again, until every scrap of food has gone.

We stand to make room for the next people and it's only when we're outside again that I realise they're separating off the children.

I grab Lilli's arm. 'Don't go with them.' And I try to stop her moving forward, but a guard is stepping towards us. 'You can stay with me.'

'It's fine,' she says. And she doesn't look frightened. If anything she looks calm. 'They give us biscuits. It's nicer in there than anywhere else.'

'But that's the point.' I've so much more I need to tell her, but the guard is shouting for me to move away.

'I'll see you later,' Lilli tells me. I know she's trying to be brave, but to me she looks like a tiny bird and I'm letting her fly right into the arms of the Traditionals.

I want to scream as I watch her join the huddle of children. I want to yell at her not to believe their lies. But all I can do is breathe in the last bit of air before I'm forced back through the door. I fill my mind and stomach with that sky, as my legs walk me back up the stairs.

Lilli doesn't come back until we're all in bed. Mum tries to hug her, but the guard shouts that the lights are going off. Lilli only has time to get on to the mattress next to me. She doesn't go head to toe, instead curling into me like we used to when we were much younger.

'What did you do there?' I whisper, as the room clicks into darkness.

'They gave us chocolate cake. And crisps.' Her voice is so quiet that I doubt Mum and Darren can hear it. 'I wanted to sneak some out for you, but I didn't know how.'

'Did they tell you stuff?'

'You know the gunshots the other night? That was actually the Cores firing,' Lilli says. 'They killed two guards and they escaped. But they've been arrested and will have to go to prison.'

'That can't be right.' Anger at her ignorance is threatening to make me shout. 'How could the Cores have got guns? We were all searched.'

'I think it might be true, Ruby. Some of the Core supporters are more dangerous than you think.' She takes a deep breath and I'm about to interrupt her but she's talking again. 'You know that protest we went to in the park? The Trads had to get us out of there quickly because the man who was speaking on that stage had a bomb. The Trads had intelligence on it and they knew that if they didn't act then lots of others would die.'

'Why would the Cores want to kill their own people? Think about it, Lilli.' I keep my hands underneath me because I want so much to literally shake sense into her.

'That's what I asked them,' Lilli says, sounding so proud and sure of herself. 'But they wanted to make an impact and then blame it on the Trads.'

The crushing and the screams claw at me from the past. They fill me with such terror that there's little space in my mind for anything else.

'You're being stupid if you believe them.'

'I'm not. They don't want to hurt us. They want to make things better.'

'How is this making things better?' I know I'm not quiet any more, but I can't help it. 'They're guarding us with guns and starving us. How is any of that okay?'

'If we want a better place to live this is what has to happen,' Lilli says.

'Girls,' Mum says and I hear her shift on the floor beside us. 'You've got to be quiet.'

'Quiet?' I shout. 'Are you hearing anything she's saying?'

'I think the whole bunk room can hear you,' someone shouts in the black room.

'You *should* all hear,' I shout. 'They're filling my sister with lies and we're letting them.'

'Ruby!' Mum's voice is a whip of anger.

'It's not lies.' Lilli is crying.

'Girls.' It's Darren I hear now. He moves out from under the bed and his voice is close. 'This is what they want to happen. They want to cause a rift between you and you can't let them. You're both free to believe what you want, but you're not free to fall out with each other.'

'But what she believes is wrong,' I say, although I'm calmer now.

'It's Lilli's choice,' Darren says. 'And we have to respect that. Just as much as she has to respect you. But don't ever let them divide you.'

'Okay,' Lilli says. 'I won't.' She sounds so innocent it

nearly breaks me.

'Besides,' Mum says quietly. 'It's an important day tomorrow.'

'Why?' I ask.

'It's my birthday,' Lilli reminds me, her voice quiet. Somehow I've let the horror around us take the important things.

'I forgot,' I say, feeling guilt creep in. 'I'm sorry.'

'It's not your fault,' Darren says. 'Everything is upside down in here.'

'I don't really want to celebrate it,' Lilli says. 'I don't want people to know.'

'We'll keep it among ourselves then and have your party when we get home,' Mum says. 'We need to sleep now, though.' I feel her hand reaching out for me and she kisses my head. 'Goodnight, my beautiful girls.'

I curl in next to Lilli again. My little sister, who'll be thirteen tomorrow. I reach for her hand and keep it tight in mine.

'Night, Lily Allen,' I say.

'Night, Ruby Tuesday,' she replies.

We haven't done that for years.

'I love you, Lilli,' I tell her.

'I love you too.' Already I know she's drifting to sleep and I have to let her. I want her to be in a safer place in her dreams.

CHAPTER TEN

'Our country will rise like a phoenix from the ashes
of past governments.' – John Andrews, leader of the
Traditional Party

When the door thumps open I think it must be the middle of the
night.

'Up,' the woman guard shouts. The light smashing on hurts
my eyes and I keep them closed. My clothes feel hard and
uncomfortable and my head hurts, until I remember the day. I
lean over and start to tickle Lilli.

'Happy birthday to you,' I sing so quietly that not even the
people in the bunk next to us will be able to hear.

She laughs and wriggles away from me, but not before I
realise how thin she already feels, her bones too clear through
her skin. Mum and Darren scoop her together in a hug and Mum
puts something in her hand.

'It's only little,' Mum says. 'Your main present is at home.' Her smile can't hide the ache of injustice in her eyes.

Lilli looks down at the tiny material heart in her palm, her name embroidered into it. Mum must have made it secretly in the sewing room.

'Thank you,' Lilli says, but she doesn't look up and I think she might cry.

'Come on,' Darren says. 'We've got to go now.' My hand feels safe in his as we let him help us stand.

Outside it's even colder than yesterday. I don't look around as we shuffle forwards and it takes all my energy just to move my feet. I wake slowly in this line, into this nightmare.

'We're okay, Ruby,' Darren whispers beside me. 'We'll be all right.' His hand still holding mine gives me strength to keep walking forwards, until eventually we get to the end of the line and I look up into the empty eyes of a guard and tell him my number.

In the dining room the benches are filled with people. There's no space, so we're lined up against the back wall. We have to watch as they eat. They have bread, two pieces and a glass of water. My world grows smaller and smaller, ending only in this. Every mouthful they have hurts my gums, my tongue and spills more cramping flames into my stomach.

'Finish,' a guard shouts. They have to eat quickly. They lick their fingers, their plates. 'Move.' And they're gone and we swarm forwards into their place. I want to check that Lilli has somewhere, but I don't manage to. I see only the bench, feel only a need to be there. The people either side are squashed tight to me, but I don't care because the food is coming.

I press my finger to two crumbs on the table and put them in my mouth. They're like grains of sand as I swallow them. Two pieces of bread are put on my plate and I grab them before anyone can take them away. *Slow down*, I know my mum will say and I try to chew enough, but my stomach is screaming, reaching up for the food.

And this is Lilli's birthday breakfast. Surely the thought of that will be enough for her to turn against the Trads?

'Finish!' It's too soon. I want to sit here. I need to rest. I drink my water and it stings my gums alive. I'm coming back to life. Maybe I'd been dying and I hadn't known. 'Move.' And so we do and I've barely stepped from my bench when the row behind us clambers in.

So many of us. So many of us caught before we could know.

Outside I'm hoping we'll be told to go back to the bunk house, but instead we're immediately divided into two sections. The men are on one side, the women and children on the other, just like they did before. Each group swells as more people finish their breakfast.

I search for Luke, but I can't see him. And I can't see Mum

or Lilli anywhere. But Destiny has found her way beside me.

'They're separating us again.'

'It'll be okay,' she says.

'What about Luke?'

Destiny links her arm through mine. 'It'll just be for a bit,' she says, sounding so sure.

We're standing in line when a woman near us starts shouting. She's clinging tight to a man as a guard rushes over to them.

'Women this way. Men that way,' he says.

'No,' the woman says.

'It's orders. You have to.'

'He's my husband.'

'Come on,' the man with her says. 'Let's do what he says.'

'Why?' the woman shouts.

The guard looks panicked as he tries to pull them apart.

'Get off me,' the woman screams and it lights a fuse of unrest among us all, spreading sparks of unease.

Another guard runs over. It's the one with the whip and he grabs the woman away as her husband tries to calm her, but she's scratching and screaming.

A gunshot shatters the air.

Its echo falls into the sudden silence.

I think they must have shot towards the sky to scare the woman, until I look again and I can't see her. And the man is standing and his arms are wide and his mouth pinned so wrong with shock. His clothes are red and I know it's blood and he howls and kneels to where she must lie and all I see is the guard raise a gun and all I hear is another shot. And it's now, in this very moment, that the edges of the world fall away.

I grip tight to Destiny's arm, needing for the woman and her husband to stand up and wipe themselves down, clean off the stage blood and the guards will say we can go. We can all go and the man and his wife will hold hands and lead us away and they'll dismantle this place.

But some children start to cry.

'Shh, shh,' a mother says and there's terror on her face as she tries to silence her child.

And I know this hell is real.

The women are sent to clean. The showers, the bedrooms, the corridors, the stairs. We have one bucket between ten of us. One cloth each. There are brooms and dustpans and brushes.

But all I see is the woman's blood. Her husband's face. The gun that killed them.

Destiny and I work together in a bunk room that's not our own and although no one has told us to be silent, neither of us speak. At each bed we take off the sheet, turn the mattress before we pull the sheet tight over it again. Under one mattress we find a diary. Destiny and I just stare at it. It feels too personal and vulnerable sitting there and we cover it quickly, out of sight.

At every moment, the memory of those gunshots follow us. At every bed I wonder if this one belongs to them. Did they sleep on this sheet? Is this their smell? I want to find just a small thing about them, to bring their lives back again.

Destiny and I shake out the next sheet.

They didn't know that after breakfast they would die.

On one bed there are two dinosaurs. One is stuffed and ragged, with the tail stitched. The other is plastic. They should be in a home somewhere, tucked into their right bed, or sticky in a child's hand. Not here. No child should be here.

It's only now that I see Conor's mum. She's on her hands and knees scrubbing the skirting board. Her skin looks grey, clinging to her cheekbones. This camp is destroying her. There's no guard in here and they never told us that we couldn't swap jobs, so I go and take the cloth from her before she knows.

'The sheets are easier,' I tell her. I think she'll protest, but she only sinks back on to her knees.

'Where've they taken Conor, Ruby?' she asks. Each word is folded in despair. 'Where is he?'

'He'll be working somewhere too,' I tell her.

Conor's mum covers her face with her hands and her shoulders are shaking. I've never seen any of my friends' mums cry. I put my arms round her and I can feel her bones jagged and pitiful and it makes me want to scream. She's Conor's mum and she's ill and she needs help, but no one is giving it to her. No one cares.

'It'll be okay,' I say. 'You'll see him soon.' I feel her nod her head in my arms and with every part of me – every cell, every heartbeat – I need this to be true.

After watery soup for lunch, the women and children are herded into the hall at the end of the camp. Lilli barely looks back as she's taken with the other children to the room next door. Mum hasn't told her that a woman and a man were shot and maybe she's right that it's better that way. I don't want that truth carved into my sister's bones.

The guard at the front is the same as before. She smiles, watching us, as the last of the children leave the room. It's only now that I realise that Mrs Jesenska isn't with us.

'Where's Violette?' I ask my mum

'I'm not sure,' she answers, but I can tell she's hiding something.

'What's happened?' I look her squarely in the eyes, giving her no choice but to tell me.

'She's been taken somewhere with her husband. And Darren noticed how another older man, the one on his own, he wasn't there this morning.'

'Silence!' a guard shouts and dread prickles my skin as I look towards the front.

We sit in our group to sew with Destiny and her mum, but there's a hollowness to the room without Mrs Jesenska here. My mind wanders down dark paths as I think where she might be and each time I dig the needle sharp into the material to stop my thoughts. The room is quiet enough for us to hear cuttings of children's laughter from the room next door and I hold on to the sound and surround myself with it.

I wonder what Luke will think of these underpants we're making, of how ugly they are, but then realise that maybe he won't even get a chance to see them and the need I feel to have him close slices through my hunger and battles back any other hurt I have, until I'm just a burning point of missing him. Missing our railway hut. Missing his skin on mine.

When we're finished, we're told to line up in rows again and wait for the children to come back. Behind us I hear the urgent whispers of a woman. 'There are at least twenty pairs of scissors in this room. And only five guards.' I don't know who she's talking to, but someone replies with angry words until the woman interrupts her. 'I'm just saying that it's an option if we need it.'

Lilli comes through the door with the other children. She looks happy and I know I'm running out of time. I have to somehow do something to get us out of here, before the Traditionals build a wall between us too high for me to climb over to reach her.

Mum hugs her when she gets to us.

'Was it okay?' she asks, her eyes searching Lilli's face for clues.

'Yes. It was good.'

Good? How can anything in this camp be good?

'They gave me these.' She holds up a pair of pink pyjamas with a bow tied over them. 'And a cake with candles.'

'They knew it was your birthday?' Mum asks, her voice failing to stay upbeat.

'Yes. They know lots of things about us.'

What are you telling them, Lilli?

'The heart Mum made you is better than some rank pyjamas,' I say. Lilli looks lost, so Mum leans over to hug her.

'The pyjamas are lovely. Think how well you'll sleep.' She glares at me over the top of Lilli's head, but I hold my ground and don't look away.

We're each given a new pair of underpants as we leave and even though they're hideous I can't wait to change into them. I hold mine tight as we march out slowly, stepping to the rhythm that the Trads set. As we get closer to the exercise yard, I can see groups of the men. They've dug deep holes in a straight line and in them sit huge posts, travelling down between two of the buildings.

Lilli pulls on Mum's sleeve. 'There's Darren,' she says pointing to a figure slamming a spade into the ground. Mum's relief makes her stand taller. I want to run and speak to him and tell him about the sewing and how Lilli went away again.

'What do you think they're doing?' I ask.

'It looks like they're building a fence,' Mum says simply.

'Just in the middle like that?' Lilli asks.

'Yes,' Mum says, as we're lined up for roll call.

Darren looks over. Mum waves, even though I'm sure she's not supposed to. He pretends he hasn't seen her, but I know he has, because he digs the spade harder into the ground as if he's not exhausted, or starving. I want to go and drag him back to be with us. We don't feel complete without him here.

'Why are they building a fence?' Lilli persists. Her new pyjamas held close to her.

Mum takes her hand. 'To separate us.'

I count each of the men as they arrive in the bunk room. Almost everyone has someone who runs to hug them when they appear, but Stan has no one. He looks beaten down by the day and even though I'm waiting for Luke, I can't leave him like that. I walk over and when I hug him I think he might cry.

'What are they doing to us, Ruby?' he asks.

'I don't know.'

And then Luke is in the doorway. He looks like he hasn't even got the energy to move, but he walks with his dad, stepping over the people sitting on the floor. I watch him for a moment and see how much he's changed since we've been in this camp, how he's definitely lost weight and the stubble on his face makes him seem older.

'Go to him,' Stan tells me.

When Luke sees me he has that change in his eyes. The look that's mine, that makes the world disappear. I don't care if there are guards outside, I don't care if they might walk in, I have to be with him.

And when I get to him he hugs me. Holding me so close that in this moment the horrors are nothing, because Luke is everything.

'Don't cry, Rubes,' he says. His forehead gentle on mine, his thumbs wiping away the tears on my cheeks.

'Mum thinks it's a fence you're building,' I say.

'It is,' he replies.

'Why?'

'Maybe more people are coming and it'll be easier with some on each side?'

'So they won't separate us?'

'No one will do that.' He looks deep into my eyes, willing me to believe it. 'What did they make you do today?'

His hope spreads to me as I step back from him. 'Well, this is when you're in for a treat.' I start unbuttoning my jeans and show him the top of the crinkly new underpants.

'What are they?' he laughs.

221

'The latest in high-quality lingerie.' I lean in to whisper, 'Do you want a closer look?' And before he can say anything I grab him and push him into the tiny toilet and lock the door.

And I know I should feel self-conscious as I haven't shaved my legs for days and I know I've got spots on my forehead and probably look scrawny, but I don't care as I pull down my jeans completely. I'm in home-made underpants and they're ugly, but they're clean. I'll take this moment and be happy.

'They're very attractive,' Luke laughs as he leans into me.

'I haven't brushed my teeth since last night,' I remind him.

'I don't care.' And he pushes me against the wall and kisses me. His hands are on me and mine are on him and I know we shouldn't but I don't think I can stop. He kisses my closed eyes, my neck, my lips and I'm alive, so completely alive.

'I didn't think you'd find the knickers so sexy,' I laugh as his touch scalds my blood.

'You'd look sexy in anything,' Luke laughs too. I try to reply, but he takes my words with his lips.

There's a thumping on the door.

'Shit,' Luke says, pulling away.

'They can wait,' I tell him, needing to keep him close.

The door bangs again.

'We know you're in there.'

It's not someone waiting for the toilet. It's a guard. I look at the boarded-up window. There's no way to escape.

'Get out. Now.'

We're both in here together. I'm in my underwear.

'I'm sorry,' Luke says. He looks physically hurt as I hurry to pull up my jeans.

'Don't be,' I whisper. I put my finger to his lips before I kiss him, until the hammering on the door starts again. 'It was worth it.'

'Get out now,' the guard shouts. 'Or I will shoot someone in this room.'

I'm doing up my button as Luke unlocks the door. The guard is standing so close and he stares at Luke and then at me. Disgust filling every part of his eyes.

'Follow me,' he says, his hand on his gun. 'Both of you.'

The room is so silent as everyone watches us. I keep my head held high, because I'm not ashamed. I love Luke. They can't hurt us for that.

Mum rushes up to the guard. 'Where are you taking them?' she asks. He stands by the bunk room door and looks through her as if she hasn't even spoken. 'She's my daughter,' Mum says calmly. 'And I have a right to know where you're taking her.'

Darren stands up and walks over. He leaves Lilli alone on the bed and I look at her and try to smile. *I'm fine*, I mouth and she nods back, her breathing too quick.

'I'll go in her place,' Darren tells the guard. 'She's just a child. You can punish me.'

The guard turns to look at him.

'If you speak one more word, I will choose three people from this room and I will shoot them.' He pulls me forward and Luke follows.

I want to hug my mum before I go. I want to tell her that I love her, but now I'm too terrified. And Luke and I are taken away.

It's just our footsteps, followed by the heavy boots of the guard as we go down the stairs. I try to hold on to the sound, feel the cold of the banister underneath my fingers. I have walked down here so many times, with my mum and Darren, with my sister.

Lilli. I want to go back to her, talk to her, tell her that I love her too. Tell her to be brave. And hug her until they pull me from her.

The door is hard against my palm. It touches my skin and I hear it close behind us.

It's dark. The night has been waiting. And now it's silent and closes its eyes.

Another guard is here and I somehow manage to walk as they lead Luke and me across the yard to the wall.

'Stand with your backs against it.' Each one of the guard's words are flat and endless to the dark horizon.

There's just the dreadful, painful beating of my heart. The cloudless sky. The solid white moon. I can hear Luke breathing beside me as we stare in front at the two guards with their guns and I don't think I can stand. My legs feel as if they are made of air and I'll fall.

'Face each other,' a guard shouts. I'm shaking as I turn until Luke and I are almost touching. 'Stand further apart,' the guard shouts again. Luke and I step back from each other. I see him there, but I don't. There's just my lungs, my blood beating.

'The person in front of you,' a guard says, 'is a vile human being. When lust is left to fester it infects everything around it. It sets rot into the whole society.' He's talking to me and Luke. He's wanting us both to believe it. So when we die we hate each other? 'The Traditionals are creating a society where procreation is for the continuation of the human race. The children created will be born within marriage and will grow within a strong family unit.'

I look at Luke and I know he thinks the same. *Our love is true and pure.*

'You will stand here,' the guard says. 'And you will look at the person of your downfall. If you look away, even for a moment, I will shoot you.'

Luke stares at me. Is this our punishment? I have to look at the boy I love?

We stand so still. I won't look away. It's Luke in front of me and he helps calm the fierce terror and slow my heart, so that it no longer burrows so sharp through my skin.

I look into the eyes I've always loved, the darkest brown just before they tip into black. I want to touch his cheekbones, feel them under my fingertips. I imagine that I do. And I wonder if he does the same to me, because it's like I can feel him, his hands on my face.

I don't move. I just watch Luke watching me. In another place, I wouldn't be able to resist kissing his lips. I would kiss him a million times and never get bored of it.

I want Mum and Darren to know that we're alive. I need Lilli to know. In that room, so close to here, their worlds will be on hold. I think of my mum crying and maybe it wasn't worth it. Just being by Luke's side should've been enough.

There's a noise from across the yard. I nearly look, but I remember just in time. Luke begs me with his eyes not to turn away from him.

'I'm not going to stand all night,' I hear one guard say. There's the sound of something being put down. Maybe a chair.

'Don't get too close to them,' another voice says. 'Their faults might be catching.' And the two guards laugh. They laugh at the dirty Core supporters who are in love.

Time sneaks on, but I don't know how fast or how slow. I look into Luke's eyes and maybe an hour, maybe a minute has seeped into the past.

There's the sound of the guard walking towards us. Neither of us look. Luke blinks. I blink back. We're okay.

The guard gets close.

'This is for your own benefit,' he says, his breath bringing with it the smell of mint. 'And to eradicate teenage lust will benefit us all.'

Lust? What about love? Is there no good in that?

I hear him walk away. Eighteen footsteps. Then maybe he sits down.

My legs are beginning to ache. And the cold is wrapping closer and closer. I start to walk on the spot, looking all the time at Luke. They haven't said we can't move. I shake my arms, needing my blood to somehow warm them.

Time yawns in front of us and moves its mouth over our heads, clamping down and shaking my mind until everything is strange. It's night-time, that's all I know. And Luke is here and I love him and I know that too.

Our first kiss was in his bedroom and I hadn't known it was coming. I think I'd hoped, but I'd pretended that this boy and this girl could be friends. No matter that he was gorgeous and funny and kind. No matter that Hannah Maynard told everyone that she fancied him and no one else should go close. So when he put Prince on and was trying to convince me to listen and he was pulling these funny moves, when he toppled over and grabbed me to stop himself from falling, I hadn't known it was going to happen. And it wasn't my first kiss, but it was my best by a million miles.

'Okay?' he whispers, his mouth barely moving. I almost look over to the guard to check he hasn't heard. I blink once, yes. And nod towards him and he blinks back once and I feel better again. We can do this. Soon the guard will need to sleep and he'll send us off and they'll never catch us together again.

The cold digs deeper. I keep facing Luke, but look up towards the sky behind him. I've never seen so many stars. When we were young, Dad would sometimes take Lilli and me to the hill in the park, just so we could see them, but they were never like this. Here, it's like bright dust sprinkled in the dark that goes on forever. Dad told us that even though we can see their light each star died millions of years ago. I couldn't understand that then and I don't now. Because they're there, clearly, watching us.

I move my eyes back to Luke. He's looking at me, but I can tell that his mind is far away. I hope he's with his dad too. And I hope his dad somehow knows that we're safe and standing here, so he can sleep.

I need to sleep. I have to keep my eyes wide and let the cold air keep them open. Every time I blink, I'm scared they'll ignore me and force themselves closed.

'There's a moon,' I whisper.

'Where?' Luke asks.

'Where do you think?' I almost laugh, but keep my face and my eyes steady.

'I wish I could see it.' Luke's words are tiny snatches in the freezing air.

'I think it's full.' It's very white against the deep black sky. It's a miracle, really, how it hangs in that space. And every day it disappears and every night it's back again. It doesn't judge us, it's just there. It makes me feel safe as it watches us now. Because it means that we're part of something much bigger, something that the Trads have no way to control.

I feel for my charm bracelet and find the crescent moon clasped on it. The first one Sara chose for me. She said it looked like a smile. I feel the top of it and the curve of it is smooth against my fingers and a wave of missing her crashes into me so violently that I nearly fall. I try to hear her voice, to feel her close, but I can't. I try to see her face, but my mind won't hold her. She's not here and I can't find her.

I don't mean to cry, but I can't help it. The missing her pushes into me, bruising my throat. Luke looks terrified as my tears fall. He shakes his head and I wipe them away as I keep looking at him. They never said we couldn't cry.

And for the first time ever I'm glad Sara is a Trad. I wouldn't want her to be here, where every part of me hurts – my stomach, my mind, my heart. I want her to be free. Even if it means being in a society with values so screwed and twisted that people can't see the truth hidden within it. I want Sara far away from here. From an evil that seems to be growing up from the ground. And from which I'm scared we can't escape.

'I love you, Ruby,' Luke whispers. He moves his hands and although I can't look clearly, I know what he's signing. *I would die for you.* I think he wants to stop my tears, but they're coming from somewhere too deep, too powerful. 'Don't cry,' he says, his mouth hardly moving. He reaches out for me instinctively.

'No touching,' the guard shouts.

It jolts me back to here, to the freezing-cold night. To my bones that are so tired I don't think they'll ever move again. To Luke, my Luke, in front of me.

Luke and Ruby.

Ruby and Luke.

I wipe my eyes and brush the backs of my hands against my cheeks.

Dad will come. He knows to save us. I can feel him moving closer over the mountain. Creeping up the back of it with an army of Core voters. They'll storm in and surprise the guards.

And Darren. Darren tried to save me. *I'll go in her place. You can punish me.* He would have done that. He would have stood in front of a bullet for me.

The night presses so heavy on my shoulders that I think I'll collapse. I can feel the sky and every one of those stars sitting on my back, pushing me lower to the ground.

'No,' Luke says. 'Stay awake, Ruby. Look at me.'

I blink and he's here.

Luke.

My Luke.

He's here.

The sky is changing. I watch the moon as it falls slowly. The barbed wire of the fence tries to pierce it, but I know it can't reach it. Our moon won't bleed.

I'm so cold that I'll never be warm again. But the sun is coming. It's on our side. It wants to heal us.

I can get through this.

There's a sound. A door opening. People are coming out. Not the guards, but many people, Core supporters, like us. Core supporters who won't be beaten.

Close footsteps. A warm breath in my ear.

'Dismissed,' the guard says.

From this world?

I wait for the gunshot. I wait for them to take me from my life, but the guard walks away.

'We did it,' Luke says, but neither of us move. I'm sewn to the earth and feel nothing.

People are walking towards us ready for the roll call. Now, I turn to look. Rusty bones inside my body. I watch the door at the flood of orderly people. Conor is there and he doesn't understand why Luke and I are waiting here like this.

I watch the door. There are people and people, until I see Darren walk out. I barely recognise him. He seems broken.

Look up. We're here.

And Mum is behind him, with Lilli by her side and they're holding each other up.

I'm alive. We survived.

Darren sees us and starts to run towards me. There are soldiers with guns, but he doesn't care.

'Ruby!' he shouts and he gets to me and gathers me up. I've never let him hug me, not properly. And here, now, I feel the strength of the world in his arms.

'Thank God,' he says. 'Thank God.'

Mum is here. She touches my face and she's crying.

'We're alive,' I whisper.

I can barely eat. Mum holds the bread to feed me and I'm her child again. Darren rubs my arms and back to make my blood find its warmth and Lilli doesn't take her eyes from me. I have too little energy to think about what's in her mind, to know if she can find a reason from the lessons they've been teaching her.

When our breakfast is finished, I think I'll be told to go to the bunk room to sleep, but I'm made to walk in line with the other women to the furthest building again. Inside, the children are taken to the other room and I don't try to fight it as Lilli is taken with them.

We find our same group. I hardly know how I hold the thread. Almost every stitch I do is unpicked by someone else. But Luke will be doing worse than this. How will he manage a day of hard labour? His dad and Darren will hold him up, as my mum and Lilli do me.

My mind takes the day and squeezes and stretches it and wrings it dry, until we walk back to the bunk room, Mum half carrying me. I almost crawl across the room to the bed. Darren folds his jumper under my head and gently puts his coat over me, before he rests his hand on my shoulder. I see Lilli, strange in her new pink pyjamas, before I close my eyes and finally sleep.

I wake in the morning and it's enough to do just that – to wake.

When the guard turns on the light I look first to Luke and he's there, on the floor with his dad, his coat as his pillow. His dad shakes him, but Luke turns away and has to be shaken again.

Darren crawls out from under the bed. I don't think he's slept at all as he pulls himself up to sit next to me on the mattress.

'How are you feeling?' he asks, as Mum and Lilli go to join the queue for the toilet.

'I'm tired,' I say.

He tucks my hair behind my ear and I leave it there. 'We'll look after you.'

'Did Mr and Mrs Jesenska come back?' I ask.

Darren doesn't look away from me as he shakes his head. 'No. There's no sign of them.'

'I'm worried the Trads will experiment on them.'

Darren closes his eyes for a few seconds, as if that could somehow take this horror away.

'I think you could be right,' he says. He glances around us before he talks again. 'I don't think we can trust anyone in here, Ruby.'

'I can trust Luke,' I say defensively.

'Of course you can. I mean anyone we didn't know before. Your mum and I were talking about it. We think there's a mole in here.'

'A mole?'

'Yes. You know, a spy.'

'In here?' I look around. I suppose that any number of theses strangers could be pretending to be a Core.

'I had my suspicions before, but since you and Luke were caught I'm convinced. Because they knew about you. The guards never could've seen you go in the toilet together, not with everyone around like they were. Someone told them.'

'Did Mum tell you that the Trads took Lilli again?' I ask. 'With the other children?'

'Yes.'

'How can we stop them?'

Darren leans his head into his palms. 'I don't know, Ruby. Maybe it's best for her to think that she's a Trad. Just while we're in here.'

'You can't be serious?'

'She'll be safer. That's all I care about.'

'You care about more than that,' I say, shaking his arm. 'You care about truth and freedom and what's right. Remember?'

'I know,' he says. 'But I want to get you out of here and if pretending to be a Trad is the quickest way...'

'I don't want to be free if they take away my way of thinking. That's not freedom. That's just being in a prison of another kind.'

Darren looks up at me. 'You're far more wise, Rubes, than I ever gave you credit.'

I want to tell him that he's far nicer than I ever realised. That I can see now why our mum chose him and that I'm glad she did. But I can't find which words to put first and the moment drifts out of my reach and is gone.

'I've been watching the coaches that come into the camp,' Darren whispers. 'They're not closely guarded when they let the new prisoners off. I think there could be a way I can get on to them.'

'You can't just sneak on to a coach.'

'I'd have to time it right.'

'It's way too dangerous.'

'It might be our only option.'

'It won't be,' I say. 'I'll think of something else.'

'We're going to have to do something soon,' he says, as he picks up my trainer from the floor and starts to loosen the laces. 'Here. You need to get these on.'

'I can do it,' I tell him, but he doesn't let me and I'm glad. My mind might still be ready to fight, but my body is so exhausted that I feel it giving up on me.

When Mum and Lilli get back she ushers me into the line before I have a chance to go to Luke. When I glance back, Zamal is holding his hand, but Luke looks beaten. I want to run to him and kiss him and tell him to keep strong, but it's too late and I'm walking down the stairs next to Lilli.

I notice the fence as soon as I step outside. It's almost complete, but we still don't know why it's there. A wound that cuts the camp in half. There are two empty coaches, so maybe it's for the new arrivals?

I look carefully at the coaches as we stand waiting in the freezing cold of roll call. There's only one guard near them. Maybe Darren is right? Maybe they're somehow our way out of here. I watch as their engines are started, how the wheels turn until they're facing the distant gate, as they start to gather speed before they leave the camp. I look over at Darren and he's watching them too.

After roll call it's breakfast. Two slices of bread with a glass of water. I want to make it last. I want to enjoy every mouthful, but they rush us through as though we're machines.

At the door I'm pulled aside.

'Number 276?' the guard asks me.

I nod to the number on my arm. 'Isn't it obvious?' But I regret it as soon as I say it and Mum tenses beside me.

'The general wants you,' the guard says, staring at me as though I'm dirt.

'It's fine,' I tell my mum, because if he wants to see me again it means I haven't messed everything up. 'I'll be back later.' She steps forward to hug me, but I'm yanked away and led the familiar route to the general's office.

I look outside the window of the corridor as I always do, but Conor's blackthorn bush has gone. There's only a silent hole watching back. And I know we could never really have used it to escape, but suddenly I feel despair choke me. I have to shake it away, push it as far as it can go as I get the cleaning things and knock on the general's door.

He seems pleased to see me and I wonder if there's a strange part of him that thinks I really might be his daughter. If he did the maths he'd realise it's impossible. I was five when she died, so there's no way I'm her reincarnation.

'What would you like me to clean?' I ask.

'I thought the floor could do with a good sweep,' he says.

'I don't have a brush.' The bread I've just eaten has helped settle the painful hunger, but my bones are so tired they feel like they're made of lead.

'Don't worry, I've thought of that.' He's too pleased with himself as he comes out from behind his desk to get a broom that's leaning against the wall.

'Thank you,' I say, as he passes it to me and I start to sweep. But it's awkward between us and I know I have to change that. 'Have you been well?'

'Yes,' he sounds surprised. 'Thank you. Yes, I have.'

'Good.' Is that what Zoe would have said? Did she even like him? 'It's very beautiful up here. The loch. The mountain.'

'It is. Indeed,' the general says. 'We're very lucky to be in such an extraordinary part of the world.'

Lucky? I press the broom hard into the floor to stop myself from screaming.

'Is there a dustpan and brush?' I ask.

'Yes. In the corner.'

I get it and concentrate on sweeping up every bit. As I walk to the bin I see that it's filled with screwed-up bits of paper. They must have things on them, even though they're discarded. They could have any kind of information about the camp. I kneel down next to the bin and glance back, but he's watching me.

'I love being outdoors,' I say, as I sprinkle the dirt from the dustpan on top of the waste paper, before I stand up again.

'My dad used to teach me the names of all the plants.'

'Is he here with you?'

'No.' I push the broom up against the base of the wall. 'He died,' I lie. I don't know why I say it. Maybe because I'm terrified that they'll track him down and bring him here. Maybe because the general might feel closer to me if I've lost someone I love too.

'I'm sorry to hear that,' he says.

'It was a while ago,' I say.

'It doesn't make it easier.'

'No. It doesn't.' I wonder how he can sit here and talk like this when people have been murdered in this camp. Did he order for people to be killed?

I sweep up more and this time I keep my back to the general when I throw the dust into the bin. I reach in before I have time to think and I've one of the screwed-up pieces of paper in my hand. Fear is clearly in my blood because I know that if he catches me now I'll have no way out of this, but he doesn't say a word so I slip it into the pocket of my hoodie.

'Would you like one of these?' I turn to see he's holding up a plate with biscuits placed on it like a fan. I'm going to have to walk over to him, knowing that I've stolen something of his, knowing that if he opens his eyes properly he'll see. I leave the broom leaning against the wall and step over the rest of my pile of dust.

'Can I take some for my family?' I ask.

'No. I've offered them to you.'

'But they're hungry.'

'Do you know how difficult it is to feed you all?' His jaw ticks with vague annoyance. 'I suppose we could always feed half of you more food and leave the other half with nothing. Is that what you want?'

'No.' There's so much more I want to say, but I'm too vulnerable here. Too close to a stranger I can't predict.

'So,' he says. 'You would come to the same conclusion as we do.' He holds the biscuits towards me again.

'Thank you.'

'They were my mother's favourites,' the general says.

I can smell the lemon in the biscuit before I can taste it. I keep each bite held in my mouth, the taste dissolving into my whole body.

'We're worried about some friends of ours who've disappeared.'

'Who might they be?' He tips his head to the side just slightly, as if he's interested.

'Violette Jesenska and her husband. They're older and we don't know why they've gone.' I press my arm against my hoodie pocket and hold it there.

'Unfortunately, elderly people are often too set in their ways to change their thinking and certainly useless for work.'

Useless? I think of the spark of light the Jesenskas bring us.

'Where are they? Are they safe?'

The general's laugh is sudden. 'Their minds are probably safer than they've been in years, now that they're in our hands.'

'Are they alive?'

'Yes.' The general smiles. 'And they're helping us to find a quicker, pain-free way to make people see the error of their ways. If it works then we wouldn't need you to be here.'

'You'd let us go?'

'Core supporters would potentially only need to undergo a small procedure and then we'd have everyone thinking in the same way. There'd be no conflict. Can you imagine that?'

'What procedure?' I try to make my stomach steel. I have to be impassive to anything he tells me.

'No need to worry yourself with the details. All we need to focus on is the fact that it works and we'll be building a world that would have been good enough for Zoe.'

The details? What are they doing to the Jesenskas?

I breathe deeply to calm myself. 'Do you have a picture of her?' I ask. I see my question balance in front of the general as he wonders which way to answer. When he smiles it somehow makes him human.

'Here,' he says, turning one of the framed photos on his desk so that I can see. And she does look like me. Even I'm a bit spooked by how similar we are.

'How did she die?' I ask.

'Cancer,' he says, the word turning him grey.

'My friend's mum has cancer,' I say quickly. 'But she's in here, so she can't have her treatment.'

'And you want me to do what?' His human mask has gone, he's the general again.

'Let her go to the hospital. Please.'

'And give her a chance to survive, where my daughter didn't?'

'Yes,' I say, but already I know my words are useless. The general might as well be shredding them in his hands and scattering them for me to sweep up and throw away.

'But then I'd be willingly prolonging the life of someone whose beliefs go against the good of society,' he says.

'She's a mother.'

'Even worse. She's raising a child with her dangerous views.' *She couldn't have raised Conor better*, I want to scream at him. *He's funny and kind and it's you who is destroying him.*

'You could help her.'

The general stares at me. 'But would that be for the good of the nation? You must see that the fewer Core voters we have, then the quicker there'll a pure society.'

'If that's the case,' I say. 'Then surely you actually want to kill us all?'

The general's eyes look even deeper into me. He has a twitch on his lips and I watch it tick.

'No one wants that,' he says, his face expressionless. 'But we will do what it takes.'

CHAPTER ELEVEN

'For too long, the wheels of our nation have been left
to rust. But now we have got them turning again and
our national pride is free to run.' – John Andrews,
leader of the Traditional Party

I sit with Luke and Destiny, huddled on the floor of the bunk
room, trying to distract ourselves from the hunger which won't
leave us alone. The soup we had for supper was so watery that it
barely feels like I've eaten.

'The general pretty much admitted that they're doing some
sort of experiments on the Jesenskas.' Just saying the word
makes me feel sick. 'And I doubt it'll stop with them.'

'Do you think that was always the plan?' It's the first
time I've seen true distress in Destiny's eyes. 'For us being
here?'

'I don't know,' I say. Luke is holding my hand, but not even the feel of his skin against mine can make any of this all right. 'But I took this.' I've got my back to the room, so no one else can see as I take the piece of paper from my hoodie.

'What is it?' Luke asks.

'I got it from the general's bin.' I try to smile, but Luke looks furious.

'You can't just take stuff out of his room, Ruby. It's way too dangerous.'

'I have to do something.'

'What's on it?' Destiny leans forwards as I flatten out the paper. It's almost empty apart from two pencil lines and numbers either side. Disappointment hits me hard. 'What do you think it means?'

'Nothing.' I screw the paper into a tiny ball. 'It was a complete waste of time.'

We sit and stare at each other as I realise that I put myself in danger for something so useless.

'It's not nothing,' Destiny says. 'We could use it to tell stuff to the outside world.'

'How?'

'With my make up pencil. We can write things on it and try to get our messages out of the camp, tell people exactly what's going on. Leave our own paper trail,' she smiles.

The bunk room door suddenly slams open and fear freezes Luke and Destiny as I hurry to hide the paper in my pocket.

Two guards come in and there are two more in the corridor behind them.

'Women and children,' the guard at the front says. 'You're to follow us.'

A man with glasses stands up. He's always been quiet, sitting in a tight unit with his wife and daughter.

'Why?' he asks. 'What do you want with them?'

'They're being relocated to a different building,' the guard says.

'Relocated?'

'It's overcrowded in here. And it's unsanitary for the mind and body to have men and women in such close quarters.'

Anger flashes quick and brutal on the man's face. 'We're married, for God's sake. This is my wife.'

'And these are my orders,' the guard says.

'Which you'll obey, even if they're wrong?'

'I obey them because I believe in them.'

The man's wife stands up. 'We'll go,' she says quietly.

'I don't want to,' their daughter says. My stomach folds as she reaches for her dad's arm and starts to cry.

Destiny scrambles to her feet. 'Let's do this quickly,' she says. 'They're not going to change their minds.'

'I'm not leaving you,' I tell Luke. 'They can't make me.'

'It'll just be for sleeping,' Destiny says. 'You'll see each other in the day and at meals.'

Does she really believe that as she walks through the chaos in the room towards her mum? Luke looks at me, despair too frightening in his eyes as he stands, still holding my hand.

But I don't move. 'They want to separate us. They don't care.'

'We're going to have to do what they say,' Luke says and he helps me up until we're facing each other. 'They don't seem human any more.'

I feel a hand on my back and my mum is standing beside us. 'I've said goodbye to Darren,' she says, her face raw with shock. 'We've got to go.'

'I'll see you at breakfast, Ruby,' Luke says and his lie makes a raft for both of us to keep afloat. I nod and he leans forward and hugs me so tight, but then he's gone, his dad pulling him away.

Mum and I walk among the people. Destiny is with her mum, Aba, in the crowd by the door, her eyes defiant. I think Lilli must be here, but then I spot her by our bed, her face buried in Darren's chest. He's crying too, his chin resting on the top of her head, his eyes tight shut against the pain.

'I'll get her,' I say quietly to Mum. I go over to them. They're a sculpture of grief. 'Come on, Lils.' They both open their eyes and look at me. 'We're not going far.'

'Why are they doing it?' She's rocked by confusion. Everything she's been taught in those lessons must be spinning apart.

'You have to go,' Darren tells her.

247

'But I don't want to.'

'I need you to look after your mum for me until I see you again. Okay?'

Lilli barely nods.

'Promise?' Darren says.

'I promise,' she whispers.

'That's my girl.' And he lets her go so she can come to me. He puts his hand on my shoulder and when he looks at me I don't know how we can be without him. He's the rope that keeps us held together.

'I believe in you,' he says to me. 'We'll find a way.' I nod at him, because it's all I can do as my chest feels crushed with it all. He doesn't wipe away his tears as he kisses my forehead. 'I love you, Ruby.' And I know he does. And I want to tell him that I love him too. I want to say those three small words, which are big enough to fill the sky, but my tears block my throat.

All I can do is drag Lilli with me to where our mum waits.

We're led out into the darkness. The guards take us through a gate in the fence, until all that's on our side is the furthest building in the camp. We go through a small door and it's black and cold in here as they lead us up some steps. The Trads have torches, which they hold in front and travel over us. Could we run now? Surely it's dark enough for them not to find us all? But when we get to the perimeter fence, then what? If we climb it they'll shoot us in the back. And if we escape, will they start shooting the men? One for every woman who's free.

Mum is in front as we go up the stairs, Rimi in her arms and Zamal holding her hand. At the top, the queue slows down and as we stop next to each door the guards push in a certain number of people. I hold tight to Lilli as we're moved further along, counted like animals and forced through another open door. A guard turns on a light before shutting us in.

There are no beds. The window is blocked shut as we're used to. There's a pile of blankets against the wall and immediately people go over and start grabbing them. There must be about forty of us in here, but I can't see how there'll even be enough space on the floor for us all to lie down.

'This is exciting, isn't it?' Mum says to Rimi and Zamal. 'A new room to explore.' Rimi nods. She has sores under her nose from where she rubs her rabbit's ear.

'Is it because of our bad blood?' Zamal asks, looking up at Mum with eyes wide enough to break me.

'No one's got bad blood,' Mum says.

'We all have and it's making us sick,' Zamal says. 'But they'll make us better.'

Mum kneels down next to him, balancing Rimi safe on her knee.

'Your blood is perfect. You are perfect,' she says.

'I'll get us some blankets,' I say. I'm wading through shock, but I won't let it suck me down.

'I'll come with you,' Destiny says.

'What if they're separating us so they can experiment on us? Or them?' I whisper, as we walk across the room.

'Don't let that thought in, Ruby.'

'They could do anything.'

Destiny links her arm through mine, but I can feel her shaking. 'We won't let them,' she says.

We manage to pull three blankets from the pile and I turn to see Conor's mum standing near us, her back close to the wall.

'Carol,' I say and she looks up, but I've never seen her eyes so empty. 'Come with us.' And she follows to where Mum and Aba have found a space in the corner with Zamal and Rimi.

We sit down as best we can and Mum puts Rimi on her lap. Destiny lies down with Zamal curled almost on top of her and Carol sits next to me, with Lilli squashed close on my other side.

'They're definitely just separating us for sleeping,' Destiny says, her words sure of themselves, steady on flat ground. 'This is an old office block or something. There won't be a dining room, or showers, or anything.'

'You're right,' Mum says.

'They better let us wash still,' I say.

Destiny pulls a blanket over her and Zamal. I hadn't realised he sucks his thumb and it makes him look even younger. He closes his eyes as Destiny strokes his hair. He must be missing his mum so much. I wonder how deep she's nestled in his mind and whether she's there in the background of every thought of his. I reach over and touch his nose. He opens his eyes sleepily and his smile makes me warmer than a million blankets ever could.

'You're very brave,' I tell him quietly.

He nods and closes his eyes again and I think that perhaps inside himself he's crying.

Destiny starts to sing. It sounds like a lullaby, but it's one I've never heard before, in a language I don't know. Her mum came from Ghana when she was young and maybe this is a song from her childhood. I imagine the notes travelling from Destiny to her mother, who runs with them to her own mother. They're like a ribbon, caught on the wind, travelling through time and sunshine until they find their roots.

If Destiny's grandmother could see now where her lullaby has come to rest, what would she think? How could she make sense of it?

I'm ripped from sleep when a guard comes in and slams on the light.

'Get up,' she says.

My bones feel like they've been shaved in the night. They're raw and painful from where I slept on the cold floor.

'It's breakfast time,' Mum tells Rimi and Zamal.

'Did you sleep at all?' I ask Destiny.

'A bit,' she replies, as she rubs her hands over her face and blinks on her mask of survival.

Conor's mum is still lying under her blanket. The shape of her body is sharp through the material. She's barely moving, but the blanket is rising and falling enough for me to know that she's breathing. I step over the two people between us.

'Carol,' I say. 'We have to get up.' She's awake, but she doesn't even look at me.

'They've taken Conor from me,' she says.

'He might be there at breakfast.'

Now she turns to see me. 'Do you really think that?'

'I have to,' I tell her.

She struggles to sit so I help her as Destiny folds her blanket. What would Conor feel if he could see how frail his mum is now? His anger would burn a hole in the sky.

We're told to walk down the stairs. At the bottom are a line of buckets filled with water. I wait in turn to be passed the mug and I drink, before we're herded into a long thin corridor. There are too many of us, so the line has to double back on itself. Somewhere a woman coughs violently. At the end is a table piled high with a stack of bread.

'We're not going to eat in the dining room then?' Mum says.

'No.' Which means there's no chance of seeing Luke at breakfast. No chance of knowing where he is, or how he is. I look at Conor's mum where she leans against the wall and I wonder if she's seen the food yet and realised it too.

'Won't we see Darren?' Lilli asks Mum.

'I'm sure we will later,' Mum replies, her face determined as we follow the line forwards. But she can't hide the empty space beside her where Darren should be.

'Why's no one from the outside coming to help us?' I ask her.

'I think the Trads are probably being very clever about what they're saying.'

'But when people find out, surely they'll do something?'

'It depends what they know. What they're told.' We move forwards again. 'What they believe.' My stomach hurts more, the closer we get to the table. 'John Andrews will be very selective about what he allows to be put on the news.'

'What about the internet though?'

'There are so many lies written there. No one will know what's true and what's not.'

'So people might not even know we're here?' I ask.

'Maybe not. The Trads shut down a lot of social media sites. And anywhere else they'll just say what they want to say.'

But I have a piece of paper hidden in my pocket and Destiny's pencil. Could we really get a message to the outside world?

Mum lets me go in front, so that I get my bread first. I start to eat it as soon as it's in my hands, but the food is awkward in my dry mouth and I cough as I swallow it. I'm still eating when I follow the line of women outside.

The rain is instant and harsh on my face, beating through my clothes. It soaks the rest of my bread, but it wets my lips and I need that. There, on the other side of the fence, are huddles of men. Somewhere in among them must be Luke and Darren. And Conor.

'They haven't said we can't go close to the fence,' I tell Destiny.

'It's not a good idea, Ruby,' Aba says.

But Destiny knows they can't stop me. 'Be careful,' she says.

I eat the last bit of my bread as I walk closer to the mesh that divides Luke and me. I spot Stan and I don't even need to beckon him over because he's coming towards me.

'You always were a brave one, Ruby,' he says, his voice warm.

'It takes one to know one.'

'How are you all?'

'We're okay.'

'And your little gay friend? What's her name again?'

'Destiny.'

'That's the one. How's she bearing up?'

'She's fine. Have you seen Luke?'

254

Stan looks around. 'He's there. I'll go and tell him you want to see him.' As he walks away he looks over his shoulder. 'Tell Destiny to keep strong.'

'I will.'

I watch Luke's dad try to pull him back, but he shrugs him off and they both hurry towards me. There aren't any guards nearby, so I step as close as I can to him, hooking my fingers into the fence. He somehow looks thinner than when I last saw him and the skin under his eyes is darker. I ache to touch him, to feel his hand on mine, but his dad holds him away.

'Where did they take you?' Luke asks.

'We slept in there,' I tell him, nodding to the building behind me. 'It's like an old office block or something. The rooms are smaller and there aren't any beds.'

'They'll get some,' he says.

'You think?'

'Maybe.'

My heart feels bruised, standing so close to Luke without being able to hug him.

'You need to look after Darren for us,' I say.

'I will.'

'He's on his own, Luke.'

'My dad and I will be with him.'

I want to tell him how Destiny and I have written on the paper I stole and are going to find a way to get the messages out of the camp, but his dad is too close and will hear.

'Where's Conor?' I ask. 'Where is he?'

'He doesn't want his mum to see him at the moment.'

'Why?'

'Because they've hurt him, Ruby.'

'What do you mean?'

'He kicked off about being separated from her, so they hit him.'

'Badly?'

Luke only nods. My mind scorches with an image of Conor needing to see his mum. The anger eating his mind until he's no sense left.

'You've got to help him, Luke. He's got to stay calm.'

'I know. I'm trying.' He starts to cough. The same violent hacking that more and more people in the camp have.

'Right,' Luke's dad says. 'That's enough now. You're both going to move away from here before you get caught.'

'I can't,' I tell him. I know I sound like a child, but I can't just walk away from Luke, not knowing when I'll see him again.

'You have to.' I've never heard Luke's dad sound so angry. But the rain is on my skin, where Luke should be. 'You've got to stay strong, Ruby.'

'It'll get sorted out,' Luke says, but already they're walking away from me.

'Ruby.' We've finished roll call and Conor's mum finds me in the line as we wait to be led to the building where we sew. Her scarf clings to her head, soaked by the rain. 'Did you see Conor?'

'No.' I don't think I can bear this conversation.

'I couldn't find him anywhere,' she says.

'There were a lot of people,' I say. 'Mum only just caught a glimpse of Darren.'

'But he would have been looking for me,' she says. Her eyes are fragile and I can't be the one to break them.

'He'll be fine,' I tell her. 'Luke told me he's with them.'

The gate in the fence is opened and we all push through it, needing to get to the other building and out of the rain. We have to walk across the exercise yard, but my bones are so cold I don't know how I move. We're slow enough to look around, needing to see the men we've been separated from, but there's no sign of any of them any more. They must be somewhere behind the boarded-up windows and the closed doors.

'When will I see my mummy?' Zamal looks up at Destiny. He has one hand in hers, the other in mine.

'Soon,' she tells him. And it seems enough for him to know this.

Mum and Lilli are standing at the entrance of the hall, ignoring the swarm of women who jostle past, until I'm with them. Mum's eyes are red and Lilli looks like a scrap of a person lost in this horror.

'You saw Darren?' I ask.

'Yes.' Mum's lips move, but I can tell that her soul is crushed.

'How was he?'

Mum nods at me as though she can somehow make all of this okay. 'He was fine.' But her hands are shaking as she hugs me.

Lilli doesn't make any complaint as she goes to stand with Zamal and Rimi at the front. A strange cloud of happiness steps close to the other children as they all walk out of the room. It's so out of place here and I hope it's just because of the extra food they're being given and not the lessons they're listening to.

The rest of us are pushed into groups of four and we cling to Destiny and her mum, Aba, as we sit down. There are more women now than there were the first time, so there's less space for us all. And there are more guards, dotted around the outside of us.

'They don't look human,' I whisper, looking at two of them standing by the door. They look like clones of each other – the same blank expression, sitting on top of insipid skin.

'You must keep seeing them as real people,' Aba says. 'Otherwise, how will they see us? If we start to think of them as less than human, then that's how they'll treat us.'

'I think they've already started on that one, Mum,' Destiny says.

'Then it's up to us to change their minds.'

'Everyone, quiet!' the guard at the front yells and our voices dissolve instantly. How must it feel to have this much control? This much power? 'Today as you work you shall hear John Andrews speak.'

I look at Mum. The leader of the Traditional Party is here?

There's a fuzzy crackle from some speakers at the front and his voice walks out among us.

'Not the real him then,' I whisper to Destiny.

'Too busy for people like us,' she says.

'*Fellow countrymen, know that a nation without good laws is a bad nation. And know that we've had the courage to instil great laws.*' It's a speech I've heard before. Or maybe different. They all seem staged as they repeat themselves. '*You are a nation of individuals. Of people who deserve better. Who deserve the best.*'

'Are they having a laugh?' Destiny says, but her mum glares at her so fiercely to make her quiet as we start to sew shapeless grey dresses.

'*The first duty of every citizen is to work.*'

Well I've got that one right at least. I puncture the material with the needle, in time with his words.

'*You had the courage to stand up and say you'd had enough.*'

I zone him out. My stitching is getting all right now but I'm not good enough to do anything like the collars.

Destiny nudges my arm. 'Look.' She nods down to the material in her hands. At the bottom of the dress, she's stitched steps going up. 'Cores forever,' she whispers. And her eyes spark so strongly that everything feels a bit better. 'I did it with the knickers too.'

'Core supporters in your pants,' I whisper back.

'So long as they're gorgeous,' she says. And through the darkness of the camp and the speech of John Andrews, she brings a line of laughter that grips my stomach too tight as I try to hold it in. 'They better not make us wear these dresses.'

'You don't like them?' I ask, poking my arm through the tube of a half-made sleeve. 'Is it the colour, or the style that you find so offensive?'

'I'll be glad to change out of my dirty clothes,' Aba whispers.

'Imagine walking down the school corridor in this.' Destiny's laugh is a shard of rainbow among us, until her mum shakes her arm hard.

'*We will heal our broken society.*' John Andrews' voice keeps squeezing through the speakers.

'We'd certainly get noticed,' I say quietly.

'For all the wrong reasons.'

'Do you think school is still going on?' I ask.

'Not a chance,' Destiny says. 'It won't open without us. We're far too important.' And she pokes me in the side.

But she's wrong. We're Core supporters. That puts us in the bracket of being dispensable and forgotten about.

'*I will not rest until you all live in the country that you deserve.*'

It's strange to think that they might be at school. Sara sitting at her desk, being told off for gum, doodling shipwrecks on her work. The sounds of the corridors are so clear, the noise of us all as we crush between lessons. Chairs scraping, windows opening, teachers talking. It's all there, happening right now, but it's too far away, far out of our reach.

Destiny nudges my arm and whispers something I can't hear. I'm confused, so she leans in closer.

'We could put one of our messages on an empty coach,' she whispers. I look at her like she's mad. 'You clean the general's office. Maybe they'll want us to clean a coach before it leaves and we could hide a bit of paper under one of the seats.'

My mind tries to shut down with the impossibility of it all, but I have to keep hoping there's a way.

'You're a genius,' I say and Destiny's laugh brings light again to the heavy air.

By the time we stop for lunch, every single part of me aches. My shoulders hurt from being hunched over and my back needs me to stand and stretch. The cold won't leave me, grinding even deeper than it was before. My eyes just want to close and sleep, but I've had to force them open and focus on the threading of the needle and the tiny stitching.

No one has the energy to speak as we hobble to our feet as though we're all old women. Someone in the line in front starts to cough and I think they might be sick. The children rush back through the crowd and everything feels so wrong as Rimi and Zamal come to us, when their mum should be here.

'You okay?' I ask, ruffling Zamal's hair. My fingers already look different, more bony. He looks up at me and nods, but he doesn't smile, that lonely silence sitting on him.

'Where's Lilli?' Mum asks him.

'She's talking to the teacher,' he says.

'Why?'

'She had a question,' Zamal tells her.

A question? What's Lilli got to ask that's more important than coming back to us?

'What was it?' I ask, but Zamal just shrugs. 'Does she talk to them a lot?'

'Sometimes.'

'Does she tell them things?'

'Ruby,' Mum says. 'Leave him be.'

'But we should know,' I tell her. 'Lilli could be telling them anything.'

'Like what exactly?'

'I don't know. Stuff, about us.'

Zamal looks up at Destiny.

'They gave me this,' he says and holds up a glove puppet of a lion. 'It's strong like me.'

'That's lovely,' Destiny says. 'What are you going to call it?'

'I want Mummy to choose a name when she comes back.' The hope in his voice pierces through me.

'She'll love that,' Destiny manages to say, just as Lilli appears at the door. She walks slowly towards us, not looking us in the eye.

'Hi,' she says, standing in next to Aba.

'Why did they keep you back?' Mum asks.

'I was just talking,' Lilli says.

'About what?'

'About things.'

I look up at Mum, but she's glaring at Lilli. 'Like what?'

'That if everyone just did what they're told then they could let us go.' Lilli is angry, but I'm not sure who with. 'They don't want to separate us from Darren, but it's difficult for them.'

'You do know not to trust them, don't you?' Mum says.

'I just want Darren to be with us again,' Lilli snaps.

I see the glance between Mum and Aba before the guard at the front yells at us all to get into pairs. And as we're herded out and back through the yard, I try to remember Aba's words – that the guards are human. That somewhere, under the uniform, under the skin, there has to be a heart that beats like ours.

We pass the men standing for roll call in the rain. They stare at us and we stare back, but it's useless to try to find Luke or Darren or Conor. There are too many of them, a bundle of unhappy faces jostling to see us, kept away by the guards and their guns.

There's a small wooden stage on their side that some of them must have made this morning. It's close to the fence, so we'll be able to see it clearly from the women's section. Maybe it's for the general to stand over us and spout more Trad rubbish to us all.

We're given soup, but no bread. I'm too tired, too hungry to even complain. We eat it standing outside, the water of the rain mingling with the water of the soup. I'd like to watch the drops of the liquids as they come together, but I need to drink it. I close my eyes as I tip up the bowl, feel chunks of vegetables and potato touch my lips before I let them in.

I eat the whole meal with my eyes closed, pretending I'm in the garden at home. We're eating outside for fun, because we can. Just to see what it's like to hear the rain on our bowls and feel the sky on our skin. I imagine Mum and Lilli laughing and Darren is next to me. He nods at me, his smile giving me strength. *I believe in you*, he says.

I tip up my bowl again, but it's empty.

In the evening, hunger and exhaustion swamps us all. Rimi sits on my lap, making her rabbit dance on the floor. She's humming to herself, in her own little world. Destiny is using a sock as a glove puppet as she plays with Zamal.

'I'm bigger and stronger than you,' he says, nudging her away with his lion puppet.

'Ah, but I can bake better cookies than you.'

'You're a bad Core,' Zamal says, hitting the sock puppet over and over. 'You're nasty and very bad.'

Rimi stops her rabbit dancing and looks up at her brother.

'How about —' Destiny's voice is filled with forced cheeriness as she takes the puppet from Zamal and holds his hand instead — 'we try something different.'

'Like what?' Lilli asks.

'Well, if they're going to make us wear those grey dresses,' Destiny says, 'we need to celebrate looking good as long as we can. I need your help though.' She stands up and pulls Lilli with her.

'I'm too tired,' Lilli says. My sister looks like a shadow.

'We're never too tired,' Destiny tells her.

'What do we have to do?' Zamal asks.

'You'll see.' The other women are watching Destiny as she goes to gather up some blankets and drops them at our feet. Mum's coat is next to us, folded as a pillow. 'Here —' she holds it out to Lilli — 'put this on backwards.'

'Backwards?'

'It'll work.'

Lilli slips her skinny arms into the sleeves and I feel so protective, so proud of her. How in the middle of the horror of this camp, she's found a way to keep her soul strong. Destiny does the buttons up Lilli's back. Her fingers are slow and stumble and I know she'd never say it, but I can tell she's struggling through her own weakness.

'It looks better than it does on me,' Mum says, from where she sits with Aba.

'It looks like a straightjacket,' another woman says, her laughing quickly taken over by coughing.

Lilli looks funny and beautiful and it should make me happy to see her smile, but it hurts my heart so painfully that I have to bite my lips to stop myself from crying.

Destiny takes off her own jumper and puts it on Zamal. It hangs past his knees, almost to his feet. It's the first time I've heard Rimi laugh and it's beautiful. Angel footsteps in the air. It makes Zamal laugh too and it feels like the whole room has somehow found the strength to smile.

'Your turn,' Destiny tells me. I stand here as she wraps one of the blankets around my waist. I have to hold it in place with my hand. 'Luke'll love it.' She hugs me. 'You'll have to show him this sexy outfit when we get out.'

Destiny layers a blanket over her shoulders, before she takes the red material wrapped around her arm and ties it as a bandanna across her forehead, the stitched number on the inside pressing against her skin. I feel fear creep in that she'll be caught like this, but her face looks with triumph through the bleakness.

'We're ready,' she says. 'Follow me.' And we step over the legs of the watching women. Someone tries to stifle her cough, but everyone else is quiet, looking at us, needing this magic. Even Conor's mum watches, although the sadness in her eyes has leaked on to her skin.

Aba starts to clap a steady beat and others copy her as we walk among them and Destiny begins to sing. I think it must be one of her church songs and I slow my pace to match it. It's about love and peace and I want to catch those words.

'Sing it, girl,' her mother says and Destiny's voice rises higher. People stop clapping to give the song its place to breathe. I stop walking and I listen.

We all listen, stilled, until the very final note. And when Destiny stops singing, none of us move. We hold the echo of her voice in each of us. And in me I feel it bloom and plant its own seeds of hope.

CHAPTER TWELVE

'Fellow countrymen, know that a nation without
good laws is a bad nation.' — John Andrews, leader of
the Traditional Party

I'm jolted out of sleep when a guard opens the door. The night
has gone too quickly and now I'm awake I can feel my bruised
bones and taste the sharpness of my hunger.

'Up,' he shouts and none of us disobey. Lilli and I fold the
blanket together.

'Do you reckon they'll let us shower today?' I ask her.

'Possibly,' she replies, but she's distant, slightly out of my reach.

At the door, the guard stops the people at the front, using his
gun as a barrier.

'Children first,' he says.

Confusion is instant. Mum grabs me and Lilli, her arms steel
around us.

'Why?' Destiny's mum asks.

'Those under thirteen,' the man says.

Under thirteen. So they won't be taking Lilli.

Zamal clings to Destiny's leg. Mum picks up Rimi and keeps her close. They are the only small children in our room. I know others have many more.

'You didn't answer the question,' Destiny's mum says, staring at the guard until he looks at her. 'Why are they going?'

'It's overcrowded,' the guard says. 'They can't help with the cooking and cleaning.'

'We can teach them,' Mum interrupts him.

'Where are you taking them?' Aba asks.

'They'll be safe,' the guard answers, his lips barely moving. 'They'll be in an environment better suited to them.'

'Where?' Destiny asks.

'Is it away from the camp?'

'They won't be far away,' the guard says. 'Hand them over now.'

Zamal starts to cry. He holds tight to Destiny's leg as she tries to bend down to him.

'It'll be okay,' she says, but I doubt he hears as he starts to wail. The sound is too painful for all of us.

Rimi's arms are tight around Mum's neck. 'I don't want to,' she says.

'You're going to a nice place,' Mum tells her, but the lie is too suffocating.

'No.' Rimi wraps her legs around Mum's waist as she starts to cry.

'You give me the children now,' the guard says. 'Or I will take them.' His words squeeze my lungs, making it difficult to breathe.

'You have to,' Mum tells Rimi.

'We'll see you again later,' Destiny tells Zamal, as she peels him away from her leg. 'It's just so we can work more. That's good, isn't it?' Her words are fast in her panic.

Zamal stands and looks at her, his arms by his side, tears relentless on his cheeks.

'But I want to stay with you,' he says.

'You will be with us.' Destiny's voice starts to crack. 'Later.'

I kneel down next to him. 'You look after your little sister,' I tell him. 'And I'll look after mine.'

'Why can't Lilli come with us?' he asks. 'She does lessons with us.'

'She's thirteen now,' I say. 'She's too old. But you'll see us all later and when you do you can tell us about your day.' I hug him quickly. It's so difficult to let him go. 'Okay?'

He nods.

Aba untangles Rimi's ankles from Mum's back. She prises her arms away from Mum's shoulders and puts her on the ground next to her brother.

The children are level with the guard's gun. It stops their tears.

'This way,' he says and they step out of the door. Zamal takes his sister's hand and in her other she holds her grey rabbit close. She looks back at us just once before the guard leads them away.

We hear screaming from the other rooms as children are taken from their mothers. It's a sound I've never heard before and even though I sit on the floor and block my ears, it's more brutal than anything I've ever known.

A gunshot shatters it all.

It thuds into my mind and cracks sudden and violent through me, leaving behind silence as we stare at each other.

Have they killed a mother? A child?

Mum sits between Lilli and me and curls us under her arms, rocking us close. Yet still I don't feel safe.

'What are they doing?' Lilli asks, over and over. 'What are they doing?' As my mind burrows its way to blankness.

Everyone around me looks stunned as the guards make us leave the room and we're lined up for breakfast. Some women are hardly able to stand, held up by others. I can tell by the shape of their bodies, how they curve forwards in pain, that their hearts really have been taken from them.

We move in line to get our bread. Lilli doesn't look like my sister. She's a stranger, lost, and my mum holds her tight to stop her drifting away. We go outside. Some women don't even eat the food. Hunger is destroying them, but they have another pain now that they won't be able to think beyond.

None of us look over to the other side of the fence, even though the day is clear enough for us to find the men we know. Today we see only the children they've taken.

'They killed two mothers,' a woman next to me says. She talks to no one and everyone. 'They shot them in front of their children.'

I close my eyes.

Where are Rimi and Zamal? We told them they'd be safe.

'Do you think they'll bring the children back later?' someone asks.

'No,' she says. 'Do you?'

Do I? Did I ever believe it? But I don't want to say it, don't even want to shake my head in case it stirs up the truth.

'Will they hurt them?' Lilli asks. But no one answers and her words drip down into her bewilderment where I know they'll drown.

I don't feel safe without my mum near me, but she and Lilli have been ordered to go with a group to sort out the dresses. I'm on kitchen duty. A male guard stands by the door, his legs splayed wide. Was it him who shot those mothers?

The steam in the kitchen makes me cough, a painful rattle in my lungs. But at least it's warm in here and I wish I could stay all day. I peel the potatoes and when no one is watching I put a scrap of the raw skin in my mouth. Its muddiness sticks to my thirst, but it's worth it. I take scrunches of peel and put them in my pockets. It's not much, but it's something for Mum and Lilli at least.

I look up at the guard. His back is turned to me, so I pull a scrap of paper from my sleeve, one with Destiny's writing explaining what's happening in this camp. I wish I could add to it that the children have been taken. I feel my blood beating too fast as I move the paper to my palm, before I tip it into the kitchen waste. Maybe someone outside of this place will have to sort through it? It could be a guard, but it's a chance I have to take.

We're allowed one glass of water each before we leave. The guards make us rush, but I want to feel every drop as it makes my gums live again. It's like swallowing gold.

Outside we're led back to the women's section and so I step from one area of hell to another. The wind digs its freezing fingers through my dress, dragging them along my skin.

'Line up,' a guard near us shouts, but we could be here for hours and I can't see Mum or Lilli anywhere. A hand grabs me and it's Destiny. Together we find a place and stand, waiting, my bones sewn with needles of ice.

We watch as the men spill into the yard on their side and are ordered to get into line. I scan them for Luke. How will he be able to spot me when they make us all wear the same dresses? I see Mr Hart, his eyes searching desperately among us. I'd forgotten about his wife and children. Does he know what happened earlier? Do any of them know?

'My mum thinks there's a mole among the women,' Destiny says quietly.

'Darren thought that. But wouldn't we be able to tell if someone in our room was actually spying for the Trads?'

'I don't think we can trust anyone.'

I link my arm through hers and squeeze it, needing to feel even a grain of warmth.

'Well, it's not me,' I tell her.

'You sure?'

'I'm sure.'

'So my deepest darkest secrets are safe with you, then?'

'Always.'

I spot Stan on the other side of the fence and he looks shrunken and desolate. Next to him is Conor, his face scorched with bruises, his eye swollen. I need his mum not to see him, not like this.

'I put one of our paper trails down the loo,' Destiny says.

'How will anyone find that?' Somehow among the terror she's still able to make me laugh.

'I've no idea, but it was worth a try.'

'Always worth a try.'

'And the next time I'm near a coach, I'll be straight up those steps to hide one in there.'

'Of course you will.' I smile and there's a part of me that believes she might.

'It's strange, isn't it?' Destiny says. 'How we weren't friends at school.'

'It is a bit.'

'How does that happen?'

'What, that we never knew we were friends?'

'Yeah.'

'I don't know. I somehow missed out on the fact about how cool you are.'

'And I somehow missed out on the fact about how cool *you* are.'

'Well,' I laugh quietly. 'We know now.'

'We'll be friends, won't we?' Destiny asks. 'When we're back at school.'

I'd give anything to be walking in the school corridor right now, introducing Destiny to Sara, sitting with her in the canteen.

'You try stopping me,' I tell her.

'My friends'll like you,' she says.

'They will?'

'Theo will fancy you, so we'll have to get Luke to sort him out.'

And then he's there, Luke. He's next to Conor, looking

to this side, and I know he's scanning the faces for me.

'I need him to see me,' I say.

'You've found him?'

'He's near the end.' I just need eye contact with him. 'How can I get his attention?'

'You'll have to get naked, girl,' Destiny says. 'Then you'll get *all* their attention.'

'I'm serious, Destiny. This is killing me.'

'I'm serious too. Give those Trads something else to think about.'

I take her laugh with me as I go closer to the fence.

The bedroom feels stripped bare without Zamal and Rimi and even with so many women crammed in here there's an invisible hole that swamps the room where they should be. I try to imagine where they are. There are rumours that the children have been taken away from the camp and there's hope that maybe they're in a better place.

I look over to where Aba and my mum sit side by side, their backs against the wall. They stare into nothing and everything. I know they won't have the answers I want to hear, so I don't go to them. Instead I step over the piles of women to reach Destiny and Lilli.

We sit cross-legged and make a circle, our knees touching, and I hold on to their hands like I would a lifeboat. Because I think my mind at least could drift and drift, through the cracks in the doors and the fence and it might never come back. If I let it, it'll get picked apart by crows, leaving the shell of me here.

'I want Zamal and Rimi to come back.' Lilli starts to cry. She doesn't let go of our hands to wipe away her tears so I watch them fall, roll down her nose and cheeks, sinking into her skin.

'Don't let them win,' Destiny tells her. 'We have to stay strong. Prove they can't break us.'

Lilli nods, over and over. I see her trying so hard not to cry, but her tears won't stop. I wonder what's going on in her head right now – how she must be more confused than any of us. Because I know that the Trads were beginning to convince her – their ideas were sneaking into her eyes. She'd blink and I'd still see the words there, pushing their way deeper inside. But now?

'I'm not going to leave you,' I tell my sister. 'I'll get you through this.'

Somewhere, in another room, a woman screams. It's not the sound of surprise, but of a deeper pain than I thought was possible for a human to feel. It scrapes inside me and I don't know how we don't all shatter. There are noises in the corridor, shouting from the guards, but no more sounds of a gun. Not yet.

'Have you ever seen a raven sat on a telephone wire when it rains?' Destiny asks.

'What do you mean?'

'Exactly that. A raven on a wire when it's really raining. I saw it once. It was a proper storm. Not just a bit of rain, but totally pouring and the wind going crazy. I was in my bedroom watching it and the raven was getting battered and I waited for it to move. But it didn't.'

'It didn't fly away?'

'No. It stayed there, calm as anything, as though there was nothing going on around it. Literally closed its eyes, stood tall and faced the storm head-on.'

'It didn't get knocked off?' Lilli asks.

'No. It was like it was testing itself. You know, that it was strong enough to withstand it. And then when the rain slowed down, it flew away.' Destiny lifts our hands and squeezes them tight. 'We're that bird. We're that raven.'

'We are?' Lilli asks quietly.

'We have to be,' Destiny tells her.

We're squashed in tight to sleep and although it doesn't make the floor any more comfortable, it's a little bit warmer at least. Mum and Lilli are already deep in their dreams, but I can't find a way to join them. My eyes keep staying open in the dark, listening to the bleak coughing of some of the women.

It's not just Zamal and Rimi I'm thinking about, it's all the other children they've taken too. Does Mr Hart know yet? How will he cope, on his side of the fence, unable to do anything?

I reach up for my necklace and pull it out from under my hoodie. My name is spelled out underneath my thumb and fingers and I press down into the letters so I can feel them printed in my skin. But now I've let Luke into my mind and the ache without him here cuts deep into me.

I turn on to my side and have to brush Destiny's hair from my face.

'Are you awake?' I whisper.

'Yes,' Destiny whispers back.

'I can't sleep.'

'Me neither.'

The darkness is so thick between us that I can't even see her outline. All around us, exhausted women sleep.

'Where do you think they've taken them, Ruby?' she asks. 'I'm so scared that they're going to hurt them. Like really hurt them. So they never come back.'

I know the Traditionals are capable of anything now. *The behaviour of young children must be adjusted accordingly*. The general's words bring bile to my throat.

'I think I'm going to be sick,' I whisper.

'Here. Put your head on this.' I hear her moving and she's pushing her coat underneath my head. But bile is climbing up my throat, my saliva hot and sticky. My stomach cramps and I try to turn away as I vomit.

'Ruby?' It's Mum's voice, but I can't reply. My body is in painful spasms as I retch. I want all the pain in my heart to go too, but that stays there as I retch some more. I feel the hands of my mum stroking my hair, someone else stroking my back.

'All done?' Mum asks.

'Yes,' I reply.

'Good girl.' She kisses my head, before she picks up Destiny's coat. She must find her way over the sleeping women in the dark as I hear her knocking on the door and people grumbling. She knocks again and it opens, shedding a line of light into the room.

'What's going on?' the guard asks.

I stay lying down. I'm shivering, even though the blanket is pulled up to my chin. Lilli strokes my hair as the door closes.

Mum has gone. She doesn't come back. I try to stay awake.

'She'll be fine,' Destiny says.

I try so hard not to sleep, but my eyes have weights that pull me down.

The guard opens the door in the morning and Mum is lying next to me. She must've swapped places with Lilli when she came back.

'How are you feeling?' she asks, moving the hair from my forehead.

'Did they hurt you?' I ask.

'No.'

My skull has nails being hammered into it. They're left in there to rust and I can't pull them out.

'Are you going to be sick again?' Mum asks. I shake my head, but the pain digs into my eyes.

'I'm not ill,' I say.

But I don't have the energy to stand.

'Come on. We have to get up.' Mum helps me to sit.

'I'm so thirsty,' I tell her. My dry tongue somehow peels the words out of my mouth.

'I know. You'll get a drink before breakfast.'

Two guards walk in. They're carrying a pile each of grey material.

'From now on,' one shouts, as though we're far away. 'You're to wear only these at all times.'

'Nice,' Destiny says. 'Our dresses.'

The guards give them to the women next to the door, before they leave and close us in.

'I need water,' I tell Mum.

'There's not any here,' she says. 'It won't be long. We'll get dressed quickly.'

But thirst is stripping me bare. It hurts to swallow.

Already Mum is wearing her dress. It looks awful. A lump of grey.

'How am I looking?' Destiny asks. She swirls in front of me, but when I try to smile my lips crack and I taste blood.

'Beautiful,' I tell her, as Mum takes the red material from my arm and pulls off my hoodie and T-shirt. I feel too naked without my own clothes, stripped of who I am.

It's freezing and the dress she puts on me doesn't warm me. I tuck Luke's necklace inside where it can't be seen.

'Can I put this over the top?' I ask, taking my hoodie from her.

'No,' she says. 'We'll ask them later, but not at the moment.'

I reach into the pocket and hold the precious pieces of paper that Destiny and I have written more messages on and my mum doesn't know as I slip them into the small square pocket on the side of the grey dress I'm wearing.

Destiny nods at me, though, and there's her smile that tells me that we mustn't give up.

'I'm sorry about your coat,' I tell her. I can see that mum tried to clean it as best she could, but now it's damp and probably won't dry before she wears it again. 'I'll buy you a new one when we're out.'

'Deal,' Destiny says. 'We'll go shopping together.'

Mum is silent as she fixes the red material with my number over the top of the grey dress. Next to us, Conor's mum gets changed and I see how her body is caving in on itself, her skin sticking roughly to the outline of her bones. Mum goes to help tie the strip of material on her arm, while Destiny does her own using her teeth, careful to keep her number on the inside.

We all stand in the same grey dresses and wait. The door opens and a male guard comes in carrying a box.

'You're to take off all of your jewellery and put it in here.'

There's a beat of a second as we all stare at him, until another guard steps into the room.

'Now,' she says.

I watch my mum take off her earrings.

'We have to do it, Ruby,' she says.

'I don't want to,' I whisper.

'You have no choice.'

I unhook the clasp of my charm bracelet and slip it from my wrist. Each part of it belongs to mine and Sara's story, together, but they want to take it away. I hold it in my palm and feel the charms on my skin. The yellow daffodil she chose so I wouldn't have to pick the real flowers. The tiny silver phone she gave me last birthday, linking her to me.

Lilli stands with her hands by her sides. She only had her ears pierced a few months ago and they've barely healed.

'I'll do it,' Mum tells her and she takes the tiny stars from my sister's ears.

'Will I get them back?' Lilli asks.

'I'm sure,' Mum tells her.

The guard walks among us with the box. When he gets to me, I have to drop my charm bracelet into it.

'Those,' he says, pointing towards my earrings. I take out the

283

small hoops and give them to him. 'And that.' He nods towards the necklace Luke gave me, the one that spells my name.

'I want to keep it on,' I say. The guard looks stunned for an instant, but quickly stands taller.

'It's orders,' he says.

His hand jolts up to my throat and I try to step back but already he's gripped my necklace and yanks it from me.

My name sits in his fist. He keeps his dead eyes on me as he drops it into the box.

I turn in time to see my mum taking her wedding ring from her finger and she lets it go, into the pile of everything they've taken from us, before the guard walks away among the other women.

Mum's face has the fire of defiance. 'They're just possessions,' she tells Lilli and me. 'They can't steal what's inside of us. They can never take that away.'

I don't know how I walk down the stairs, yet I do. It's the thought of water that pulls me there. And when I get the cup in my hand, each sip is more precious than anything I've ever owned. Just the one glass softens my headache, soothes my lips and makes me feel like I can walk again.

But outside, now we're all in grey dresses and with our jewellery gone, something has changed. You can tell it in the eyes of the guards as they patrol past our line. Before, we were holding on to scraps of being real people, but now they don't see that. To them we are below animals.

In front of me a woman drops her bread. When she bends to pick it up the guard stamps on her hand. She screams as he grinds his heel deeper.

But none of us help her.

'Please,' the woman gasps up at the guard, so he pulls her up and hits her so hard that she falls to the floor. I just look at her curled helpless there and I do nothing.

The guard makes us step over her. I take my bread before I lift my feet over the woman. I don't talk to her. I don't kneel down to her. I step over her as everyone does and walk away with my food.

The cold wipes my thoughts. It grinds its way across my face, down my throat. My fingers freeze motionless around my bread, but I manage to push it into my mouth.

We stay huddled together and I beg for the sun to come out. When Mum's finished eating she puts her arms around Lilli and me and tries to make us warm.

'They can't make us stand out in this for too long,' Aba says. None of us answer. She starts to walk away and I glance up too late to see her talking to a guard. He brings back his arm and thumps her so hard in the stomach that she folds and falls heavily to the ground.

Destiny sees it the moment I do. I try to hold her back, but when the guard walks away she struggles free from me.

How can this be happening?

I look up at the sky, but all that's there is the cold white.

The day passes in frozen words and hunger. I don't warm up. An empty window in the sewing room tunnels cold air into us and it freezes my fingers and numbs my brain. For the first time I'm actually pleased that Lilli has been taken to the other room, even though the younger children aren't there with her and The Trads will have more chance to get to her. At least she'll be warm.

She doesn't come back for lunch and I hope they're feeding her something better than what we get. When Destiny and I take our food outside I see Darren, standing right up to the fence that divides us, so I weave quickly through the women to get to him. But now I'm facing him I am shocked by how gaunt he looks.

'Ruby,' he says and his smile is still his own. 'How are you all? How's Mum?'

'She's fine.' I see her walking over and Lilli has joined her now, so I know I haven't much time. 'But they're still taking Lilli to that room and I don't really know what they're telling her or what she's saying to them.'

'What she's saying to them?'

'I know she wouldn't do it on purpose.'

'Darren,' Lilli says, as she rushes up next to me and she looks so pleased to see him that I'm surprised she doesn't scale the fence. I can tell Mum is trying not to cry as she touches her palm as close to Darren's as she can get.

'Ruby.' It's Destiny beside me. 'Luke wants you.' I look further along and he's there and now he's all I see. I push through the women until I'm facing him and I try to smile but my heart hurts so much.

'Nice dress,' he says.

'I made it myself,' I say, pulling the material to the side. 'We're working on your outfits now.'

Luke raises his eyebrows. 'Lucky us.' And I see his hunger and his sunken cheeks. There's a sudden tension in his eyes as he bites his thumb. 'We've heard rumours that they're doing things to the women. The male guards are.'

'No,' I tell him. 'There's nothing like that.' But how can I be sure?

Luke's shoulders relax just slightly.

'How's Conor's mum?' he asks.

'Not well,' I say.

'They managed to find each other,' Luke tells me. 'At the end of the fence.'

'You're going to have to stay with him later. I don't know what he'll do.'

Luke nods. 'I drew you something.'

I feel desperate suddenly because the seconds are ticking by and I need to fill them with him. I want to touch him and have

287

him hold me and I have to breathe so deeply to stop myself from screaming.

'Ruby?' Luke looks at me. 'I'm going to drop this on the ground by the fence and then I'm going to walk away. If you want to you can pick it up. But only if you think it's safe. Okay?'

'I love you, Luke,' I tell him and he smiles, his fingers moving silently in reply. He's signing the words to our Prince song. *I would die for you*. I take each beat, each letter and hold them in a place where the guards can never find them.

Luke throws a piece of paper as close to the fence as he can get, before coughing shakes his body and he turns and walks away. I don't even look for guards as I dart forwards, wriggle my hand through the fence until my fingers sweep the ground the other side. I grasp the paper, pull it back through and go to join Destiny so we can move into the crowd of women, becoming one of the grey mass again.

'What is it?' she asks.

I open it up. It's the size of my palm, torn from his sketchbook. A pencil drawing of Luke and me when we had to stand together the whole night. His face is silhouetted against the white moon, mine against the black sky that's dotted with stars. We're there together. There's no fence, no guards, no fear. Our hands are joined, our bodies so close that even light can't shine between us.

'That boy loves you, Ruby,' Destiny says.

I fold my picture and put it in my pocket.

When I get home, I'll put it on the wall of my room. And I'll lie on my bed with Luke and I'll kiss him beneath it.

We line up, our grey dresses doing nothing against the freezing cold. It slides its way beneath my skin, turning my blood to ice before it eats into my bones. We chant as we move forwards, slower than ever, before Destiny and I finally get to the front.

'Number?' the guard asks blankly.

'276,' I tell him.

'Move on.' I step away.

'Number?' I hear him ask Destiny.

She answers quietly, so that only he can hear. There's a pause. I stop and look back to see the guard drumming his pen on his paper, a strange smirk on his face.

'Sexuality?' he asks her.

'Excuse me?' She looks him straight in the eyes, but I can see her panic too clear.

'Do you like boys?' he asks. 'Or girls?'

How can they know anything about Destiny? *Don't answer*, I silently beg her. But she stands tall. *Just lie.*

'I like girls,' she says.

The guard looks at her as though she's infected.

'Wait to the side,' he tells her.

'No,' I say. 'She's with me.'

'*With* you?'

'She's just my friend,' I say. 'But we're staying together.'

'No,' the guard next to him says calmly, tapping his finger on the trigger of his rifle. 'You're not.'

'I'm okay,' Destiny tells me, yet her hands are shaking. I step forwards to hug her, but the guard blocks me.

'I'm only protecting you,' he sneers. 'It might be catching.'

'There's nothing wrong with her,' I say, anger spitting from me.

'Leave it, Ruby,' Destiny says, as the guard starts to pull me away.

'I can walk on my own,' I tell him, before I look back and see Destiny there, her hand over her mouth, her breathing fast. 'Be the raven on the wire, Destiny,' I shout, before I yank myself free from the guard and run. My feet pound the ground and I wait to hear a gunshot. Wait to feel the bright red pain piercing my back. But it doesn't come.

I push past the women, knowing only Destiny standing terrified, the guard's hand gripped on her shoulder. I run up the stairs and count the doors until I'm at our room. I burst in and the first thing I see is Aba. Somehow, she's smiling. She's with Mum and Lilli and Conor's mum and they're all laughing, the sound so wrong in the air.

They stop the moment they see me.

'They've got Destiny,' I say. Aba staggers to her feet.

'What?' she steps over women to get to me. 'Where? What do you mean?' The panic around her is fierce.

'At roll call.' My breathing is struggling.

'Ruby.' Aba shakes me. 'Where's Destiny? Where is she?'

'They made her stand to the side.'

She runs down the corridor.

'Aba,' Mum calls to her, but she won't stop. 'Keep Lilli with you here,' she tells Conor's mum.

By the time I'm outside, Mum's caught up with Aba. She's trying to hold her, but Aba is kicking herself free.

'Where's my daughter?' she screams.

'Help me, Ruby,' Mum says. And I have to grip Aba's arms, cradle her head as the line of women still waiting for roll call stare at us. 'Destiny will be all right,' Mum struggles to say.

Two guards close to us stand with their legs far apart, watching as though we're some form of entertainment.

'What have you done with my daughter?' Aba shouts at them, as we try to hold her. 'No!' she screams and she's fighting against us.

I never thought I'd see her cry. Destiny's proud, strong mum, who's made of love and steel, is falling apart bit by bit in our arms.

'I want her back,' she cries.

'You'll get her back,' Mum says and we start to lead her towards the door, almost carrying her.

Suddenly Aba breaks free. She runs and we can't catch her, a flame of anger burning across the ground. The guard looks shocked when she reaches him. He flinches, but stands firm.

'Where is Destiny?' she snarls. Now she's the animal they want us to be.

But the guard just laughs.

I watch Destiny's mum raise her arm.

'No, Aba.' Mum's voice is a bullet through the air.

Everything slows as Destiny's mum hits the guard. I see his mouth twist and his hand is on his gun and death walks from his face as he forces back the trigger.

Aba's arms reach up and there's blood, too much blood as she falls. We can't get to her in time. She's bleeding and my mind can't make this real as I kneel next to her and Mum strokes her forehead and I hold her hand. Her breath is just a violent jolt and she stares at us and tries to speak.

But now she's still. Everything is still.

Apart from my heart and my body that's shaking.

'Get up,' I hear the guard shout. He must be talking to us. His voice is so close, yet it's somewhere far behind the mountain.

The light goes from Destiny's mum.

The light goes from our world.

I'm kicked in the side and I fall.

'Now,' the guard's voice tells me. Mum is pulling me up.

'We can't leave her here,' I say.

'We have to,' Mum says. And she pulls me away, back towards the building.

I glance at the crowd of men watching through the fence. And I see Darren, his hands raised to his head, as if he's trying to tear from his mind what he's seeing. But I know it'll always be there. Aba's blood will stain us forever.

Lilli stands in the doorway of the bedroom, Conor's mum's arm tight around her.

'What happened?' she asks.

Aba's blood is on our hands. It soaks the front of Mum's dress, sticking the material to her skin. Lilli stares at it. 'They shot you?' her words are too small, too simple.

'No,' Mum says. We step into the room. Women are sitting on the floor in silence, needing to know but not wanting to. It's better that they have a world with Destiny's mum still in it.

'You're bleeding,' Lilli says.

'No.' Mum's legs give way beneath her and she sinks to the floor. 'They shot Aba,' she whispers.

Conor's mum opens her mouth, but there are no words there. How can there be? How can there be questions when there are no answers? No reason?

My whole body is trembling as I sit down. Lilli stays standing. She doesn't move.

'Where's Destiny?' she asks.

'I don't know,' I say.

'Did they kill her too?'

'I don't think so.'

But they've taken her. They've murdered her mother.

I lie down, my head on the bare floor. I hold Mum's hand. Someone puts a blanket over us. And this is how we stay.

CHAPTER THIRTEEN

'With a total shutdown on anti-social behaviour,
we will clean up our streets, we will clean up our
nation.' – John Andrews, leader of the Traditional
Party

Mum wakes in the morning with Aba's blood dried on her dress.

'You need to change,' Conor's mum tells her. Mum nods.

Conor's mum goes to talk to a guard and a new dress is passed through the door. Mum changes into it, but she won't let go of the old one.

'I want to keep it,' she says.

'You can't,' I try to tell her. But Aba's soul is caught in the spread of blood.

'I have to,' Mum says defiantly. 'When we get out, I'll show people. It's proof that it happened.'

'You won't need proof,' I say. 'People will believe us.'

'Will they?' She looks around, searching for someone she doesn't find, before she folds the dress and puts it under her blanket.

We line up and drink from the shared glass of water. Today I hate it. It makes me feel sick. I have to force my throat open to swallow it.

Lilli and I are in the line in front of Mum. We shuffle forwards, our hands so tight in each other's.

'How did they know Destiny was gay?' Lilli asks me quietly. 'Who else knew apart from us?'

'Did you tell anyone?' I hate doubting her, but it's still there, nagging at me.

'No.'

'If there's someone spying, they could have overheard her,' I say.

Any of these strangers around us could be Trads. But would they really starve themselves along with us, for bits of conversations that might mean nothing?

'We can't trust anyone,' I tell Lilli, as we move closer to the front. 'You mustn't speak to anyone but us.'

We eat bread. And then we sew.

We line up.

We give our numbers.

We clean.

And we sleep.

In the morning it's difficult to wake Conor's mum. When she opens her eyes, I see how the whites have crept yellow. Her skin looks thin enough to tear.

'You have to get up,' I tell her. 'It's breakfast.'

'I can't,' she says.

'You can. You have to.'

She lets me and Mum lift her and even though she's so light I don't know where I get my own strength from. Thirst has taken off the coating of my mouth and replaced it with sand. My swollen tongue licks it, needing water. It's like torture, imagining a tap turning on, the drip, drip of it.

It's not long before I'm in the queue and given the glass and I can drink. The relief blinds everything else for these few seconds, as it slides cold down my throat.

We stand in line.

'Why is this happening?' Lilli asks, more to herself than to me. Her blood nestles in the cracked skin on her lips and I feel useless that I can't heal them for her.

We move forwards until I have bread in my hands and I want to eat it, but it hurts to swallow. I don't know if it's something real or imaginary that's blocking my throat.

And we're outside in the bitter cold. The sun is there, but it

297

doesn't reach us. It's turned its back on the camp and lets the blistering blue sky pierce us with ice.

'Number?' the guard asks me when it's my turn.

'276,' I reply. He looks up, bored.

'You're to go to the general's office.' It's been days since I've been there and I thought maybe the general didn't want to see me again. I say a silent thank you to Zoe as I start to move away in the direction I'm meant to go. 'Wait.' He grabs my arm enough to hurt. 'You'll be escorted.'

As we walk, I scratch through the reserves of my energy but there's nothing there. Every movement of mine is slow. My eyes see through the window as we go down the corridor. Outside, there are piles of men working, digging trenches, but I can't see Luke or Darren.

'What are they doing?' I ask the guard who leads me.

'A new shower block,' she says, pulling me towards the cleaning cupboard.

How will I work when I can hardly stand up? I'm kneeling down to pick up the bucket when she turns to talk to someone in the corridor. I can rest, just for a moment.

'They're bloody barbarians the lot of them.' It's a man speaking, his voice chiselled from fine china. The guard laughs and she's no longer watching me. She's now simply a woman flirting with a man. 'The sooner we get rid of them all the better.'

I walk out of the cupboard and it's Stan standing close enough to touch her. I look around him for the man who was speaking but there's no one else here.

'Stan?'

He looks so shocked and I'm worried that by saying his name I've got him into trouble.

'Ruby,' he says, but it's not his voice, not Stan's.

'What's wrong?' I whisper. 'What's happened?'

I don't blink, waiting for some sort of sign from him. But he just does a stranger's laugh.

'I suppose you were bound to find out sooner or later.' There's no trace of Stan's voice that I know.

'Find out what?' My mind is knotted. Nothing is making sense.

'I'm a Traditional.'

'You can't be,' I say.

'Can't I?'

And I see it, there in his sneering eyes, that he's telling the truth. The flint of his betrayal rubs against my heart, striking it again and again until sparks of anger appear.

'You tricked us,' I whisper. 'You bastard.'

But I'm just the dirt on his shoes, the dust in his eye.

'A vulgar Core,' he says to me. 'You're nothing more, nothing less.'

'I *am* more,' I say, standing straight. 'I am so much more, as we all are.'

'I haven't got time to waste on you,' he says, turning his back to walk away.

'I'll tell the men on your side of the fence,' I say. 'I'll find a way.'

He stops and looks at me. 'If you do,' he says calmly, 'if even one person finds out who I am, I shall have your mother shot. And I'll line up Luke next to her, for good measure.' He tips his head to one side, twists his moustache. 'And you wouldn't like that would you, dear little Ruby? Especially when your sweet gay friend has already been taken away.'

Destiny. It was never Lilli. It was me who told Stan.

I can hear my breathing, as biting pains start in my stomach and find their way to my chest. But he just laughs and touches the guard gently on her shoulder, before he finally walks away. I watch the gap he leaves behind. The empty space. Stan doesn't exist, he never did and he never will. Whoever this man is took our trust and crushed it. He took Destiny.

'You really are stupid, aren't you?' the guard beside me says. It takes every part of me to ignore her as I walk towards the general's office. I wait for the guard to catch up with me, before she knocks on the door.

'Enter,' the general says.

The guard steps in before me. 'Number 276 to see you, sir.'

'Ah,' the general says and I step inside and close the door in the guard's face.

It's the first time I've been in here since they put us in grey dresses. If the general notices, he doesn't say. He only seems pleased to see me as I stand here with the ghost of Stan too thick and heavy in my mind.

'I got you these,' he says, stepping out from behind his desk. In his hand is that same plate, but this time there are biscuits coated in chocolate. 'They're shortbread.' It's a strange eagerness in his voice. 'They were Zoe's favourite.'

'Thank you.' I hope he doesn't see my hand shaking as I take one.

'What can I teach you today?' The general's eager voice drifts in from far away.

'Today?'

'Yes,' he says. 'I feel that we're making progress.'

'We are.' I'm so calm, when really I want to scream until my lungs disintegrate. 'I'm interested to know where the children have gone.'

'We noticed during their classes that some weren't advancing as we would have hoped. They still seemed too attached to their parents and we needed to separate them from that influence.'

'Where are they?'

'They're in good hands.'

'Are they still in the camp?' I ask. The general drifts his fingers along his closed mouth, forwards and back, before he breathes in, his knuckles under his chin.

'Most of them have been moved to a separate unit, but you have my word that they're well.' *Most?* He sits down on the edge of his desk, yet still he looms too large in the room. 'You seem to have adjusted well to your new clothes.'

'We could've just washed our old ones. And you took our jewellery.'

'That's not a bad thing,' the general says, as he smiles at me. 'We're doing it for you. Would it help if you saw it as a rebirth?'

'Maybe,' I lie.

'It's about us trying to wire your brain correctly,' the general says, boosted now. 'Unplugging the lies you've been told and retraining your thoughts the right way.'

'Do you really think that's possible?'

'Of course. But we also see the need for the process to accelerate, so we've recently begun using a neurosurgical treatment called leucotomy. It's very clever and hopefully very effective.'

'Are you operating on people?' I hold my hands together behind my back. He mustn't see that I'm shaking.

'No. Nothing like that.' The general leans forwards, his hands on his thighs. 'It's all done through electrical stimuli. Electric currents to the brain, to sever connections in the prefrontal cortex.'

It isn't hunger that makes the floor fall from me.

'Am I making it difficult to understand?' he asks, his voice talking to a child.

'It's a lot to follow,' I say. 'But it's interesting.'

'They don't feel a thing,' he assures me. 'It's all done under anaesthetic.'

'So they don't suffer?'

'Not at all. We're using it alongside deep-sleep therapy. When they wake up they don't know how long they've been asleep, or what treatment they've been given.'

'So they do wake up?' I don't know how I form each word.

'Of course. The ones who we think are ready.'

'Are they all right?'

'Absolutely. Their minds are wiped clean, ready to start again.' He looks at me with a strange concern. 'Would it help if you saw them?' the general asks.

'Yes.' My voice is numb.

'Come. I'll show you.' He stands up from the desk and automatically holds out his hand to me, before he seems to remember who he is and pulls it back. 'I want to put your mind at rest.' He walks past me towards the door.

We're going now. It seems so simple as I'm following him down the corridor, one step behind. But out here, he's no longer Zoe's dad. I'm no longer a shadow of his daughter. Here, he is a man in control, his boots heavy on the floor, his shoulders broad, his arms big enough to snap me if he wants.

We go past the cleaning cupboard, further down to a door at the end. Is this it? Have the people who've disappeared been this close all along?

The general opens the door and I follow him in.

The smell of disinfectant is so strong that I nearly retch. Bleach tangled with false ferns and petals. A man in a white coat looks up and when he sees it's the general he salutes clumsily.

'Sir.'

'Which beds are the leucotomy patients in?' the general asks him. The room is so long, cordoned off with cubicle after cubicle.

'The first six are for sterilisation. You need the further end of the ward.'

Sterilisation?

'This way,' the general tells me. And I have to follow him, one step in front of the other, past curtains that hide secrets I don't dare imagine.

I keep my eyes to the floor, but it's now that I see them. Children's shoes lined up, three pairs in each section. Are they sterilising them? Is this what's happened to the children who've been taken away?

'Keep up,' I hear the general say and beside me the man in the white coat has joined us and I know now that I walk with the devil.

He stops us in front of a grey plastic curtain. But I'm not

ready. His fingers pull it back, but I don't want to see.

'Doctor,' the general says. 'Talk us through what's happening here.'

My eyes focus on Destiny. Her head is clamped back on the bed. Her bottom lip is sunk down, her teeth exposed and rigid.

Above her, on the wall, is the number 198.

I know I'm breathing too quickly now, the sound raised in the quiet around us.

'Do you know her?' the general asks me. I stare at her bruised and swollen eyelids.

'No,' I tell him, as the doctor comes to stand next to me, so close that I feel the rub of his white coat on my arm.

'Yes. Number 198. We think she's responding well,' the doctor says. He puts his hand on the sheet over Destiny's leg, but she doesn't flinch. 'We're trying her in an insulin-induced coma, so that we can better administer the lobotomy.'

I hang Destiny's personality on each of his words and cling tight to it to stop myself from falling.

'This is the homosexual?' the general asks.

'Yes. Hence the increased dose. The plan is to leave her with an infantile personality.'

'Surgically induced childhood?' the general asks.

'Exactly. She'll then get the chance to start again. We'll be able to teach her the right way to be.'

'You see –' the general turns to me – 'it's completely pain

free. I think it really could be the answer to everything. Would you agree?'

I nod.

'We feel it's quite a breakthrough,' the general says.

'Would you like to see more?' the doctor asks. 'We've had particularly fascinating results with the twins.'

I shake my head.

'Maybe another time.' The general smiles and pats the doctor on the top of his arm, his palm curving round the white coat.

Doctors are meant to save lives. Their white is the colour of angels.

The general is speaking, saying something else. But all I hear is Destiny's silence.

And I'm being ushered away. I have to pretend that I don't know her, I don't care, that I can leave her here without looking back. Leave her in a room with rows of hidden children whose futures are being destroyed.

'Has that settled your doubts?' the general asks.

I have to reply to him. I have to somehow search for the right words through the darkness.

'It's very clever,' I say.

'I'm glad that you thought so.'

But I'm hollow now. There's nothing left.

*

I wait in the cleaning cupboard on my own. I can't go out, not yet.

Destiny is a number.

They have taken her and she is number 198.

Do you know her?

No.

I disowned you.

I have left you there.

The cupboard air is too tight, too dark. I can feel it eating through my skin.

I left you there. And I can't breathe. I find the door handle and twist it and I run. Away from you, Destiny. They're stealing your soul and I'm running away from you.

We're walking in pairs to the sewing block. I'm with Carol and behind us are my mum and Lilli when we see a new coach pull up, filled with more Core supporters. They stare out at us, their healthy faces behind the glass. And all I see is Destiny, her spirit falling on to the clean pillowcase.

'Stand to the side,' a guard tells us, as they start to unload the new people. The first person to come down the steps is a man with a boy on his hip, another clutching his hand.

I think there could be a way on to the coach, I hear Darren say as clearly as if he's next to me. *You have to time it right.*

The moment the guard has his back to me I lean to whisper to Carol. 'Tell Mum I'm going to be okay.' I don't give her time to understand before I slip away from her, through the chaos of new people and slide under the coach. I have to be quick. I have to find a place to hold before anyone sees me. There's somewhere for me to grasp my hands away from the wheels and I lift up my feet until I'm balanced, my back on some kind of ridge. My muscles begin to shake, but I make them forget. And I wash my mind clear of where I am and what I'm about to do.

The noise beyond the coach eventually begins to drift away. A guard is shouting. Always shouting. There's the sound of shoes walking and children crying. One is screaming. I take the sound and wrap it in the blackened floor of the coach above me. Into the grease and nuts and bolts, flattening the sounds of human suffering into the metal, until I can bear it.

Until the engine starting rocks terror into me, rolling in waves through my body, almost shaking my arms free. And the wheels must be turning because we're moving. The ground underneath me begins to run, faster. It stops suddenly at the gate. Will they even think to check? If they find me, I won't have time to blink before a bullet hits.

The ground moves backwards again, taking away my mum, Lilli, Darren. Taking Luke. I suddenly want to let go. I want to go back inside. I need to be near them, to know that Luke is almost close enough to touch, but we're on a road, moving so quickly. My muscles hurt to hold on and I keep my eyes closed tight to what I've just done.

I know I'm going to fall. Every jolt in the road loosens my grip. My skin burns with the effort. But if I let go, Mum will never know. I'll have just disappeared. Or will they take back my body and lay it out for everyone to see? Will they force Luke to look?

I won't let go. Not yet.

Hold tight. Forget the road. Forget the speed.

'I did more than sneak a note on board,' I whisper to Destiny and I laugh, but I start to cry and I have to stop. I have to stay strong.

The sound of the road fills my world, the heavy hum, the engine beating out its rhythm. I try to sing quietly with it, but it takes too much energy when I need every drop.

Hold on, Ruby. It's Darren's voice I imagine I hear. *Hold on.*

Right now he must be digging the hole for the shower block, the spade hitting the earth. I see him wipe his eyes and look up to the sun. *I'll get you free*, I tell him.

And I'll save Destiny's soul.

But the weight of the number they gave me is dragging me down. 276. It makes my bones lead and it's too difficult to carry. So I let each of them drop. One by one the numbers fall from me, get caught by the tarmac of the road and roll away. And now I know I can hold on. Because I'm not a number. I have a name and it is Ruby West.

The coach slows and stops. I'm able to turn my head a bit to the side, enough to see long grass, a ditch.

Now.

I let go. The ground bites into me, but I push it away, crawling into the daylight, a snake in the grass. I roll into the ditch and don't move. Wait for the shouts as I'm found. But the coach starts to drive away. It goes and leaves me.

I lie in total silence. From here, I can see the sky, a faint blue with clouds pushed into it. The type of clouds that have clear edges, as though drawn by hand. I lie and stare at them, at the leaves that stretch above me, clinging to their trees.

I want to sleep. To close my eyes in the comfort of this crushed grass. It's cold, but I'm alive. And I'm beyond the fence.

Get help, Lilli tells me.

I turn on to my stomach and on to my hands and knees. I look above the ditch to the road at the small empty roundabout that slowed the coach and let me fall. *Thank you*, I tell it, before I scramble into the trees behind me. The forest is thick and dark and if I go deeper I might get lost, when I need someone to know what's happening, to get us free.

I go back close to the road and start to crawl, but I'm too slow, the ground sharp and wet beneath my knees. I know I haven't got much time before the next roll call. After a few hours of sewing, the women will be back in line to have their numbers checked. There's not long to get help into the camp

310

before the guards realise I've gone. I stand up, stoop low and start to run.

I hear a car coming. It's getting closer as I scramble up through the ditch and I'm here and shouting and waiting for them to see me. A blue car appears and I'm crying because they'll stop. I try to call to them, but no sound comes out and they're nearly here, so close that I can see the man driving, he's young and he'll know what to do. But he barely glances at me. A brief glimpse of his eyes and a refusal to help.

'No!' I scream after him, running as fast as my shattered body can, my calf bleeding, a bruise on my shoulder digging deeper.

I want to fall back into the grass and curl up and get taken by the earth. Find a place where the world stops turning. But I hear my mum's whisper on the wind. I feel Luke's hand in mine and he pulls me further and further along the road.

There are buildings, a small street. I stagger towards the few people on the pavement. I feel hope, I feel terror and my mind struggles to find sense. A woman is scattering something on the ground and there are pigeons pecking with their petrol necks. I see their eyes and I see their wings and I hear Destiny as I run towards them.

But in the distance there's a flash of green, a red slash, shining boots and I fall towards the nearest door. Inside the shop it's warm, a heat that's too hot and a fear that's too close. Three people are in the post office queue. They all stand and stare.

'Help me,' I say, but they don't move. There are three women and none of them step forward. None of them speak. 'Please. They stole me. They stole us all.' And I'm shouting as I rush towards the nearest person, so old she'll fall, and I pull on her arm. 'Please. They're coming. Please get help.'

'Okay, love.' A door pushes open at the back of the shop and a man walks through, taking off his glasses so that they fall on a string around his neck. 'I'll have to ask you to leave.'

'Please, no, no. They'll take me back.' Thirst sticks to my words, each letter made of rust.

'Take you back where?' He's gentler now, but I know there's a Trad soldier on the street. Before the man can stop me I run past him, to the door he came from and I'm through and in a room and the man is grabbing me by the arm, but I pull away from him and fall against a wall.

'They're killing us,' I whisper.

He steps forwards and kneels down next to me. 'You're not in trouble. Just let me know where you live,' he says. I look into his eyes and I want to trust him, but that word is dust to me now. 'Tell you what.' He gets a pen and a small notebook from his pocket. 'If you pop your mum or dad's number on here I'll give them a ring and they can come and get you.'

The paper is useless in my hands.

'My mother is in the camp. It's not far away,' I say.

'We could phone her. I'm sure she wouldn't mind.'

'They took our phones,' I tell him.

'Did you fall out with her? I know how you young feel about your phones, but it's not worth running away. Your mum will be worried.' I shake my head.

'They put Core voters in a camp, for a trial.' But he doesn't understand. How could he? How can anyone believe that such a place exists?

'What's your name?' he asks calmly.

'Ruby,' I say. 'Ruby West.'

'Well, Ruby, I've never heard of this camp. And I would know if something like this was happening close by.'

I reach out to him, but he leaves his hand by his side. 'I promise,' I say. 'They shot Destiny's mum.' Aba's blood mingles with my own and pours fire into my veins. 'They've taken the children somewhere.'

The man rubs his hands over his eyes, before he looks at me again.

'You're very thin. Have you not been eating properly?'

The door suddenly kicks open. A Trad soldier is standing in the doorway, taking the light. I duck down behind the table, but he knows I'm here. I see his boots stepping towards me and I've hardly time to write my dad's number on the notebook before the soldier grabs me and I try to crawl away, but he pulls me up. I scream, just as a hand clamps my pain back inside.

Another Trad is here and I kick out and try to fight, but I'm nothing against them.

The man from the post office tries to step in.

'Now look here,' he says to the soldiers. 'You're being a bit rough.'

'She's a danger to society,' I hear one of them say and I bite down hard on his palm until his hand moves and I can breathe.

'The camp's in an old army barracks,' I shout, before the hand is on my mouth again.

'The old barracks?' The man looks confused as I throw his notebook on the floor, my dad's number hidden in the pages as they drag me out of the door.

The soldiers haul me through the shop, past people gawping who must see the Trads' fingers too tight on me. Must see as I'm forced into a car, as I'm folded up, thrown inside. Too terrified to cry.

I close my eyes the whole way back. I know I should watch the trees, the grass, the freedom just outside the car, but it's too painful. I've destroyed it all.

I feel empty of everything but fear. It touches every speck of my bones, every drop of my blood and it's so dark that I can't see beyond it.

I keep my eyes closed even when I hear the gates open and we drive into the camp. And when they pull me out of the car I keep them closed as they drag me with them. I hear groups of people murmuring, but I can't look at them.

I could have set you free.

I only open my eyes when we're in a corridor whose smell I recognise, strong enough to almost make me vomit.

The guard knocks on the general's door.

'Yes,' I hear him say, before they open it.

'Number 276,' one guard says.

'Thank you. You may leave her here,' the general says. 'One of you wait outside. I won't be long.'

The general sits behind his desk, looking at me. I'm no longer Zoe.

'Number 276,' he says.

'No,' I reply. 'I am Ruby.' But I'm betrayed by the shake in my voice.

'What a disappointment. I thought I could trust you.'

'You can,' I tell him.

'So, you're a liar as well. I shouldn't have been so foolish to think otherwise.' Anger swarms from him, stinging my exposed skin.

I look to the painting of the horse, the one nearest me, and try to let it calm me. The fine lines of its mane, its chestnut-brown fur. But it makes me want to cry and I have to bite back the pain in my throat. I won't let the general have the satisfaction of even one of my tears.

'Who were you working with?' he demands.

'No one.' I turn to stare hatred into his eyes.

'Whose idea was it?'

'Mine.'

'You expect me to believe that you contrived all that on your own?'

'I'm capable,' I say.

'I don't believe you.'

'There was no one else.' Desperation is weaving in and out of my breathing and I know he notices it. 'I just did it without thinking.'

'It was impulsive?'

'Yes.'

The general puts back his shoulders and tips his head so I see his nostrils flare.

'A dangerous trait,' he says. 'Not one we'd like in our country.'

'Are you going to put me in that room with the doctor?'

'To experiment on you?'

'Yes.' I feel the blood too strong in my heart.

The general leans forwards and picks up his cup from his saucer. His eyes don't leave mine as he drinks, before he puts it back down, the sound of china rubbing on china.

'I wouldn't waste precious resources on you,' he says. 'No, you'll be punished.'

I feel my lungs rip apart as I try to swallow.

The general stands up and walks around the desk until he's in front of me. I flinch as he reaches out and wait for the pain, but he's undoing the red material around my arm. He's taking my number from me.

'Turn around,' he says.

I do. And now I'm facing the door. His breath is too close as I hear his arms move. They're either side of me, the material in front of my face. He clasps it over my eyes and spins my world to darkness.

I raise my hands but he slams them away, as he tightens the material, enough for my hair to burn.

'You disgust me,' he says, his wet lips on my ear.

And the door opens and I'm being led. Someone else pulls me by the elbow, the sound of footsteps either side of me as I stumble and am dragged up, hurried along a tunnel I can't see.

More doors bang and I'm led outside, cold air covering me. The ground is rough and I'm sure this is the path I've been on so many times before.

Further, until the silence is strange and heavy and I know there are people watching. I must be on the men's side as they lead me and we stop and there's the sound of the gate opening and I'm pulled through. To the women's side? I can hear someone crying.

'Lilli?' I call out.

I'm dragged nearer to the sound and hands are on my head,

my hair is twisted and pulled until the blindfold and darkness are taken from me and sunlight burns my eyes.

My sister stands next to my mum in front of the crowd of women in our camp. How so many of them are so silent, yet there are Lilli's tears as she reaches out and clings tight to my dress.

Mum touches the dried cut across my cheek. 'What did they do to you?' But a guard pushes her back and she falls against the fence. I look past it now to the other side. To where there are gallows on the stage, nooses hanging down.

No no no no no no.

The Trads are leading two people towards the steps and I know who it is. I know who it is. I know who it is.

My scream rips my soul in two.

'Luke!' I see my hand reach out for the fence, feel my fingers distant as they grip the metal. 'Darren.'

They stand together, horror tight on their mouths.

I was meant to save them.

'They can't make us watch,' a woman says, as my blood burns holes in my chest.

'They won't do it,' my mum says.

'Luke,' I shout again, but he's staring at the sky. 'Luke!' And he's trying to find me as I rip at the fence, try to claw it from the ground. He sees me and I stop as he closes his eyes and opens them, his chest rising and falling too quickly. I put my hand to my heart, but he's suddenly dragged up the steps. Darren stumbles beside him, but they pull him up too. The guards force them to stand on the stools beneath the ropes. They put the nooses around their necks.

'No,' I hear Mum whisper.

'Let them go,' I scream.

'Kelly,' Darren calls to my mum and she looks up at him. His breathing is strong, catching in the air that he needs. 'Ruby. Lilli. Don't be frightened.' And it crushes my soul. I want to speak to him but the words are buried in the rubble of myself. They can't find their way out.

'276.' It's the general's voice, warped through his speaker, spiralling into me. 'This is on you. One of these people will live. One must die. You will choose.'

'Dear God,' I hear someone behind me say.

'276, you must decide, or they will both die.' The general's voice rips into the air, leaving behind a suffocating silence.

I don't move. I can't.

I need fragments to breathe.

'276.'

Luke doesn't look at me. He stares straight ahead.

'I can't,' I whisper to my mum and I'm shaking her and she's trying to calm me. 'I can't choose.'

A gunshot cracks.

There's screaming and a gunshot again, but it's the guard next to the general and he's firing towards the sky.

everyone is quiet, too quiet

Lilli shaking violently in my arms I can barely hold her

The clouds choose now to break a place for the sun and it shines down on the gallows. Darren holds himself steady in the light as he looks over at us.

'I love you,' he shouts. And he kicks away his stool.

CHAPTER FOURTEEN

'There's a shadow hanging over our country. We
alone can bring you, our nation, into the light.'
– John Andrews, leader of the Traditional Party

The world is a splintered place I don't understand. Just air that
holds the echoes of Lilli's screams.

As they cut down Darren's body.

How long have we been standing here?

I stare at the sky as it slowly turns black.

My mum's eyes don't waver from the empty gallows.

On the other side of the fence, the men's faces slowly drift
into darkness. I see Luke, standing on the ground now, until he
almost disappears, swallowed by time moving on. By an evening
that Darren will never know. Because of me.

*

They tell us to walk back inside and we move across the yard, up the stairs and into our rooms. No one says a word. We fall where we stand. Mum is between Lilli and I and we pull a blanket over her, covering her shoulders so that only her face can be seen. Her cheeks are sunken in, her lips bitten to bleed. I want to stay awake to look at her, to hold her in my memory.

But the light goes off. I'm in a sea of black and I'm sinking.

The morning is here too soon and instantly I see Darren standing at the gallows. I push it and push it away and try to bring him back alive, but I can't.

Lilli sits up, the blanket falling to her knees, her eyes red from crying.

'It's my fault,' I whisper. I feel the weight of that rope on my own neck, pulling me down.

Mum grabs my wrist, the fire of grief and injustice lit in her. 'This is *not* your fault, Ruby.' I hang my head as Mum brushes away my tears. 'You didn't kill Darren.' But she's crying too. '*They* did. Do you hear me? *They* did. The Traditionals led him up those steps, *they* put that noose on him, not you.' Her breathing is rushed with fury. 'Not you.'

I squeeze my eyes shut tight, blocking away the truth.

'Look at me,' Mum says, but I can't. I don't want to see the pain I've carved so deep into her face. 'Look at me,' she shouts.

I've no choice and when I do, I see the defiance in her eyes. 'This is what they want you to feel. They're trying to break us and if we let them, then they've won. You must understand that.' I nod my head. 'Tell me. Tell me that you understand.'

'I do,' I say.

'Good.' And she puts her palms on either side of my face so I look at no one but her. 'You know Darren would tell us that we mustn't let them win.' I want to stop her tears, but she lets them fall. 'They can try, but they won't destroy us.'

'That's right,' a woman nearer the door says.

'So we're going to stand up now,' Mum says. 'We're going to take our courage in our hands and we're going to walk down those stairs and fill our stomachs with their bread. And we're going to go outside with our heads held higher than ever before. Okay?' She nods, just once. 'And we're going to do this for Darren.' When she says his name, I feel her heart break, but she holds her arms still.

'Yes,' Lilli says.

'And you, little miss,' Mum says, turning to her, 'will dry your eyes. We won't give them the satisfaction of seeing us cry.' Lilli brushes away her tears, but more come. 'We're alive and we're going to stay alive,' she tells us. 'Do you hear me?'

'Yes,' Lilli says again.

'Ruby?'

'Yes,' I say. And Mum takes our hands.

We exist on a line between life and death, between hope and despair. And every day we get to choose which side we'll walk. Some mornings I wake with life and hope by my side, but most days I have to claw my way through thick clouds to find them. When Mum or Lilli begin to fall, I save them, as they do me. We are somehow strong enough to hold each other's souls in place.

We try the same for Conor's mum, but often she's so lost when she wakes that we can't find her. It's a shell of herself that walks beside us.

Darren's spirit is everywhere. Mum has hold of it so tight and she won't ever let it go. She talks of him and Lilli talks of him and I try, but my words get caught in guilt and regret too complicated to untangle. It burns me every moment of every day, a searing red line that cuts through everything.

We cook, we wash, we clean, we sew. My mind is turned inside out until it's a flat sheet that I grip in the wind. There's nothing on it. I stand for roll call and see only the mountains, with snow now on their peaks. So life has gone on. The world is turning and the seasons keep walking, even though our lives have stopped.

We're settling down to sleep when the door opens. A female guard is standing in the light from the corridor.

'Sit up,' she tells us. There's confusion among us. Under our blanket, Lilli reaches for my hand. 'Who can tell me the rules that we, as Traditionals, should abide by?' the guard shouts.

A panicked silence stifles us. I know their rules, I've heard them enough times, but somehow my mind can't reach any of them.

'To not be promiscuous,' a woman finally says.

'To work hard,' says another.

'What else?' the guard demands.

'No alcohol in a public place,' someone says.

'And . . .?' The guard asks, but no one answers. 'You must not *steal*.' She stretches the word through her teeth.

I want to look around at the other women, to see if anyone knows why the guard is saying this, but I keep my eyes firmly on her. I'm not guilty of whatever she's accusing and she mustn't think I am.

'How,' she continues, 'can we have a fair society if people steal? How can there be trust? Tell me that.' Our silence stays with us as she glares into the room. Her eyes rest on Lilli and I feel my sister squeeze my hand. 'Tell me – is stealing right, or wrong?'

'It's wrong,' Lilli answers. Has she done something? Please God no, not Lilli.

'Louder,' the guard commands.

'It's wrong,' Lilli repeats.

'And people who steal should be punished.' The guard's eyes leave my sister and find a woman near the door. 'Is that correct?'

'Yes,' the woman answers.

'Earlier, we caught a woman stealing potatoes from the kitchen.'

Relief floods me. Lilli and Mum were on sewing duty with me. None of us have set foot near the kitchen today.

'We know that you contaminate each other. If there's one thief among you, there'll be hundreds.'

That's not true.

'As a punishment,' the guard says. 'Tomorrow, before dawn, every woman in camp will be lined up and every tenth person shall be shot.' Her voice is tinted with eagerness, so I know I must have heard it wrong.

'But I don't steal,' a woman behind me says. 'I've never stolen anything in my life.'

'Then this will be a deterrent to make sure you never do.' The guard smiles. She *smiles*. 'Sleep well,' she says before she closes the door. The darkness is sudden and complete.

'Mum?' Lilli whispers.

'Yes.'

'I don't understand.'

'There's nothing to worry about,' Mum tells her.

'Are you mad?' a voice nearby shouts at her. 'Tomorrow they're going to use us as target practice.'

'They're going to shoot us?' Lilli's asks.

'It won't be you, Lilli,' I tell her. If I think it hard enough, I can convince myself.

'If we stand together,' Mum says, 'and the number lands on one of us, then the other two will be spared.' Mum's voice is balanced, as though she's working out a sum.

Somewhere in the room, a woman starts to weep. Around me, I hear whispered prayers. What do you do if tomorrow you might die?

'Ruby,' Mum says, her hand in mine. 'Tell me something I don't know about you.'

'What do you mean?'

'Anything. Just something I never knew before.'

The dark whittles into my bones and tries to take me.

'I don't like your shepherd's pie,' I say.

'My shepherd's pie?' She sounds confused.

'Yes,' I admit.

'But it's one of your favourites.'

'I just pretended because I didn't want to make you feel bad.'

And Mum laughs. In the crushing horror of this night, she's able to laugh.

'My secret,' Lilli says, 'is that I've never kissed a boy.'

'What about Paul Jenkins?' I ask her.

'I made it up.'

'But in the alley by his house. Sharon told me about it.'

'It was all a lie,' Lilli says simply.

'That's okay,' Mum says. But she sounds so sad and I feel her mind wandering to a bleak place and I need to keep her with me. We've all got to stay on this side of hope.

'Mum, what's your favourite smell?' I ask her.

'Smell?'

'Yes.'

'Yours and Lilli's hair.'

'Still?'

'Always.'

Sorrow sweeps in and grabs my breath. Mum holds me tight.

'Don't cry,' she says. 'Don't give them your tears.'

But how can I not? I want to live. I want us all to live. I want every woman in this room to live, every person in this camp.

I must have slept somehow, but now I'm awake. I don't know what time it is, or how long it'll be before the guard opens the door. I hope I still have hours. But then I also hope it's just minutes. There's a cruelty in waiting that fills me with poisoned thoughts.

We will stand, our backs to that wall.

One in ten of us will die. Just because we believe in different things to them.

My heart beats so hard that it must bruise my ribs and the pain rattles around my body, to my feet, my neck, scalding my skull.

Breathe, Ruby.

Will they make the men watch, as they made us when they murdered Darren?

His name drifts through my fingers. I try to clasp it, but it's too painful and I let go.

Help us, I beg him.

I grasp the blanket tight to me, my fingers on my forehead follow the line of my eyebrows, touch my eyelashes. I'm Ruby. And I'm alive. I feel the bones in my cheeks, bring my fingertips to my lips. It's my skin, with my blood underneath it. I bite enough to feel pain and know that it's my brain that feels it.

I've got fifteen years of memories spread within me. They're my very own. I have Luke. I have his arms and his voice and his kisses and they're mine.

I won't feel the guards' madness. I'll stay stronger than steel and face their bullets. They'll count to ten again and again, but even if they take me I'll always have lived. In other people's minds, I'll be here.

I am the raven on the wire.

Everyone is awake. Somewhere outside the sun must soon be rising. It will keep going even if we don't. It will look down on empty spaces where some of us should be.

The guards herd us out of the bunk room. A swarm of us. We're only insects to them as we shuffle along the corridor in pairs. I'm with Lilli. Mum insists we stay together. I hold my sister's hand and feel the stair rail in my other. I watch my mum walk, see how she's tied her hair into −

An explosion throws me into the air. The walls have disappeared, the ceiling is falling.

I'm on the floor. There's a pain in my head. My brain must be bleeding.

I'm crawling over bodies.

There's no sound, only the ringing in my skull.

'Mum!' I can't hear me calling. 'Lilli.'

I breathe a grey cloud and swallow it and it wants to choke me.

There's blood as I drag myself away.

I cough so much that I sick murky bile on to the ground.

'Lilli?'

I'm outside and it's still dark, only lights by the fence. People are walking, running. There are people not moving.

Where are the guards?

Another explosion breaks through my silence. It's close by, but I've nowhere to hide. I lie on the ground and try to cover my head.

My eyes, my throat, they're burning.

My arms won't protect me.

I feel blood on my leg.

'Ruby!' I can hear Lilli. She's calling me. I look for her, but there's just thick dust and bodies. 'Ruby.' I stand up and follow her voice, run towards it.

'Lilli!' I have to wade through the screaming. 'I'm here.'

I see her standing alone, her arms by her side. Her face is bleeding, the blood falling on her shoulder.

'Where's Mum?' I ask her.

She shakes her head, but has no expression, no pain, no fear.

We search among the people, but everyone is calling out and Mum won't hear me shouting. I hold Lilli's hand and we search, but I can't find her. I can't find my mum.

'We need to look in the building,' I say, but it's no longer there, not as it should be. The stairs stick out like bones in the ruins and I run towards them. There're so many bricks. I let go of Lilli and start to pick them up, one by one.

'Mum,' I call. My fingers lift the dark rubble. Everywhere there's dust. 'Mum.'

There's an arm and I move the bricks, but it isn't her. She's not my mother, this woman, her eyes staring into hell.

Everywhere there's screaming, the sounds growing and fading, binding tight around my skull. It's hard to see through the dust because I'm crying when I don't want to be.

Don't let them see you upset, my mum says. But who is here to see? There's no sign of the guards, no guns at my back.

'Help me, Lilli,' I say and together we dig through the bricks, moving everything we can, but it's a mound in front of us. The air is still thick with clouds of shattered wall. If Mum is under this, how will she be able to breathe? 'Hurry,' I say and I force my arms to move.

The dust begins to lift and Lilli walks away from me.

'Mum?' I hear her say. I look to where she stands by the body of a woman lying on the ground. I don't want to get up, but I do. I see myself step closer. She lies on the ground, on her side, as if she's asleep. One of her arms is stretched out. There's a wound on her forehead, the blood from it spilling into her hair.

I kneel down next to her. 'Get up, Mum,' I whisper. But her eyes are closed. 'We've got to go.' Her mouth is slightly open and there should be a word there, but she doesn't reply. I wipe the dirt from her fingers. 'It's time to go,' I tell her, but she doesn't move.

'She's breathing,' Lilli says and she's shaking our mum's arm. I think I should hold her back, but now I see it too, the slow rise and fall of Mum's chest.

'Mum,' I cry and I'm wiping her blood and pulling her to sit as a helicopter above suddenly takes the sounds of the world around us. Lilli says something that I can't hear as our mum opens her eyes. She sees me and she sees Lilli and she reaches out to touch my cheek, but the helicopter is circling and I don't know who it is or where the guards are. It flies away and the shouting comes back.

'What happened?' Mum asks, looking around.

'I don't know.' I try to wipe the dust from her face, as everywhere around us people are screaming. 'We have to go. Can you stand up?'

Mum nods, but she's so confused as she leans on me and takes Lilli's hand.

Her body staggers, but her eyes are strong.

'I'm fine,' she says. 'I can walk.'

The gate into the men's section is open and people are pushing, running towards the entrance of the camp.

'What about the guards?' Lilli asks. We look around at the jagged ruins, the choking clouds disintegrating to let the shapes of suffering through, yet there's no one here to shoot us.

'This is our chance,' I say. But at every step I wait for the earth to explode and take us.

I see now, through the fence, there are vans arriving, yellow steps painted across them. The yellow steps of the Core Party.

'Take Mum with you,' I say to Lilli.

'Where are you going?'

'I won't leave Destiny,' I say.

'Ruby!' It's Mum shouting to me, but already I'm running against the tide of panic, through the waves of broken people, to the door I need. I find the light switch and the corridor blinks into life.

Inside here it's so quiet and I stop, seeing only the closed doors. Where is the general? Will he be in his office while the other guards flee and his camp falls apart? There's a noise behind me and I whip round, arms raised, but it's my mum, her face sharp with distress as she stands holding Lilli's hand.

'Where's Destiny?' she asks, her cough violent, rattling into the silence. And so I take them with me, leading them, knowing that at any time a gun could be aimed at us. I barely breathe as we walk past the general's room and I wait to see him standing here, but he doesn't come. We run past the cupboard and no one tries to stop me as I open the furthest door.

There's the same strong smell of disinfectant, the same taste of despair.

'What is this place?' Mum whispers as she pulls aside the first grey curtain. Three children lie in separate beds, staring terrified at us. 'What have they done to them?' Mum tries to lift the nearest girl, but she cries out in pain.

I go to stroke back the girl's sweat-stained hair. 'We won't hurt you,' I tell her. 'But you have to be brave.'

She winces as Mum wraps her naked legs in the sheet and gently picks her up. 'How many more?' Mum's voice is still ribbed with dust as Lilli rips back another curtain.

'Zamal,' she says. And he's here. One of the sterilised. A wave of nausea hits me, but I breathe deep enough to push it away, to stay strong for him. He doesn't speak as I lift him from the bed.

'Is Rimi here?' I ask, but he only looks at me with wide eyes and I know the answer. 'Can you stand up?' He nods, but his legs buckle and Lilli has to break his fall.

'I'll carry him as well,' Mum says. 'You find Destiny.'

'But what about the other children?' Lilli asks.

'We'll come back for them, I promise,' Mum tells her, as I run to the curtain at the end.

Destiny is strapped to the mattress. Her head is locked back, headphones clamped to her ears and a screen plays so close to her face that it touches her. I yank it all away but she barely flinches.

'Help me,' I tell Lilli and we untie the leather straps and I lift Destiny. She falls against me, her head rolling back until only the whites of her eyes are showing. 'Destiny, it's me, Ruby.' She blinks slowly, a strange groaning coming from her. 'You're safe now,' I tell her.

She's only bones, but still Lilli and I struggle to carry her between us, her feet dragging on the floor. I find my last grains of strength to hold her as we leave the building, into the chaos of people searching, crying.

'Get to the gate,' Mum tells us, blood tangled deep in her hair as she clutches Zamal and the little girl tight.

Someone pulls me back. I turn and Luke is standing in front of me.

'Ruby,' he says. And it's all I hear.

His dad is beside him, his shirt torn.

'Help us,' I say and his dad takes Destiny from me, holding her as a child.

'I've got you,' he tells her.

There's the sound of a helicopter returning, somewhere deep in the sky. 'We've got to hurry,' Mum says, as Luke reaches out to carry Zamal, shielding him from everything around us. I keep Lilli's hand in mine.

It's like this that we find our way to freedom.

SIX MONTHS LATER

My name is Ruby West and I am not a number.

I do exist.

I have courage and I have hope.

But I will never forget.

I wake as I do every day, in Mum and Darren's bed. Lilli is curled next to me, her hand linked around my wrist even though she's still asleep. It's barely light outside, but it's enough to see her eyes locked tight against the nightmares that haunt her. I should wake her. Sometimes I do. But I think that reality might be even worse than those dreams.

Instead I lie back on the pillow and pull the sleeves of Darren's jumper further over my hands. *I'm sorry*, I whisper to him. *I'm sorry, I'm sorry, I'm sorry*. I rub the arms of his jumper over my eyelids again and again, not caring if I scratch my skin raw. I need it to wipe away the pain inside me, but it never does.

I hear movement close by. I know it's Mum getting up from the mattress on the floor.

'It's okay, I'm here,' she says and I feel her stroke my hair from my face. But I want it left there, covering me, hiding me from the world.

'It's not,' I reply and when she hugs me I pretend that it's Darren's shoulder my tears fall on to.

Mum makes us breakfast as she does every day. I don't want to eat it but I must, because Lilli copies everything I do.

When we first returned – after the assessments and prodding and probing and questions, questions, questions – I couldn't be anywhere. I couldn't be in our home without Darren. And I couldn't be outside where terror peeled me back, layer by layer. So I sat and existed in burrows of memories. Deeper I went every moment, down tunnels of gunshots, seeing the general's face at every turn. Deeper, even when the earth from above began to drip down, filling my eyes, my nose, my mouth until I was choking and Mum would have to drag me back, shake me free.

Always, Lilli would be sitting, staring at me.

Mum picked the earth from my ears until I could hear and swept the mud from my eyes until I could see how my sister was fading in front of me. And so now, every day, I eat my breakfast. And every day Lilli eats hers too. I put on my school uniform because then I know she will. I do my shoes and hold on to my bag and take her hand before I open the front door and together we walk each step.

Our dad phones us as he does each morning now. It's nice to hear his voice, but it hurts so much too because it makes me miss Darren even more. Dad comes to visit us as much as he can, but Darren isn't here and the hole that's left sometimes burns too bright to even think.

At school, Luke waits by the gate – never inside where he used to be. I want to feel happiness when I see him, but I'm not there yet. One day, maybe. For now having him by my side is enough. We go into our school knowing that the Traditionals are not here. They're no longer in power, but they've left behind a shattered country that can't quite find all the pieces to make itself whole again.

Lilli's Tight-Knits meet her and take her from me and will protect her for the day.

Sara is by my locker.

'Hey,' she says. And I nod and try on a smile as she links her arm through mine.

She's asked about the camp, but understands that I can't speak of it yet and is careful with the scars she can't see. One day I'll find the courage to tell her the truth about Darren. About how he died because of me. And maybe I will tell her how I hid under a coach to escape. How I met a man in a shop who phoned my dad and set off a chain of events that led to the bombing of the camp. The bombing that the Cores on the outside carried out before dawn because they thought we'd all be sleeping. The bomb that killed so many innocent people as they walked down those stairs. That made the general and his guards run for their own lives. The bomb that also set us free.

Sara knows about the children who were taken, because the world talks about them. Of those who were brutally sterilised. And of those, along with Rimi, who were found safe in a home not far from the camp, their indoctrination only just begun, the damage reversible. She knows too of the vanished twins. At night I sometimes dream of them. I like to pretend that they are living in the mountains, waiting for us to find them there.

Conor is lost to us too. He spends his days and nights sitting next to his mum as she struggles for each breath. Her treatment started again when she left the camp, but she's too frail, too ill. Conor is riddled with an anger that seeps from his skin and though I try to find a way through to him, he's so far away that I don't know if he'll ever return.

Mr Hart has not come back to school. I have heard that his wife did not survive. I wonder if there's reason enough for him to wake every day. I'd like to think there is.

Destiny isn't in the corridors. She isn't in the classrooms or the canteen. We don't walk along arm in arm, meeting each other's friends. Instead I wait for the minutes to tick by until I can visit her. Later, Luke and Lilli and I will go to the place where she's looked after. We'll sit and talk to her and hold her hand. Lilli will do her make up and I will paint her nails. Maybe today she will recognise us. Maybe it'll be today that she raises her head on her own and says my name with a smile.

Every day I tell her that she's loved. I tell her that our society is being rebuilt. I tell her that there is kindness and that it outweighs the bad. That the sky is still blue and the sun still rises. I tell her that we are no longer numbers. That we are free. I tell her this, because I have to believe it myself. The more I say it, the more it is true.

Luke will sit in the corner of that room and he'll open his sketchbook. Every day the raven he draws becomes stronger. The feathers form on the curves of its wings, its eyes shine. It gives me hope and strength. Strength to live and strength to speak. Because in time I will tell all who will listen that prejudice is poison. That power can turn people ugly and it disintegrates souls, but love's roots are stronger than hate. And if we let love grow taller and wider it'll be all that we can see.

I'll tell how each second is precious, each moment is a gift.

In time I will.

In time.

AUTHOR'S NOTE

Ruby's story has its roots in the unbearable horrors of the Holocaust, where it's estimated that 12 million people died in Hitler's concentration camps. Prisoners were subjected to unimaginable suffering, including starvation, hard-labour and barbaric medical experiments. My book is set in the present day and it is, of course, a work of fiction. And yet when I was writing *I Am Not a Number* I had a sense of life imitating art. The influence of fascism on global politics is undeniable, from Europe to South America and the USA. Today, too often, we hear echoes of the past in the words of politicians; words of prejudice, racism and nationalism spoken from those who are meant to be leading our world. We mustn't be the ones to tolerate this, to turn our backs. Above all else my intention is that this book carries a message of hope – hope that love and tolerance will prevail. I truly believe that, guided by the younger generation, who show such courage through their actions and protests, we can learn to replace division with unity, fear with friendship and the language of hatred with that of respect.

ACKNOWLEDGEMENTS

My biggest thank you is for my beautiful mum – in your determination to live, you showed me that every day is a gift. I'll treasure this knowledge always and be forever grateful that you were mine.

Thank you to Miles for holding me along bumpy paths and smooth tracks, through mountains and moonrivers. And to our wonderful boys Arthur, Albert and Frank - you are my sunshine. To Philip, Lara, Emma and Anna - thank you for always being by my side. I love you all.

To my brilliant agent, Veronique Baxter – thank you for your endless wisdom, your kindness and your friendship – I'm so lucky to have you guiding me.

To my amazing editor, Sarah Levison – a huge thank you for your insight, your incredible intuition and the care you have given to Ruby and her story. I'm so grateful that I was paired with such a talent as you. Thank you also to Amy St Johnston for working closely on this book. And, of course, to Ali Dougal – thank you for keeping a keen eye and being a constant for Ruby. And to all the team at Egmont - especially Lisa Holton for my stunning cover, the inimitable Cally Poplak, Tiff Leeson, Ingrid Gilmore, Laura Bird, Siobhan McDermott, Hilary Bell, Sarah Garnham and Jasveen Bansal. I'm very proud to be published by you. And thank you to Susila Baybars and Becky Peacock for your enviable copyediting and proofreading skills.

Thank you to my very first readers – Samala Bernstein and Ronika Banerji – your encouraging words made me believe in this book. And to Audrey Bennett for answering random questions. And a big thank you to Brian Conaghan for reading under time-pressure and having nothing but kind words.

To my writing group – Nikki, Allie, Sandi, Debs, Suzanna and Lucy – thank you for pushing me to be the best writer I can be. And my reading group Jo, Babs, Jackie and Catherine. To Jules, Abie, Jess, Jen, Tash, Sarah D, Sarah C and Jane for sharing this strange new world. And to all the bloggers who spread the love of books – especially the stars who are Carmen Haselup, Michelle Toy and Grace Latter.

To the brilliant, sparky, interested and interesting teenagers who I'm lucky enough to meet on school visits. You are the future. Keep using your voices and know that each and every one of you counts. To librarians everywhere – thank you for working tirelessly to bring books to children; it means the world to me that you're championing mine. And thank you to Ness, Jules and Naomi for running the best shop ever – The Book Nook at First Avenue, Hove.

I'm so lucky to have amazing friends – whether I sing with you, swim with you, laugh, talk, or pray with you, every one of you is an irreplaceable part in my life – especially Toots, Lucy, Wally, my school friends and Rolle College Alumni, The wonderful Whinneys, my forever NCTers, The Cameroons, my Pub Quiz team extraordinaire, school-gate mums and dads and Gospel choir friends.

To my writing spirit – thank you for leading Ruby, Luke, Destiny and Lilli to me. It's been heartbreaking, but an honour, to write their story.

Finally and most importantly – I read many books on the Holocaust while I was writing *I Am Not A Number*. Each one seared me in a way that I hope will never diminish: *I Have Lived A Thousand Years*, by Livia Bitton-Jackson; *Freedom and Justice*, by Zbigniew Drecki; *Charlotte*, by David Foenkinos; *If This Is A Woman*, by Sarah Helm; *If This Is A Man*, by Primo Levi; *Night*, by Elie Wiesel. They had the courage to write, so that we will never forget.

HIGH VOLTAGE READING

FROM ELECTRIC MONKEY